DEATH AT CROOKHAM HALL

AN IRIS WOODMORE MYSTERY

MICHELLE SALTER

Boldwood

First published in Great Britain in 2023 by Boldwood Books Ltd.

Copyright © Michelle Salter, 2023

Cover Design by Lawston Design

Cover Photography: Lawston Design

A CIP catalogue record for this book is available from the British Library.

Paperback ISBN 978-1-83751-040-5

Large Print ISBN 978-1-83751-036-8

Hardback ISBN 978-1-83751-035-1

Ebook ISBN 978-1-83751-033-7

Kindle ISBN 978-1-83751-034-4

Audio CD ISBN 978-1-83751-041-2

MP3 CD ISBN 978-1-83751-038-2

Digital audio download ISBN 978-1-83751-032-0

Boldwood Books Ltd
23 Bowerdean Street
London SW6 3TN
www.boldwoodbooks.com

For Mum and Dad

PROLOGUE

WALDENMERE LAKE, WALDEN, HAMPSHIRE

She wore a linen cloak that was too thick for the warm August night, but it hid her features.

She stood at the end of the wooden jetty; the water was inviting. She wanted to jump, to feel the cold of the lake, submerge, float upwards and drift away. Her body ached with tiredness.

The noise of a train pulling into the railway station roused her. She drew the hood over her head, touching her unfamiliar cropped hair. A short dark bob had replaced her long blonde locks. She took a lingering look at the silver-grey water then emerged from the shadows and strolled towards the station.

She walked to the end of the platform and boarded. It was the last train of the night and no other passengers joined her in the carriage during the journey.

When she reached her destination, she waited for a few minutes before leaving the train. She stepped down and the platform was empty. Panic gripped her. What if they weren't here? Where would she go? She had nothing but the clothes she was wearing.

She walked through the deserted concourse, taking deep

breaths and tasting burning coal. A tall figure emerged from behind a kiosk at the far end of the station. Arranging the cloak to disguise her features, she moved towards the person.

'Did anyone see you?'

It was a familiar voice. Her panic subsided.

'I don't think so.' She pulled back her hood. 'If they did, they wouldn't have recognised me.'

'Good.'

'I hid by the lake until the train pulled in.' She still longed to be immersed in the calmness of the water. 'It's strange to think I may never see Waldenmere again.'

'You will never see it again. You must *never* return to Walden.'

She nodded. She had no choice but to agree.

'There's a taxi outside. I've paid him. He'll take you to where you're going to be living.'

'Aren't you coming with me?'

'I can't. I'll be missed.'

'Why are you doing this?' She took the purse she was handed.

'Because I was once helpless. And I remember the fear.'

1

1920

'Mrs Siddons has invited me to listen to a debate in the House of Commons.' I hooked my coat on the hatstand, dumped my bag on my desk and went through to the boss's office.

Elijah Whittle, editor of *The Walden Herald*, commanded his empire from a smoke-filled den. I say empire, the newspaper's headquarters consisted of two rooms above Laffaye Printworks. My desk was in the main office whilst Elijah sat in a small adjoining room.

From his desk, he could keep an eye on the main office door, the large railway clock on the wall and me at work. I was the only permanent reporter; he mainly used freelancers, and the rest of the newspaper staff were housed downstairs in the printworks.

'Is that a good idea, Iris?' He stubbed out his cigarette and ran his nicotine-stained fingers through his grey hair.

'I can't avoid the place forever,' I said with a flippancy I didn't feel. 'You must have seen debates there?'

'Many times, when I worked for *The Daily Telegraph*. I can't promise you'll enjoy the experience.'

'Is *The Walden Herald* going to support Mrs Siddons?' I didn't think he'd commit before the other candidates in the by-election had been announced, but it was worth a try.

'I'll see what she has to say on the hustings, then make up my mind.' He reached for his cigarettes and I cranked open the window.

'What do you think about women in Parliament?'

Elijah held progressive views on many things, but there was a traditional streak running through him. 'I think women MPs will vastly improve our parliamentary system. But I'll judge each candidate on their merits, irrespective of their sex.'

I couldn't object to this infuriatingly reasonable response. 'Do we know who the other candidates are yet?' So far, only Mrs Siddons had been declared for the Liberal Party.

He gave me a wry smile. I flopped into the nearest chair. 'What have you heard?'

'Lady Delphina Timpson is standing for the Conservatives.'

'What? Another woman's standing?' This ruined my vision of Mrs Siddons' triumphant victory over the male opposition.

'What are you going to do now?' He regarded me with amusement. 'With two women to support?'

'I'll judge each on their merits.' I repeated his words back to him, but I was lying. Mrs Siddons had become my friend after my mother's death. Six years and the Great War had passed since then, and I wasn't about to switch my allegiance.

'The first constituency ever to have two women standing against each other in a by-election.' He took a contented drag of his cigarette.

This was heady stuff for our corner of north-east Hampshire. But I wanted Mrs Siddons to be the third female to take her seat in the House of Commons. Not some other woman.

'Who's the Labour candidate?' I asked.

'Donald Anstey. I don't know much about him. He supports

women becoming MPs but I bet he never thought he'd be standing against two of them.'

'Will we get to interview them all?'

'That's the plan. I've put in a request to Lady Timpson's office.'

'I know her daughter, Constance. She was at Miss Cotton's Academy at the same time as me. I haven't seen her for years. What about Donald Anstey?'

'He's looking pretty dull compared to the mighty Mrs Siddons and the wealthy Lady Timpson. I expect he'll do what he can to gain a few column inches.' He stubbed out his cigarette. 'This won't do our circulation any harm.'

My emotions were doing battle. I was irritated that another woman was standing against Mrs Siddons. But this was a story that was likely to generate national interest, especially with a candidate as famous as Lady Timpson.

'Do some research and draft notes on each candidate. I want impartial information. I know who you favour, but I don't want any bias coming through yet. We may decide not to support any of them.'

'We?' I'd already made up my mind to do everything in my power to ensure Mrs Siddons became the next MP for Aldershot.

'I mean Mr Laffaye and me.'

'Does Mr Laffaye ever tell you what to write? Or what not to write?'

As editor of *The Walden Herald*, Elijah was responsible for the newspaper's content. But Horace Laffaye owned the paper and held the purse strings. I often wondered how much influence he exerted.

'He offers advice. Which I can regard or disregard. Fortunately, we tend to agree on most things. And I'm sure we will over this.'

I wondered what would happen if they didn't.

* * *

At five o'clock, I left the office and went downstairs and out onto Queens Road. It was a still, damp evening and the smell of ink hung in the air, rising through the grate above the printworks.

Further down the road I took the footpath that led to Walden-mere. One of my favourite walks was to follow the meandering route of Grebe Stream down to Heron Bay, where it flowed into the lake.

Wood sorrel and lesser celandine were in flower on the banks, and dog violets were peeking out along the edges of the footpath. The trees were still bare, but it wouldn't be long before their leaves unfurled.

As I'd hoped, I spotted an easel propped up in a glade near Heron Bay. Alice Thackeray's distinctive red hair stood out against the watery grey backdrop. I pushed through the ferns to join her in the clearing.

Although it was mild for March, there was still a chill in the air and she was wrapped in a thick, green woollen coat, her bare hands delicately dabbing a paintbrush onto canvas.

I examined the watercolour. She'd started with a rough sketch of the shoreline and had just begun to colour the reedbeds. The more she progressed, the more the reeds appeared to be swaying in the breeze. 'I wish I could paint like that.'

She smiled. Then frowned. 'Iris, you're wearing trousers again.'

I ignored this. 'Guess who's standing against Mrs Siddons in the by-election?'

'Some chap called Anstey. Father says he's a communist.'

'No, not him. Lady Delphina Timpson.' I perched on a nearby log, but it was too damp, so I got up again.

'Constance's mother?' I had her attention.

'She's standing as the Conservative candidate. She announced it this morning from Army HQ in Aldershot. Lord Tobias Timpson by her side.'

'Two women standing? Father's going to be furious.' The light was fading and she began to wash her brushes.

'Lady Timpson's hoping for the military vote.'

'She won't get Father's. He disapproves of women in politics.'

'He'll have to vote for the communist then.' I took great pleasure in Colonel Thackeray's predicament. 'Have you seen Constance since school?'

'During the war she gave us donations of food and clothes, the Walden Women's Group, I mean. We used to distribute them to local families in need.' She carefully covered up the canvas and I helped her to pack away her paints.

'Ever been to Crookham Hall?' I asked.

'A few times, for dances. The Timpsons used to hold them to entertain the troops. It's very grand. Are you going there?'

'Maybe. Elijah wants to interview Lady Timpson.'

I was unlikely to be invited to the hall in any other capacity. Alice had the advantage of being a Colonel's daughter, whereas I was further down the social scale.

We waded through bracken to join the lake path and I told her about my invitation to the House of Commons.

'Isn't that where your mother...'

'Yes.'

'I'm surprised Mrs Siddons wants to take you there.'

'So am I,' I admitted.

'Is she trying to influence how you'll write about her in the paper?'

'I'm not sure she'd risk taking me to Westminster if that was all she wanted,' I snapped.

'I suppose not. Are you sure you want to go?' She linked her arm through mine.

'Yes,' I said untruthfully. I wasn't sure at all. 'I'm going to stay with Gran and Aunt Maud.'

'Just for a visit?' she said in alarm. 'I'd hate you to move away again. I missed you during the war.'

'I'm only staying with them overnight as the debate might not finish in time for me to catch the last train,' I reassured her. 'I missed you too. And Waldenmere.' But I avoided meeting her eyes. I had missed Alice, but I hadn't wanted to leave our home on Hither Green Lane. The truth was it had been Father's idea to move back to Walden. He'd persuaded me to return by getting me the job with Elijah. They were old friends from their days at *The Daily Telegraph*. It hadn't been how I'd imagined launching my writing career, but I'd tried – and failed – to get a foot in the door of any of the London newspapers. All I'd managed to do was sell a few of my articles to ladies' magazines. *The Walden Herald* had seemed as good a place to start as any.

And now, sleepy old Walden had a story on its hands that would be of national interest. For once, I seemed to be in the right place at the right time.

2

I left the house early. Too early to catch my train to London.

But dawn was the only time I could guarantee having the lake to myself. Even on this dull March morning, Waldenmere had an eerie beauty. At first light, there was a stillness about the lake that became diluted as the day progressed. To be by the water at this time reassured me that the storm had passed, and we were at peace.

During the war years in the city, I often dreamt of being back at Waldenmere. It represented something constant in an ever-changing world.

I was watching the light shimmer on the flat silvery water when the sound of the newspaper train pulling in made me look up. I realised I wasn't alone. A man was standing on the wooden jetty by the railway station. He gave me a sad smile as though he knew who I was.

There was only a short distance between us, but a low mist hung in the air, and I had to squint to get a better look at his face. I didn't recognise him. He appeared to be holding some flowers, which he dropped into the water.

I pulled my coat tighter around me and walked away. I glanced back to see if he'd moved, but he remained on the jetty.

After breakfast, I headed to the railway station, carrying a small suitcase. I half expected to see the man still on the jetty, but no one was around. I walked over to where he'd been standing and peered into the water. Half a dozen bedraggled purple flowers were clinging to the banks. They looked strangely out of place. These weren't the common dog violets that grew in abundance around Waldenmere.

They were sweet violets – the flower of the suffragettes.

* * *

That afternoon, I walked through the Central Lobby of the Houses of Parliament, a nervous tension tightening my stomach.

I strolled in a circle, making a pretence of examining each painting and reading each inscription. But they were all a blur. I wanted to appear as though I was casually sauntering, but I knew exactly where I was heading. As soon as I'd entered the lobby, my eyes had sought out the ornate metal grilles set into the windows.

The grilles had once sat in the stone arches of the Ladies' Gallery, but after my mother's protest, they'd been cleaned and moved to the Central Lobby.

My heart beat a little faster as I got nearer. I checked no one was watching and reached out to touch the cold metal. The grilles were still impressive, though I suspected they wouldn't be quite so tarnished if my mother hadn't painted them. I ran my fingers over the latticework, imagining her in action. Had she been scared? Or exhilarated?

'Are those the ones...?' Mrs Siddons appeared by my side, making me jump.

I nodded.

The grilles had been designed in the 1830s to screen the ladies in the gallery from the men below. MPs weren't to be distracted by women watching them at work. The problem was, they restricted the view of the debating chamber and made the Ladies' Gallery extremely hot. My mother hadn't been the first suffragist to target them.

In 1908, Helen Fox and Muriel Matters of the Women's Freedom League had chained and padlocked themselves to the grilles whilst my mother's namesake, Violet Tillard, had pushed a large banner through the latticework on the end of a rope.

'How did your mother's protest come about? It was the day Emmeline Pankhurst tried to petition the King, wasn't it?'

'Yes, the twenty-first of May 1914. We didn't know what she was planning. We thought she was marching to Buckingham Palace with the others.'

'But she came here instead?'

'She knew there'd be no police around. They'd all be at the march. Somehow, she managed to get into the Ladies' Gallery. She painted the grilles suffragette green and lowered a Women's Social and Political Union banner into the chamber below.'

Mrs Siddons smiled and touched the tarnished metal. I took a last look before she led me away to the Strangers' Gallery, where the public sat. Several MPs I recognised greeted her cordially – I couldn't help wondering how much support they'd give her if she were taking to the floor with them instead of spectating.

In the chamber, my eyes were drawn to the Ladies' Gallery. It hadn't been used for years. Knowing my mother had been there shortly before she died made my skin prickle.

I turned my attention to the speakers when the Equal Franchise Act came up for debate. Lady Astor faced an all-male audience and gave a vigorous but uninspiring speech on why women must have the vote on the same terms as men. Winston Churchill retaliated with a forceful and vociferous argument against the bill. Heated exchanges followed with numerous interjections from the Speaker.

'I wish Mother were here to see this,' I whispered to Mrs Siddons. 'Though I expect she would've done something embarrassing to get us thrown out.'

'I feel like doing that myself.' Mrs Siddons laughed but shook her head. 'This is getting us nowhere.'

The Representation of the People Act in 1918 had given the vote to all men over the age of twenty-one but only to women over the age of thirty who met a property qualification.

At twenty-one, I wasn't eligible to vote. My mother wouldn't have been satisfied, and neither was I. As expected, the bill was rejected and the discussion moved on.

I emerged with relief from the smoke-filled gallery into the cool evening air. 'I'm surprised any women stand for election. They get patronised by their fellow MPs and ridiculed by the newspapers.'

'Most of my press coverage does tend to focus on what I look like rather than what I have to say.'

I smiled, glancing at her attire. She was wearing a full-length, dark green silk dress that hugged her matronly figure. A matching silk cap rested on her perfectly curled dark hair. And despite disparaging comments in the press about her fondness for expensive jewellery, she wore an emerald necklace and matching earrings. In a country still on its knees after a bloody and costly war, ostentatious displays of wealth were frowned upon by some.

'They've moved on from Lady Astor's hats to your earrings,' I commented as we strolled towards Westminster Bridge.

'No doubt Delphina and I will be pitted against each other in the fashion stakes as well as the political ones. As for Mr Anstey, apart from passing comment on the type of hat he wears, I don't think they'll worry too much about his clothes.'

Delphina? So, Mrs Siddons was on first-name terms with her opponent.

'How do you feel about Lady Timpson standing against you?'

'I welcome more women playing a part in politics. I'm just not sure of her motives.'

'How do you know her?'

'We were friends when we were young. I haven't seen much of her in recent years.'

I wanted to find out more, but I knew we were nearing the spot where *it* happened. Mrs Siddons must have sensed my anxiety because she took my hand.

'Would you like to go a different way?' We were by the corner of Parliament as it joined Westminster Bridge.

'No.'

She glanced at me but said nothing.

I wanted to go to the exact place. I couldn't help myself. I didn't know why, but I had to. 'It was here.' I stopped abruptly. 'Mother went into the water here.'

We stood under the shadow of Big Ben.

'She came out through Speaker's Court over there and onto the Green.' I pointed. 'She must have been heading towards these steps up to the bridge when she fell into the river.'

The Thames was black and fetid. I shuddered, trying to block out the image of my mother sinking into its filthy darkness, swallowing putrid water.

'Come away.' I felt Mrs Siddons tug my hand.

'I'm surprised the WSPU didn't put up a plaque.' I forced a laugh. '*Suffragette Violet Woodmore fell here – another martyr to the cause.*'

'She didn't fall,' said a gruff voice, startling me.

An old man with a weathered face was watching us. He wore the scarlet uniform of a Thames waterman.

I stared at him, feeling a chill of foreboding, knowing I didn't want to hear what he was about to say. I had an impulse to run away. But I stayed rooted to the spot.

'I saw her, that suffragette.' He rubbed the grey bristles on his chin. 'She didn't fall, she jumped.'

3

'She came out of nowhere and threw herself in the river.' The waterman pointed to where my mother had entered the water.

'No,' I said. 'She fell.'

'If she were hurrying, she might have tripped.' Mrs Siddons tugged at my arm.

'She jumped. I'm sure of that.' The man removed his cap and twisted it in his hands.

'She must have fallen and it looked like she jumped.' Scenarios of what could have happened flitted through my mind. 'Was she running? Was someone chasing her?'

'Not that I could see. She was standing there one minute and the next she was in the river. I've worked this stretch of the Thames for forty years, and I've never seen anything like it.'

'What did you do?' Mrs Siddons asked.

'I got her to the shore, and the Serjeant-at-Arms hauled her away.'

'The Serjeant-at-Arms must have been chasing her.' My anger rose at the thought of my fragile mother being dragged around like a sack of laundry.

The waterman shook his head. 'I had to call him over. He wasn't there before she went into the water.'

'She wouldn't have jumped.' I tried to sound calm. 'She couldn't swim.'

'I could see that. Mad thing to do, it was. She nearly got hit by a boat. I don't know what possessed her.'

'Perhaps you didn't see what caused her to fall?' Mrs Siddons suggested.

'I could see it all clearly from my boat.' He wasn't to be dissuaded.

I shivered, feeling the chill of the night air. My head pounded, and when Mrs Siddons pulled on my arm, I let her lead me away.

She steered me across the road to St Stephen's Tavern, where she ordered two brandies. I'd expected the barman to ask us to leave as we were unaccompanied by a man. Instead, he greeted her like an old friend.

'You've always believed your mother fell?' Mrs Siddons found us a small table in the corner. The tavern smelt of beer and cigars.

'We thought she'd been spotted on her way out and panicked and slipped into the water.'

'Is it possible she could have jumped? As a form of protest, I mean?' She pushed the brandy towards me.

I took a sip, the liquid burning my throat. 'No. She wouldn't have done that, she couldn't swim. She never bathed with me in Waldenmere. She would only paddle in the shallows.'

A Liberal MP I recognised nodded at Mrs Siddons as he passed our table. She gave him an almost coquettish smile, then turned back to me. 'She wasn't arrested, was she?'

'She was taken to St Thomas' Hospital. The police came, but they were told she was too ill to be questioned. Do you think one of them chased her? Forced her to jump into the river?'

'Some policemen were heavy-handed on occasions, but...'

'They were rough with those women who marched on Buckingham Palace.' I thought back to newspaper reports of that day. 'They grabbed their breasts and forced them to the ground and lifted their skirts.'

'Some policemen behaved appallingly towards suffragettes. The rumour is they were encouraged to. But I'm not sure they'd force a woman to jump into a river.' She touched my arm. 'Don't take what that waterman said too seriously. He was probably exaggerating.'

I wasn't convinced – he'd seemed so certain. I sipped my brandy and took in my surroundings for the first time. I noticed how many MPs were huddled around tables in the dimly lit tavern.

Mrs Siddons followed my gaze. 'More decisions are made here than they are in Parliament.' She clearly knew how things worked in this world. And how to play the game.

My family had known Sybil Siddons as a passing acquaintance in Walden but lost touch after our move to London. A few days after Mother's death, she'd turned up on our doorstep with the offer of help.

At the time, Mrs Siddons had been a suffragist, a member of the National Union of Women's Suffrage Societies. Their aim was to achieve women's suffrage through peaceful and legal means by introducing parliamentary bills. My mother had been a suffragette, a member of Emmeline Pankhurst's more militant Women's Social and Political Union. Their motto was 'Deeds not Words', and they lived up to this by carrying out campaigns of vandalism and civil disobedience.

How I wished my mother had taken Mrs Siddons route of using her wits to gain a position of power rather than throwing herself physically at the problem.

'What did they say when you went to see them?' I asked.

'Who?' Mrs Siddons looked at me in confusion.

'The WSPU.' My thoughts drifted back to the aftermath of my mother's death. 'You went to their headquarters at Lincoln's Inn House afterwards, didn't you? What did they think happened to Mother?'

'They didn't know. They assumed she'd fallen in her haste to get away.'

'Did they think someone was chasing her?' I regretted not going to see them myself.

She shook her head. 'They would've told me if they thought she'd been forced into the water. You know what they were like. They would have shouted it from the rooftops if someone in authority had caused her death.'

This was true. 'The year before Mother died, I walked with her in Emily Wilding Davison's funeral procession. I'd just turned fourteen and had to wear a white dress with a purple sash and carry a handful of white lilies.' I still recoiled at the memory. 'I wanted to honour Emily, but I hated it. The crowds were overwhelming.'

The suffragettes had planned a similar event for my mother's funeral. But Mrs Siddons had managed to keep them at bay. She'd also persuaded Reverend Childs to allow Mother to be buried at St Martha's Church in Walden. 'I don't know how we would have managed them without you.'

'They were becoming too militant. Even some of their own members thought so.' She drank the last of her brandy. 'Occasionally I spoke to Emmeline about it, usually when the WSPU was overstepping the mark.'

'Which they often did.' I let my anger show. 'I'm so glad we were able to take her back to Walden. Away from them.'

'I know you hold them responsible for what happened. But they felt they had no choice. It's thanks to women like your mother we now have some political representation.'

'Do you think she was willing to die for the cause?' My hostility wasn't just directed at the WSPU. As soon as that gruff voice had said my mother didn't fall, I'd known what was coming next.

'I think you're giving too much credence to what that waterman said.' She sighed. 'I'd hoped today would make you feel less angry with your mother. You should be proud of her.'

I didn't reply.

* * *

'Did the police ever speak to Mother about what happened at the House of Commons?' I asked Aunt Maud that evening.

It was the first chance I'd had to speak to her alone. After interrogating me about my trip to Westminster, Gran had finally gone up to bed at ten o'clock, declaring that green silk on a woman of Mrs Siddons age was vulgar.

'They had enough on their plates with the demonstration at Buckingham Palace. They charged nearly seventy women at Bow Street. Even Mrs Pankhurst was arrested. Violet was one less suffragette to deal with.' She placed two mugs of cocoa on the small parlour table. 'I think they knew she was damaged beyond repair and unlikely to cause them any more problems.'

Mother had always been a slight woman, and her two prison sentences had made her even thinner. Hunger strikes and force-feeding had taken their toll, but we'd managed to nurse her back to health. This time had been different. The filthy Thames water had entered her already-weak stomach. Her body began to shut down, and her pale skin took on a strange blue tinge. I spent hours sitting by her bed, holding her limp hand. The pain that seared through me when she died evolved into resentment and anger.

Aunt Maud had tried to give me Mother's medals – the portcullis brooch she was awarded after her first time in prison and her hunger strike medals – but I'd told her to throw them away. I wondered what had become of them.

'When we left the Commons, we stopped at the place where Mother fell into the river. A waterman said he'd seen her jump. He helped her get out of the water.'

'What?' My aunt looked incensed.

'He said she didn't fall. She jumped.'

'No, that's not true. You know she wouldn't have done that.'

'What made her go to the House of Commons? Who came up with the idea?'

'It was something they cooked up at Lincoln's Inn House. With the police out of the way, they thought it was their chance to have another go at the Ladies' Gallery.'

'She can't have gone alone. Who went with her? Why didn't they help her?'

'I think there were two or three of them.' She stirred her cocoa.

'What were their names?'

'I believe one was Rebecca Dent. Do you remember her?'

I shook my head. 'Do you still see her?' I needed to talk to this woman. Even though it may not be true, I couldn't ignore what the waterman had said. I had to know why my mother had ended up in the Thames.

'I haven't seen her for years. When I helped out at the soup kitchens during the war, I came across a few of your mother's old friends. One of them told me Rebecca had gone missing.'

'Missing? What do you mean?'

'She disappeared. At the start of the war.'

4

'Was she killed during the bombings? Her body not found?' I thought of the Zeppelin raids on Hither Green in 1917.

'No, nothing like that. Rebecca didn't live in London. She lived in Walden.' Aunt Maud pulled her shawl around her. The fire was nothing but embers, but we'd face the wrath of Gran if we put more coals on at this time of night.

'Walden?' I thought my mother had become involved with the cause after we'd moved to London. I couldn't imagine a Walden branch of the WSPU.

'She was a servant to that lady you mentioned the other day.'

'What lady?' I shivered and sipped my cocoa. I was longing for the warmth of my bed but curious to hear more.

'Lady Timpson. The one who's standing in the election.'

I almost choked on my drink. 'A suffragette worked for the Timpsons?'

'I don't suppose she told them. She'd have lost her position if she had. Though I suppose it must have come out later.'

'But what happened to her?'

Aunt Maud shrugged. 'She just disappeared. I don't know anything beyond that.'

'Who else was with Mother that day? You said there were three of them.'

'I think one of them might have been Rebecca, but I'm not certain.'

'Could we go to Lincoln's Inn House? Try to find out?' I needed to know more, and this seemed the best place to start.

'The WSPU disbanded during the war. I'm not sure how we'd contact them now.'

'When did you hear Rebecca was missing?'

'She'd been gone for about three years when someone told me. I think it was 1917. The Pankhursts were involved in the war effort and I went along to a few of their fundraisers.' She took a poker and bent down to try to stoke the coals back to life. 'I must admit, I avoided meeting your mother's suffragette friends after she died.'

'I would have too.'

'I tried not to be bitter. But seeing them go about their lives as if nothing had happened upset me. We'd lost Violet, and I was angry.' My aunt kept poking the grate. 'But as the war went on—'

'They suffered losses too?' I finished her sentence. My grief and anger had gone through a similar transition.

'Fathers, husbands, sons. All that waiting and not knowing. Dreading the arrival of a telegram. I couldn't stay angry.' She sank back into her armchair. 'It's funny, now it's all over, I see the same resentment in those who lost loved ones in the war when they talk to people who came through it unscathed.'

I knew what she meant. Not for the first time, I felt the overwhelming sense of relief that the war had finally ended.

* * *

Early next morning, I crept downstairs, careful not to rouse Gran. I stepped out onto Brightside Road, looking up at the windows of the soot-covered house before walking up to Hither Green Lane. I passed Glenview Road, where there was still a gaping hole in the landscape. Three homes had been destroyed in a Zeppelin raid in October 1917, killing fifteen people, ten of them children.

On Hither Green Lane, I stopped outside the terraced house my father had sold the year before. It had once been our happy family home. That seemed like a lifetime ago. I crossed the road and walked alongside the high wall surrounding the Park Fever Hospital.

When I reached the iron gate, I peered through at the hospital campus and the water tower. A few months after my mother's death, war was declared, and I'd been sent to Exeter to stay with my father's parents. When I was seventeen, I joined the Voluntary Aid Detachment and returned to Hither Green Lane. I got a posting at the Park Fever Hospital, which was being used to accommodate some of the thousands of refugees that had fled occupied Belgium.

The following year, I'd been transferred to Lewisham Military Hospital. I was considered too young for nursing duties but could do menial tasks such as clearing up blood and vomit and washing out bedpans. I'd been unprepared for the relentless stream of casualties. Those long days on the wards had forced me to bury my grief and concentrate on work. But now I worried I'd buried too much. My memories of my mother were beginning to fade. That scared me. Sometimes I struggled to picture her face.

Like many others, I lost my sense of purpose when the war ended. I only regained it when I started to work for Elijah at *The Walden Herald*.

* * *

I returned to Brightside Road, closed the door on the war-ravaged streets and followed the trail of my grandmother's gardenia scent into the dining room.

'You could have asked Mrs Siddons to come here, you know.' Gran lowered herself slowly into her chair whilst my aunt put a cushion behind her back.

'She had to attend to some business in Westminster.' I lied.

'Probably for the best.' Gran sniffed. 'There have been rumours about her and Lloyd George, you know.'

This was why I'd arranged to meet Mrs Siddons at the House of Commons. You never knew what my gran was going to say.

Aunt Maud placed a rack of toast on the breakfast table. Shorter, rounder, and kinder than Gran, her soft brown hair and smiling eyes were the same as my mother's. This relieved me. I examined her figure and wondered whether Mother would have grown plumper as she got older.

'Was your father happy about you going there?' Gran watched me over the top of her spectacles.

'No. But he understood. He said we must learn to move on.'

My grandmother's nostrils flared. She had no intention of moving on.

'You were right to accept her invitation.' My aunt put a boiled egg in front of Gran. 'How's the election going? Do you think Mrs Siddons will win?'

I could tell she wanted to move the conversation away from the painful subject of Mother.

'I'm not sure. She's popular in Walden but not so much in Aldershot. Lady Timpson's been making generous donations to army charities, and the military holds the most sway in that area.'

'Who's the Labour candidate?' She began to slather jam onto a slice of toast.

'Mr Donald Anstey. We don't know much about him. Elijah's arranging an interview.'

'Hasn't that old rogue smoked and drunk himself to death yet?' Gran interrupted.

'Two women standing in one constituency is a major step forward,' my aunt commented.

I was about to reply, but Gran cut in again.

'Isn't it enough to be a wife and a mother? Violet would still be alive if it weren't for all this nonsense.'

'Don't belittle what she fought for,' Aunt Maud snapped.

'No, it's not enough.' My words didn't come out as forcefully as I'd intended. Because in a private corner of my heart, I wished it *had* been enough for my mother.

After breakfast, I escaped upstairs to what had been Mother's childhood bedroom. Although it was a comfort to sleep there, I felt oddly displaced. Just as Walden was starting to feel like home, my trip to Westminster had dragged me back into the past. I was no longer sure where I belonged.

* * *

'Did you know where Mother was going that day?' I'd returned to Walden in an unsettled mood. Over dinner, I couldn't resist tackling my father on the subject.

'I thought she was marching on Buckingham Palace with the others.' He adopted the patient tone he always used when discussing my mother. Or, to be more accurate, my mother's death.

'Did you try to stop her?'

'Of course I did. I knew the police would be out in force. I was worried the demonstration would turn violent.'

'What did she say?'

'She told me not to worry. She said she'd be miles away from any danger. I didn't think she meant at Westminster.' Father tried to focus on his dinner.

'Were there others with her? At the House of Commons, I mean?'

'Probably.' He continued to eat.

'How many? Who were they?'

He paused as he finished his mouthful. 'I don't know.'

'A waterman told us he saw her jump into the river.'

Father went to eat again but stopped. His brow creased. 'You know she wouldn't have done that.'

'Why did he say it then?'

'No doubt the story's become exaggerated over the years. This man probably wasn't even there. Violet wouldn't have jumped.' Father pushed his plate away. 'She died in a tragic accident. There's nothing more to say.'

'How do you know it was an accident? You weren't there. You don't know what went on, and it sounds like you never bothered to find out.' I regretted the words as soon as they left my mouth.

'Iris.' He screwed up his napkin. 'Your mother could be reckless. I tried to keep her safe, but she made it very difficult.' He closed his eyes and rubbed the bridge of his nose.

Mother had been stubborn. She wouldn't argue, she simply ignored what anyone said. She'd kiss Father and me on the cheek and then disappear on her latest crusade. It had been pointless pleading with her.

But what had been her intention that day? Why had she ended up in the river? Had it been part of her plan to make the protest more radical?

'I'm sorry.' I was being unfair, taking my frustration out on my father. 'I just want to find out what happened.'

'I can understand that, but there's nothing I can tell you.'

I decided to try a different approach. 'Did you know Rebecca Dent?'

'Yes. She was a friend of your mother's. Why?'

'She went missing. In 1914, around the time war was declared.'

'I never heard about it when I was in Walden in '16.'

Father and Elijah had been recruited into the Intelligence Corps because of their contacts with overseas news agencies. For a while, Father had been billeted at Mill Ponds, a large mansion on the edge of Waldenmere. Its owner, General Cheverton, had given his home over to the war effort, and it had been used as a training academy.

'Her disappearance doesn't seem to have caused much of a stir. If Constance Timpson had gone missing, the whole country would know. Yet a servant from the same house doesn't warrant a mention.'

'The war dominated the headlines. But I'm still surprised I didn't hear about it,' Father said. 'Shame we didn't have a local newspaper back then. Elijah would have put it on the front page of *The Walden Herald*.'

He was right. Elijah would have investigated it. And kept it in people's minds. Could I persuade him to do anything about it six years on?

'How did Mother and Rebecca become friends?'

'They met at a WSPU meeting in London.'

'I thought they must have known each other here in Walden.'

'Only by sight. When Rebecca realised your mother had recognised her, she asked her not to tell anyone she was a suffragette. She said she'd be turned out of service if her employer found out. She didn't want anyone in Walden knowing.'

'I don't remember ever meeting Rebecca.'

'We didn't socialise with her when we were here. It might have raised eyebrows. But once we moved to London, Rebecca sometimes came to our house. She did the most beautiful embroidery. She once showed you how to sew.'

'I remember,' I exclaimed. I'd sat at the dining table with Mother, Aunt Maud and Rebecca, embroidering violet flowers onto purple and green sashes. 'She was tall with long, blonde hair.'

'That's right. An attractive woman. And intelligent. She had no formal education, but she was well read.'

'She was quite young, wasn't she?'

'She was around twenty-five last time I saw her, early in 1914.'

'I can't believe she's just been forgotten.' Now I could put a face to the name, I was even more determined to find out what had happened to her.

'Nor can I. It sounds like none of the papers bothered about her at the time.' He waved a finger. 'Too busy demonising the Germans.'

This was a familiar theme of my father's. He'd become exasperated with the propaganda circulated by the government and military. And, particularly, newspaper proprietors. After the war, he'd left *The Daily Telegraph* to become a freelance writer. He now worked for various news syndicates.

I wondered if I could persuade Elijah to publish an article on Rebecca. It was the only way I could think of to reignite some interest in the case. Her disappearance could be linked with the House of Commons protest – and if I found out what happened to her – I might discover more about my mother's death.

* * *

'I've never heard of Rebecca Dent.' Elijah leant back in his chair. 'But the war had just started. I don't suppose the story made it onto the front page.'

'I don't think it made it onto any page. But Lord and Lady Timpson must have reported her disappearance to the police.'

'Talk to Ben Gilbert.' Elijah waved his cigarette at me. 'It was before he became a constable but he can have a dig around. I'd be interested to know what the police found out. It doesn't sound like there was much of an investigation, but we can't jump to conclusions.'

'Can we put something in the paper?' I flapped away the smoke that was wafting into my face.

'Not now. Not with the election coming up. It might look like we were trying to somehow discredit Lady Timpson. See what Ben finds out first.'

I was disappointed, but I could see his point. I went back to my desk.

'Forget about this Rebecca for the time being,' he called. 'And start doing your homework. We're interviewing Donald Anstey at ten tomorrow. He lives on Church Road, so come straight to my cottage. We can walk from there.'

* * *

The following morning, I knocked on the front door of what had been my childhood home.

Elijah had bought the cottage in 1895 to use as a weekend retreat. At that time, he was living in London but escaped from the city when he could. He was sent on an overseas assignment in 1898 and rented the place to my newly married parents. I was born there a year later. When we moved to London in 1913, Elijah came back to live in the house.

Donald Anstey's home was further down Church Road, past St Martha's Church. It was only a short walk, but Elijah was quickly out of breath. I slowed my pace, struggling not to stride ahead.

He stopped outside a red-brick cottage and rapped on the front door. When it opened, I experienced a jolt of recognition.

Donald Anstey was the man I'd seen on the jetty by the station, dropping sweet violets into Waldenmere.

5

'I think I saw you the other day. On the jetty by the station?' I could examine Donald Anstey more closely now. He was a pleasant-looking man with light-brown hair, greying slightly at the temples. At a guess, he was in his mid-thirties.

'I often walk at Waldenmere. It helps me to arrange my thoughts.' He gave me that same sad smile, as though he knew who I was.

We were standing in a narrow hallway covered in faded green wallpaper and hung with a series of watercolours of Scottish lochs. The cottage was compact for such a tall man, and he had to stoop to pass through the door into the parlour.

I expected him to say more regarding our encounter, but he was silent. I wanted to ask about the flowers. But I could hardly demand to know why he'd dropped some sweet violets into the lake.

'What made you want to enter politics, Mr Anstey?' Elijah sat down heavily in one of the shabby armchairs. The parlour was decorated in the same green wallcovering with more Scottish scenes, this time watercolours of highland glens.

I perched on the edge of an armchair and took out my note-book. I was inexperienced at recording meetings and hoped the conversation wouldn't move too fast.

'Before the war, I was a clerk for the Board of Agriculture and Fisheries. I saw first-hand how government operated. It's all old boys. Lord this and Sir that.' He spoke with a soft Scottish accent. 'Rich aristocrats with no idea about the lives of normal working people. Then I heard a speech by Keir Hardie. He was a great man. Suddenly my vocation became clear, and I joined the Labour Party.'

Instead of talking about the local area, Donald explained his party's politics and how working people, trade unions and social-ists should unite to force change.

'Do you support women's rights?' Elijah asked.

'Oh yes.' He nodded.

'Do you welcome more women in Parliament?'

'Yes.'

'How do you feel about standing against two women?'

He paused. 'Humbled.'

'How long have you lived in Walden?'

Longer pause. 'About a year.'

I soon realised I wasn't going to struggle to keep up with this conversation. Donald took his time to consider each question before giving a slow, measured and usually brief response.

'What made you come here?'

'I used to live in London, but when I came back from fighting overseas, I wanted to be somewhere quieter.'

'What specific plans do you have to improve the lives of your constituents?'

Another long pause. 'I'd like to see more provision for the care of vulnerable and elderly people as well as our war veterans. And we desperately need to provide housing for poorer families.' He stopped, seeming to reflect on what he'd just said.

I drummed my fingers on the arm of the chair. I couldn't help thinking Donald Anstey was going to be a disaster at public speaking.

'When you say more housing is needed locally, do you have a particular location in mind?' Elijah looked determined to pin him down on something. When the inevitable silence followed, I smirked at his exasperated expression.

Eventually, Donald spoke. 'I'm drafting plans for quite an ambitious project. If I'm elected, it will be my top priority.' He stopped, seemingly worried that he'd said too much. My pencil hovered in mid-air.

'Whereabouts?' Elijah persevered. We had to write something that would be relevant to local people, not generic Labour Party policies.

Donald finally took the plunge. 'There are a number of slum dwellings on the Basingstoke Canal, opposite Crookham Hall – caravans and shacks around the Moffats' farmhouse. The facilities are a disgrace, and young children are living there. These people need proper houses, and this is where we should build them.'

The vigour of his answer took me by surprise, and I hurried to scribble it down. Samuel Moffat had inherited the farmhouse when his parents had died a year earlier. And he was no farmer. I'd heard some of his wartime comrades had found themselves homeless, and Samuel was letting them camp on his farm. The place was in a terrible state, and this unofficial campsite had spilt over onto council land.

'Interesting idea.' Elijah perked up. This could be controversial. 'But one that's likely to generate opposition.'

'I know the Timpsons want to clear the site. But where do they expect these people to go? It's mostly council land they're on. I believe we can raise enough funds to build decent homes that these families can rent. They're living in poverty and squalor, and in this day and age, that's unacceptable.'

'The Moffats still own the farmhouse and a bit of land,' Elijah said.

'They'll be glad to be shot of it. The place is falling down around them.' He clearly wasn't to be deterred from his plan.

'Lord and Lady Timpson are unlikely to welcome the current tenants as permanent neighbours.' Elijah smiled, probably imagining the tension this would create between the two candidates.

'My manifesto is about building a fairer society with greater social justice and more rights for workers. I've no interest in the feelings of the aristocracy.'

Although he'd become more animated as he'd outlined his plan, I still wasn't sure Mr Anstey was going to be forceful enough to compete with Mrs Siddons or Lady Timpson on the hustings. But I didn't doubt his integrity. I was beginning to warm to him – then, as we were leaving, he said, 'I'm sorry for what happened to your mother. Such a tragic loss.'

His words took me by surprise. I nodded but didn't reply.

* * *

'How does he know about my mother?' I demanded as we strolled up the lane. For some reason, mention of her had caused my feelings of goodwill towards Donald Anstey to evaporate.

Elijah took out his cigarettes. 'He probably recognised your name and put two and two together. He's an interesting chap. There's merit to his plans for building new houses near Crookham.'

'He's boring. We can't support him.'

'Thank you for your unbiased opinion.'

I ignored his sarcasm. 'When I saw him the other day by the lake, he was throwing sweet violets into the water.'

'Sweet violets?'

'Don't you think that's strange?'

'Maybe they were in memory of someone he lost.'

'I think he's odd.' I stopped outside St Martha's Church. 'I'm going to visit Mother's grave.'

'Iris.' I could see he was trying to find the right words. 'Don't dwell on the past. You're a bright girl. You should be looking to the future.'

As a child, Elijah had been like an uncle to me. But when my mother died, he'd been unsure how to deal with an angry four-teen-year-old. In hindsight, I realised it couldn't have been easy for him. He'd never married or had children of his own. I hadn't seen much of him during the war, but now he was my boss we were starting to form a new relationship.

He walked away, calling over his shoulder. 'Don't be long. I need you back in the office.'

* * *

After work, I went in search of Ben Gilbert and found him in the town hall, helping his mother and Alice clear up after a meeting of the Walden Women's Group.

When I'd moved back to Walden, I'd been shocked to find the little blond boy I'd played with as a child had become a police constable. He was now a burly young man with a shock of sandy hair. He was also attractive. Something that hadn't passed Alice by.

'Did you want me?' He was in the middle of dismantling a trestle table. 'I was about to walk Alice home.'

I saw the sharp look his mother gave him and could guess the reason for it. If he was spotted too often in Alice's company, her father might get wind of it.

'We can talk on the way.'

It was a chilly evening but still light. I was keen to leave the hall as I could see Mrs Gilbert eyeing me up. She and Alice wanted me to join their group, but I wasn't ready for committees just yet.

We left Mrs Gilbert to lock up and took the canal towpath that led to Waldenmere. 'Have you ever heard of a woman called Rebecca Dent?'

'No, I don't think so,' Ben replied. 'Why?'

'She worked as a maid for Lord and Lady Timpson. She went missing in August 1914, I think.'

'I remember,' Alice said. 'Everyone was talking about it at the time. But with the war, it was forgotten.'

'Did anyone look for her?'

'I think Lord Timpson organised a search of the grounds.'

'What did people think happened to her? What did the gossips say?'

Alice smiled. 'That she'd left because she couldn't put up with Lady Timpson any more. There was a rumour she was seeing a man and had run off with him.'

I was curious to see Crookham Hall. To search the estate would indicate there were concerns something bad may have happened to Rebecca.

'What's Constance Timpson like now? You said you went to dances at the hall?'

'I like her,' Alice replied. 'She's frightfully clever, but she isn't condescending or anything like that. She must have found us locals pretty dull, but she didn't show it.'

'I would have been about thirteen the last time I saw her. It was just before we moved to London.' I was wondering if I could renew my friendship with Constance. 'What's Lady Timpson like?'

Delphina, Lady Timpson, née Hinchcliffe, came from a wealthy industrial family. She'd inherited Hinchcliffe Holdings at the age of twenty-one after her father's death in 1889. Contrary to expectations, she'd single-handedly run the business and made it even more successful than it had been in her father's day. At the age of thirty, she'd unexpectedly married Lord Timpson and moved from her home town of Barnsley to his ancestral home, Crookham Hall. She renamed the business Timpson Foods, and it went from strength to strength.

'She is condescending.' Alice laughed. 'Lady of the manor. Very domineering. She bosses poor Constance and Daniel around terribly.'

'Daniel?' I asked.

'Constance's older brother. I saw him a few times at the beginning of the war, but then he joined up. He's rather sweet but the outdoors type. He doesn't say much. Constance apologised for him. Said he was happiest running the estate and wasn't comfortable with social chit chat.'

'What about Lord Timpson?'

'He's lovely. Completely different from his wife. Very charming. I don't know why he married her.'

'Money?' I speculated.

'That's the rumour,' she admitted. 'Crookham Hall is an expensive place to maintain. And she wanted a title.'

'So a matrimonial deal was done? Why couldn't he sell the family jewels? Doesn't he own some famous sapphire?'

'He couldn't sell the Star Sapphire.' Alice looked shocked. 'It's been in the Timpson family for a hundred years. One of his ancestors acquired it in Burma during a war in the 1820s, I think.'

By *acquired*, I presumed she meant that soldiers had taken it during the conflict.

'Have you ever seen it?'

She shook her head. 'I was hoping Lady Timpson or Constance would wear it to one of the dances. But I suppose it was considered too ostentatious during wartime. Though Lady Timpson doesn't seem the sort to let that bother her.'

Lady Timpson sounded like a fascinating character. I hoped I'd get to meet her.

'Look, Ben. The kingfisher's back.' Alice pointed to a flash of turquoise on the other side of the bank.

We followed the kingfisher's route along Grebe Stream until we reached Heron Bay and watched the bird swoop low as it searched for prey. I wondered how much time Alice and Ben spent alone together by the lake.

'How did your mother know Rebecca Dent?' Ben asked as he pushed away the tendrils of a willow that were threatening to become entangled in Alice's long hair.

'She was a suffragette.'

'Rebecca Dent was a suffragette?' Alice exclaimed. 'No one said anything at the time.'

'I bet that didn't go down well with the Timpsons.' Ben held back more overgrown willow to allow us a clear route to the footpath. 'How did you find out?'

'Rebecca was with my mother when she broke into the House of Commons.'

His eyes narrowed. 'And no one knew this at the time of her disappearance?'

I shook my head.

We stopped at the foot of the hill that led up to Sand Hills Hall. Ben knew better than to accompany Alice any further. The hall overlooked Waldenmere from the top of a slope on the eastern side. Running down the hill were the remains of a wooden jetty used to launch floatplanes. A few wooden posts were all that remained at the top, but the lower half still jutted out into the water like an abandoned pier. We stood under it, looking out at the grey water.

'I'll talk to Superintendent Cobbe in Aldershot. He'll remember the case. He might let me look at the records.'

'What has made you curious about this Rebecca?' Alice asked.

I hesitated. Then I told them what the waterman had said about my mother.

'It may not be true.' Ben frowned. 'Why would she jump?'

'She couldn't swim. I can only think...' To my shame, my voice cracked. 'I can't help but wonder if she decided to jump as a form of protest. Even if it meant...'

I left the sentence unfinished.

6

I was typing an article on the by-election when Ben poked his head around the office door.

'Have you seen the files on Rebecca?' I asked before he could say anything.

Elijah was in his den with the door open.

'I don't want to interrupt your work. I can meet you later?' he whispered.

'Come in here, the pair of you,' Elijah called. 'I want to hear what you've found out about this Rebecca Dent.'

We did as we were told, immersing ourselves in a cloud of smog as we sat in front of his desk.

Ben took out his notebook. 'She went to work at Crookham Hall at the age of fifteen after her mother died. She had no other family. She started as a laundry maid and then became a housemaid. In May 1914, she was promoted to Head Housemaid. She was twenty-five when she disappeared during the night of thirteenth of August 1914. The housekeeper said that Rebecca would normally get up at 6 a.m. and make sure everything was in order before the family came down to breakfast. On Saturday the fourteenth, there was no sign of her. The cook thought she must have been taken ill, and a maid was sent up to her room, but she wasn't there.'

'What did she do the day before?' I wafted away cigarette fumes.

He skimmed his notes. 'She'd gone up to London, which she often did when she had a day off. She came home at around five-thirty and had dinner in the kitchen with the other staff, then retired to her room.'

'Then what?' I got up and opened the window, despite Elijah moaning about the draught.

'No one knows. She hasn't been seen since.'

'She must have left the hall again,' Elijah said.

'Her bed hadn't been slept in. Everything in her room was as usual.'

'Did anyone hear her go out?' I asked.

'No. Lord and Lady Timpson were in London that weekend. The rest of the family had retired to bed at about ten o'clock. The staff were mostly in their rooms – a few were still doing duties around the house. Since becoming Head Housemaid, Rebecca had a bedroom to herself.'

Elijah frowned. 'Nothing was missing?'

'The housekeeper reported the matter to Lady Timpson on her return, and Rebecca's room was searched. Nothing seemed to be out of the ordinary. Her clothes and personal possessions were still there.'

'Who reported her disappearance to the police?' I was curious to know how the Timpsons had reacted.

'The housekeeper. This was a few days later.'

'The Timpsons did nothing? Weren't they concerned? This was a woman who'd worked for them for years.'

'There was nothing to suggest anything untoward had happened to her. On the other hand, it didn't seem like she'd run away either. At some point, Lord Timpson organised a search of the estate. Then later, when there'd been no progress, he wrote a letter to an acquaintance of his at Scotland Yard asking him to investigate the matter.'

'He's the only one who seems to have shown any concern for her,' I remarked.

'Did you talk to Superintendent Cobbe about it?' Elijah asked.

'He showed me the interview notes he made at the time. It seems Rebecca was a private person. The servants couldn't tell him much. There was a rumour she was seeing a man, but no one could say who he was.'

'He could have been a cover for her suffragette activities,' I suggested. 'A made-up boyfriend to explain her regular trips to London?'

'Literature in her room indicated she had sympathies with the suffragist movement, but nothing linked her to any group,' Ben said. 'She kept that side of her life hidden from the other servants.'

'Did the police look into the suffragette angle?' Elijah asked.

'They did some digging. Rebecca joined the Women's Freedom Movement in 1908, so she'd been involved for some time.' Ben flipped over a page of his notepad. 'It appears she switched her allegiance to the WSPU in 1912.'

The year she'd met Mother at a meeting. 'What happened to Rebecca's things?'

'There's a note to say the housekeeper packed all her possessions in a trunk and stored them in the attic in case Rebecca returned.'

'Could we go and look at them?'

'No. The Super doesn't want to pursue the matter. Not after all this time.' Ben closed his notebook and replaced it in his pocket. 'He'd never agree to me approaching the Timpsons about it.'

'When are we interviewing Lady Timpson?' I asked after Ben left.

'Early next week.'

'Where?'

'At Crookham Hall.' Elijah eyed me warily.

'Could we ask about Rebecca when we talk to her?'

He lit a cigarette and frowned. 'I'm not sure.'

* * *

Crookham Hall lived up to my expectations of what a stately home should look like. I'd read that most of the hall was Georgian, built in 1728. It was a typical three-storey country house of the time, with rows of symmetrical windows and two tall pillars at the entrance. In the nineteenth century, new wings were constructed to form a three-sided square enclosing a courtyard.

I loved it when my job gave me access to people and places I wouldn't normally come into contact with. I certainly didn't move in the same social circles as the Timpsons. I knew Constance from our days at Miss Cotton's Academy, but that was purely due to the lack of schools for girls. Daughters of upper and middle-class families mixed at the academy as there was no other place for them. When Constance had rebelled against having a governess, she'd ended up at Miss Cotton's.

'Mr Whittle and Miss Woodmore.' The butler showed us into a vast reception room.

Tall windows framed the rolling pastures to the side of the hall. It gave me the impression of being outdoors – then I realised the room was decorated to complement the landscape outside. One wall was covered in silk paper patterned with trailing wisteria and the other three painted a pale green. The sofas were upholstered in green velvet and the windows draped in flowing silk-damask curtains. The furniture was mahogany, and the polished wooden floor stained a dark brown.

To my surprise, the whole family was present. We'd expected to interview Lady Timpson on her own. Elijah appeared as taken aback as I felt at being thrust into this formal social setting.

Lord Timpson was standing by the mantelpiece smoking a cigar. He was a handsome man with light blue eyes and soft grey hair. His son, Daniel, was next to the window, staring out at the fields in the distance, while Constance was seated beside her mother on the sofa.

'Iris, how lovely to see you again. Mr Whittle, so good of you to come. Please take a seat.' Constance gestured to the small sofa opposite. When I last saw her, she'd been a thin, serious-faced girl of thirteen, always reading a book. She'd grown into an elegant young woman with long brown hair and dark blue eyes. She wore a mauve satin dress that accentuated her slender figure.

Lady Timpson leant forward on the green velvet sofa and beamed at us. She was wearing a rather sombre business suit consisting of a fitted navy jacket and full-length skirt in the style of Lady Astor. In the newspaper photographs I'd seen of her, Lady Timpson was always wearing a stylish dress. Evidently, like Lady Astor, she'd decided to adopt a new look to mark her political career. Presumably, to avoid some of the commentary on her fashion choices.

'Welcome to Crookham Hall. So kind of you to come,' she said. 'You may be surprised to find us all here to greet you, but my husband and children insisted on joining me this morning.'

I didn't think this was true. Daniel Timpson looked as though he'd rather be anywhere else. He smiled obligingly at his mother, then went back to gazing out of the window. Surrounding the hall was three thousand acres of farmland, woodland and pastures. From what Alice had said, this is where he would rather be.

'They're as keen as I am to talk about how we can help those in need in our community,' Lady Timpson continued. 'We're a team. When people vote for a Timpson, they don't just get me, they get my whole family.'

It was a shrewd move. Male voters were more likely to vote for a woman if they thought there was a man behind her.

'Mother is a great believer in social reform.' Constance appeared more at ease than her brother. 'We want to support her in her efforts.'

Lord Timpson smiled at his daughter. 'The Timpsons have always been generous benefactors to our less fortunate neighbours.'

'Perhaps, Lady Timpson, you could explain what social issues you intend to tackle?' Elijah asked.

'I feel we must do more for our war veterans. After all, Aldershot is the home of the British Army. We should be setting an example to the rest of the country.'

'How do you intend to support ex-soldiers?'

'By increasing the employment opportunities in this region. Having fought for their country, our brave boys should be coming home to jobs. I have some ambitious plans in this respect.'

'Could you share those plans with us?'

'All will be revealed in good time, Mr Whittle. I'm still negotiating certain aspects. However, I can reveal that I intend to use my food production business to purchase more land to help local farmers. Now the war is over, it's time to start investing again.'

'I recall that you acquired many parcels of lands just before and during the war. Land that had been earmarked for protection by the Society for the Promotion of Nature Reserves?'

I glanced at Elijah in surprise. I knew nothing about this.

'I do understand the concerns of societies like the SPNR.' Lady Timpson sighed as if this were a tiresome subject. 'But with the war looming, the priority was to ensure our country didn't go hungry. That's why the Board of Agriculture and Fisheries decided to give the land over to food production.'

'But—'

Lady Timpson interrupted. 'Now the war is over, it's time to focus on the future. The people of Britain should be proud of their country and proud to be part of its workforce. I intend to use my position as head of one of this country's most successful companies to help my constituency. I know people in high places, and I'm not ashamed to use my influence. As worthy as my fellow candidates may be, especially dear Sybil, they simply don't have the resources I have.'

Despite her years in Hampshire, there was still the hint of a soft Barnsley accent.

'It could be argued that becoming an MP will lead to a conflict of interest,' Elijah said dryly. 'How will you vote on matters that have a direct impact on your business? For instance, Mrs Siddons would like to see children between the ages of twelve and sixteen still in school. Not working in factories.'

'Dear Sybil is an old friend of mine. We agree on many issues, and I admire her stance on education. However, she needs to take into account the reality of working people's lives. Many households are reliant on the income their children provide. I refuse to take the bread from the mouths of hungry babies by not allowing young people to work in my factories. Instead, I ensure all my workers are paid a fair wage and are well looked after.'

Elijah continued to give examples of proposed labour laws that could financially impact Timpson Foods. I watched the family's reaction.

Lord Timpson inspected his manicured fingernails, while Constance contemplated her teacup. Daniel paid no attention to the conversation and stared at some horses in the distance.

'I will, of course, declare a conflict of interest when these debates come up for discussion in Parliament,' Lady Timpson replied. It was clear she wasn't going to offer any further comment, so Elijah moved on.

'There's one other matter I'd like to touch upon.'

'By all means.' She showed relief at the change of subject.

'One of your servants went missing in 1914. Miss Rebecca Dent. Have you had any news of her?'

There was a noticeable change in the atmosphere. Daniel's attention switched back to the room whilst his parents and Constance appeared startled by the question.

Lord Timpson was the first to recover. 'No, we haven't. Not a word.'

'Why do you ask, Mr Whittle?' Lady Timpson's brow creased. 'Have you heard anything of her?'

Elijah shook his head.

'Sad business.' Lord Timpson leant against the mantelpiece. 'We've never been able to find out what happened to Miss Dent. I'm not sure the police paid it the heed they ought, what with the war and all.'

'If *The Walden Herald* had existed, we would have publicised it to our readers. Now we have the benefit of a local newspaper, we could try appealing for information,' Elijah suggested.

Lord Timpson nodded. 'That's extremely decent of you.' His wife looked appalled.

'Perhaps after the election's over,' Elijah said, to Lady Timpson's obvious relief.

'We did everything we could to find that wretched woman. That's how we found out she was a suffragette,' Lady Timpson muttered in disgust. 'We had no idea what was going on.'

'Mother. There's nothing wrong with being a suffragette.'

Constance shot me an apologetic look. I wondered how much she knew.

'She deceived us. We don't owe her anything,' Lady Timpson continued. 'We should let sleeping dogs lie.'

'I liked Rebecca.' It was the first time Daniel had spoken, and everyone turned to look at him. 'I think she's still alive. She just needed to get away from here.'

A silence followed this odd statement.

Daniel's eyes rested on me. I met his appraising gaze, and he looked away. A year older than Constance, he was a good looking young man of twenty-two with long dark lashes and a youthful face.

'What Daniel means is, we searched the grounds after she went missing. But we didn't find anything.' Lord Timpson shot his son a reproving look. 'We think it's more likely she ran away.'

'Good riddance. Those women were criminals.' Lady Timpson was back on the subject of suffragettes. 'To think, we let her live under our roof, and all the time, she was one of those harpies.'

'We appreciate your concern, Mr Whittle.' Constance placed a warning hand on her mother's knee.

But there was no stopping Lady Timpson. 'Rebecca Dent probably ran away because she was involved in some ridiculous demonstration and was scared of being arrested.'

My cheeks were burning. But I had to admit there was a possibility Lady Timpson was right. Someone could have found out Rebecca had participated in the House of Commons protest and threatened to tell the police.

7

'I don't understand how someone in her position can be scathing about suffrage. So much for sisterhood.'

'I'm not surprised Rebecca ran away.' Elijah took out his cigarettes. 'Lady Timpson clearly didn't care for her.'

'We don't know that she did run away.' I gazed out of the carriage window at the pastures and woodland surrounding the hall.

'What's the alternative?'

'Lord Timpson ordered a search of the grounds after she'd gone missing. What was he expecting to find?'

'That Rebecca tripped and twisted her ankle while taking a stroll?' He struck a match. 'Or that his wife murdered the maid and dumped her body in the rose garden?'

I pulled down the carriage window. 'How did you know about Timpson Foods acquiring those parcels of land?'

'Mr Laffaye told me. There's a rumour she paid someone in Agriculture and Fisheries to give her a list of the sites the SPNR had earmarked for preservation. She used the information to buy up land cheaply.'

'That says a lot about her business ethics. Constance and Lord Timpson seemed embarrassed.'

'It's probably a feeling they're used to. Lady T has a reputation for flattening any obstacles in her path.'

'She didn't like it when you said you were going to mention Rebecca's disappearance in the paper.'

'That's not surprising. She plans to run a campaign based on the integrity of her family. Missing servants won't help her to portray a happy household.'

'She's hiding something.' I leant out of the window.

'First Anstey, and now Lady Timpson. You're not warming to Mrs Siddons' opponents, are you?' Elijah smirked.

I ignored him and watched Crookham Hall disappear from view. I had the feeling Lady Timpson knew more about Rebecca than she was letting on. And I intended to keep coming back to the hall until I found out what it was. To do that, I'd have to revive my friendship with Constance. In the meantime, I intended to sniff out everything I could on the Timpson family.

* * *

The following day, we headed to Grebe House to interview Mrs Siddons.

Of the four houses that overlooked Waldenmere, Grebe House was my favourite. It wasn't as imposing as Mill Ponds or Sand Hills Hall to the north of the lake, or as stylish as neighbouring Heron Bay Lodge, home of Horace Laffaye, but I loved its rustic charm. Ivy trailed over its gable roof and row of gabled windows. And it was in the advantageous position of overlooking Grebe Stream as it flowed into Waldenmere.

'Iris, Mr Whittle. Good of you to come.' Mrs Siddons was still resolutely ignoring newspaper comments on her love of jewellery and fine fabrics. Today she wore a full-length amethyst silk gown with a matching marcasite amethyst necklace.

We'd been invited for morning coffee, but this was no social call. Mrs Siddons got straight to business, outlining how she intended to establish six new schools in the district.

I belatedly realised I should have warned Elijah about the red velvet sofa. It was perfect for flopping into and pouring out your woes – it wasn't ideal for conducting an interview. He'd sunk into its depths, and I wasn't sure I'd be able to retrieve him. I wondered if it was a ploy by Mrs Siddons to keep visitors at her mercy whilst she looked on from a highbacked armchair.

'Do you know how many young soldiers recruited during the war couldn't read or write? Many were glad to enlist because it gave them a wage and three square meals a day. But how have we rewarded them for their service? Did they all have homes to come back to?' She carried on, clearly not expecting an answer to these questions. 'We have relatively high employment in our corner of Hampshire – what we need is more housing. Decent homes for families. Not makeshift shacks and caravans. I intend to ask the government for funds to build homes on the outskirts of town, maybe even create a new village between Walden and Aldershot.'

It seemed the shacks on the Moffats' land were set to become a political issue.

'What about the facilities needed to support these families?' Elijah managed to ask. In previous interviews, he'd attempted to guide the candidate through a series of questions. Mrs Siddons had her own agenda.

'I've covered the issue of schools, but medical provision must also be considered. I'd like Walden to have a cottage hospital to support the larger military hospital in Aldershot. I have a building in mind, but it would need to be connected to the main drainage and have central heating installed. If we can connect to the electricity supply as well, then we could try to raise funds to buy some x-ray equipment.'

I scribbled fast to record all of this. She'd carried out extensive research, and the speed and detail of her answers was in stark contrast to Donald Anstey's brief responses. It was nearly lunchtime before I extricated Elijah from the sofa, and we made our escape.

'Impressive, isn't she?'

We emerged from Grebe House to find the lake bathed in sunshine. I admired the view from Heron Bay whilst Elijah rummaged in his pockets for his cigarettes.

He grunted. 'I need a drink.'

I persisted. 'Mrs Siddons gave us enough material to write a forceful argument for why she has more to offer than the other candidates.'

He lit a cigarette. 'When it comes to education, I believe Mrs Siddons has the right approach,' he conceded. 'But Anstey had some good initiatives too.'

'One good initiative,' I answered. 'Not some.'

'Oh, Mr Whittle.' Horace Laffaye was waving at us from his front gate. Dressed in a well-cut suit with a homburg hat covering his closely cropped white-grey hair, his pristine appearance matched his home. Tucked in a copse of trees behind the bay, Heron Bay Lodge was a stylish wooden-clad house painted a soft shade of grey. It had a high-level veranda that overlooked Waldenmere. 'Would you care to join me in a nip of brandy? It's a special one I've had imported from France. It's not too early for a drink, is it? I'd feel so much more civilised if you'd take a glass with me.'

Elijah waved back at Horace. 'I most certainly would.'

He turned to me. 'I've got a task for you. Write a brief impartial profile of each candidate and their key pledges. I don't want to catch the slightest whiff of bias. Facts only, no rumours or tittle-tattle.'

I nodded. I'd liked to have seen inside Heron Bay Lodge, but I knew when I wasn't wanted.

In the office, I typed up the candidate profiles alongside their key pledges. By mid-afternoon, Elijah still hadn't returned. To while away the time, I put a fresh sheet of paper in the typewriter:

Lady Delphina Timpson – Conservative

Lady Timpson, 53, is a successful businesswoman with food production factories across the country. Rumour has it her father became rich by flouting labour laws and giving backhanders to corrupt local officials. It appears his daughter has carried on this family tradition by bribing an MP to help her buy up sites that had been earmarked for legal protection as nature reserves. Gossip says she married her husband for his title, and he married her for her money. She plans to use her wealth and position to buy votes. Although she's pledged investment to bring employment to the area, it's more likely to be another one of her money-making schemes to line her own pocket.

Mr Donald Anstey – Labour

Mr Anstey is 36 and single, probably because the only thing he's passionate about is the Labour Party. Apart from politics, he seems to have no life. He supports everything under the sun: women's rights, free healthcare for the sick and elderly, homes for war veterans, but has no idea how to achieve any of this. It's said his supporters bring camp beds to his public speeches as they know how long it takes him to reach the end of a sentence.

Mrs Sybil Siddons – Liberal

Mrs Siddons, 51, entered politics in 1901 after the death of her husband in the Boer War. She became an Alderman for Hampshire County Council and was instrumental in ensuring free schooling was available in all areas of the county. She campaigns for better education and tackles businesses that fail to adhere to child labour laws. She gets things done rather than endlessly pontificating like her male counterparts. I've heard it said she's on intimate terms with Prime Minister Lloyd George, but my grandmother may have made that up.

Hearing Elijah's heavy tread on the stairs, I took the paper from the typewriter, placed it on his desk and returned to my chair.

I smelt brandy and cigars as he walked past me into his den. A few minutes later, he gave a snort of laughter.

'In here,' he barked, waving the paper at me. 'Good job the printer didn't spot this and put it in the next edition. Now let me read the real profiles.'

I handed them to him and waited whilst he scanned the text.

He grunted a few times. 'They'll do.'

I was happy with that. 'Has Mr Laffaye indicated a preference for a particular candidate?'

'Not as yet.'

'Have you known him a long time?' I was curious about their relationship. To look at, they could hardly have been more different. Elijah cut a shambolic figure next to Horace, in his dapper suits.

'Our paths crossed over the years when I worked for the *Telegraph*. Then he settled in Walden in 1913.'

Like Father, Elijah had decided not to return to Fleet Street after the war. He'd intended to retire, but then Horace came up with the plan to launch *The Walden Herald*.

'What did Mr Laffaye do before his retirement?'

'He was a banker, though not your run-of-the-mill regional bank manager – as some locals thought when he first moved to the town.' He gave a short laugh.

'What do you mean?' *How did he become so rich* was what I really wanted to know.

'He's well-travelled. Name a country; he's been there. He spent a lot of time in America. They know Horace's name on Wall Street,' he said with pride.

'But he ended up in Walden,' I mused.

'It's as good a place as any.'

'I suppose so.' I hovered by the door. 'I'm going to London to get my hair cut on Saturday. I noticed the Society for the Promotion of Nature Reserves is giving a talk at the Natural History Museum. I might go along to find out more about them.'

'Hmm, well, don't stir that particular pot too hard. I'm not sure the paper needs to get on the wrong side of Lady Timpson.' He scrutinised me. 'Why can't you get your hair done here?'

'The bobbed cut hasn't reached Mrs Maskell's salon yet.'

'Is that what it's called?' He regarded my head as if seeing it in a new light.

'What do you know about the society?' I wanted to change the subject. My appearance was considered too modern for Walden. Until then, Elijah hadn't commented on my hair or clothes, and I wanted to keep it that way.

'Not much. It's just something Horace told me. I shouldn't have mentioned it.'

'It could have something to do with Rebecca's disappearance. After all, it was around the same time.'

'It's unlikely the two things are connected.' He eyed me warily. 'Be careful what you say. We can't afford any libel suits.'

'I'm only going to listen to a talk.' And perhaps ask a few questions whilst I was there.

'Since when have you been interested in nature?'

'I believe we should protect areas of natural beauty.'

'Hmmm,' he said suspiciously.

I didn't tell him that I also intended to go back to Westminster to see if I could speak to the waterman again.

8

I sniffed. The smell of setting lotion took me back to the first time Mother had brought me to Dolly's Salon in Lewisham when I was a teenager.

'Your Aunt Maud was in here again last week,' Dolly said. 'I'm sure she has her hair done so she can have a rest. Your gran runs her ragged these days.'

I gave a rueful smile. Even Dolly had noticed how demanding Gran had become. I picked up some magazines from the table and sat down in front of the mirror. A trip to Dolly's gave me a chance to read the beauty weeklies, ones that I pretended to my father I wasn't interested in. Flicking through the pages, it occurred to me how well Dolly Dawes knew my family. She'd been my mother's hairdresser for many years.

'I went to the House of Commons the other week to listen to a debate.' I watched her in the mirror as she started to trim my hair.

'Ah.'

'I went to the place where Mother fell into the river.'

She shook her head. 'That was a tragedy.'

'It's made me want to find out more about that day.'

'You're best off leaving things in the past, love.' She stopped cutting and gazed back at me. 'I knew your mother well enough to know she'd want you to be getting on with your life, not fretting about her.'

'Did any of Mother's suffragette friends come here?'

'A fair few. I sometimes went over to Lincoln's Inn House myself. I never joined, but I helped out when I could. If one of them came out of Holloway in a bad way, I'd go and do their hair for them. Try to get them looking right again. Shocking what they did to them in there.' She shuddered, then realised what she'd said. 'Sorry, love, you don't need me to tell you that.'

'It's alright.' I pushed the image of Mother's emaciated body from my mind. 'Did you know someone called Rebecca? Rebecca Dent.'

'I remember Miss Dent. She had a fine sheet of blonde hair. Always wanted me to make it look shiny for when she was meeting her fella.'

'When was that?' So the boyfriend had been real, not just a cover for her suffragette meetings.

'I haven't seen her for years. She stopped coming, I'm not sure why. Before the war, I'd see her regular once a month, usually on her day off on a Friday. She'd go and meet him afterwards before she went back to Walden.'

'Do you know who he was?'

'She never said much about him, which was unusual. Most girls can't stop gabbing on about how wonderful their bloke is. Made me suspect this chap was married.'

'My aunt thinks Rebecca was with my mother when she broke into the Commons.'

'That's right. Her and Kathleen Hooper. I remember them talking about it at Lincoln's Inn.'

Kathleen Hooper. Aunt Maud was right: two people had been with Mother. And Rebecca had a boyfriend, possibly married, who she met in London on her day off. It was a start.

'The three of them broke into the House of Commons together?'

'I'm not sure. I don't think Kathleen went in.' Dolly paused to look at me in the mirror. 'I know you miss your mum, love. But you shouldn't be worrying about all this now.'

'I'm curious.'

She stood back to admire her work. 'You suit a bob. Lovely thick hair, like your mother. Same can't be said for some of the young ladies that come in here. I try to talk them out of it, but they will insist.'

'Do you know where I could find Kathleen?' I barely glanced at my hair.

'I've not seen her for years. She used to live in Catford, but that was before the war. Your aunt might know where she is now.'

* * *

After lunch, I took a bus to the Natural History Museum in South Kensington. In the entrance hall, I picked up a leaflet.

One of the Society for the Promotion of Nature Reserves' aims is to identify sites of importance to wildlife in need of preservation and encourage others to acquire the sites and look after them.

'May I help you?' I turned to find an eager young man watching me.

'I've read about the society and thought I'd come along to find out more.' I gave what I hoped was an enthusiastic smile. 'Has the talk started?'

'Not yet, but I was about to close the doors. I'm sure I can find room for one more.'

'Thank you, I'd be so disappointed to miss it.'

'You've picked a good one. Mrs Juliet Rendall is speaking today. She's a founder member of the society and the only female on the committee. Some of the old duffers tend to drone on a bit, but Juliet knows how to pitch it. Come on, let's find a seat.'

I followed him through a set of double doors into a large auditorium that was nearly full. I'd imagined an audience of serious-looking older men with beards. Instead, there were chattering groups of young people, male and female.

'Shall we sit at the back? Away from the regulars,' my new friend whispered.

I nodded. I didn't want to find myself thrust into the midst of a group of nature enthusiasts when I didn't have any knowledge of the subject.

'Here will do.' He motioned to a couple of chairs in the back row. 'I'm Percy Baverstock, by the way.'

'Iris Woodmore.'

'Iris, what a pretty name. May I call you Iris? You can call me Percy.'

'Do you belong to the society, Percy?'

'Oh yes. Sorry, should have said. I'm not just some idiot rolled up off the street. Well, I am an idiot, of course.' He pushed his hair away from his brow. 'But I'm supposed to be here. I help out at the door. Meeting and greeting, that sort of thing. Probably because I never stop talking.'

I smiled. He had intelligent brown eyes and wavy hair that kept flopping down over his forehead. I had the feeling he'd be good company even if he didn't offer up any useful information.

'Here's Juliet.' A hush fell over the hall.

A tall, dark-haired woman who looked to be in her thirties took to the stage. For the next hour, she explained how agricultural and industrial developments had damaged the countryside over the last hundred years. As she spoke, she fixed her intense blue eyes on the younger members of the audience in the front row, and they seemed captivated.

Her fervour was infectious as she emphasised why it was imperative to introduce laws to preserve places of importance to wildlife. I found myself scribbling a few notes on some of the sites the society wanted to protect. It occurred to me that Waldenmere fitted the criteria to be one of them. At the end, the members of the audience who asked questions seemed as knowledgeable on the subject as the speaker. I struggled to follow some of the discussions.

'What did you think?' Percy asked afterwards when we were queuing for tea in the small canteen adjoining the hall.

'Fascinating. I knew how destructive the railway companies had been, but I hadn't realised the damage other industries had caused.' We took our cups and found a table.

'Most people don't.'

'The rest of the audience seemed to. I must admit, I didn't understand some of their questions.'

'They're regulars. That's why it's nice to see a new face. Especially a young female one. Juliet hoped that by giving talks herself, she'd attract more women to the society.' He pushed his unruly locks back off his forehead. 'Your hair's jolly pretty. Have you had it done?'

'Yes.' I tucked a strand of my shingled hair behind my ear. 'Do I smell of setting lotion?'

'Just the slightest whiff.' He wrinkled his nose.

I laughed.

'Do you like dancing?'

'I'm sorry?' I was taken aback by this abrupt change of subject.

'Dancing, you know...' He waved his hands and tapped his feet.

'I'm not very good. I don't know any of the modern dances.'

'I can teach you. There's a super club in Soho with a band that plays all the latest tunes. We could go there tonight. After all, you've just had your hair done. It would be a shame to waste a perfectly good hairdo.'

'I've got to get back to Walden.' I could picture the look on my father's face if I came home late and told him I'd been dancing in a club in Soho.

'Walden? I know it well. I'm from Winchester,' he exclaimed. 'Waldenmere's beautiful. I've made many studies there.'

'What sort of studies?'

'I work here at the museum. Mostly cataloguing stuff for the herbarium. But sometimes I visit sites to take records. Waldenmere's one of my favourites. Lovely to see it flourishing now the army camp's gone. Took a girl there on a picnic last year. She didn't like insects, ended up getting stung by a bee. Never saw her again. Jolly difficult to find a girl who likes wildlife, you know.'

'I'm not terribly fond of insects.' I tried not to smile at his disappointed expression.

He abruptly changed the subject again. 'You have two women standing in your by-election, don't you? Which one do you support? Mrs Siddons, I bet.' His grasshopper mind was disarming.

'I've interviewed all of the candidates for the newspaper I work for. Mrs Siddons was the strongest of the three.'

'A reporter? I saw you with your notebook. I hope you'll write good things about the society.'

'When I say interviewed, my boss, the editor, asks the questions. I take notes,' I admitted.

'But you're a reporter?'

'Sort of.'

'What did you make of Lady Timpson?' His expression was thoughtful.

'Opinionated. Insincere.'

He smiled.

'Do you know her?' I belatedly remembered Elijah's comment about not being able to afford a libel suit.

'I know her son, Daniel. We were at Winchester College at the same time. He's younger than me, but we played rugger together. Not a bad winger, considering his size. He flunked his exams, like me. But when your father has a huge estate for you to run, that doesn't matter too much.'

'Have you been to Crookham Hall?'

'Many times. Beautiful, isn't it? Daniel loves nature. That's how we became friends. Lord T is a good sort. When I'm studying aquatic plants at Waldenmere, he lets me take samples from the streams and the stretch of canal that runs through his estate.'

'What about Lady Timpson? Do you know her?'

'I know of her.' His fingers tapped the side of his cup. 'And some of her business dealings.'

I decided to be frank. I couldn't think how else to approach this. 'When we were interviewing her, my boss asked her a question concerning a land acquisition scandal. It was the first time I'd heard of the society.'

'So you thought you'd come along today and have a sniff around?' His tone was still friendly, but his demeanour had changed. As garrulous as he may be, Percy was no fool.

'Do you know about the scandal?'

'I know what went on. Does your boss want to run a story on Lady Timpson? Dish the dirt on one of the candidates?'

'No. I came of my own accord.'

'Why?'

I thought for a moment. I liked Percy, but the story of my mother and Rebecca wasn't one I was about to share with a stranger. Besides, if he was a close friend of Daniel's, he wasn't likely to reveal much about Lady Timpson.

'It doesn't matter. I'm sorry for bringing it up,' I said.

'I'm curious to know why you're interested in it now. It was six years ago.' He was still tapping the side of his cup.

I decided to make my escape.

'Thanks for the tea.' I stood up, feeling stupid. I should have prepared an explanation in advance for why I was asking these questions. So much for my skills as an investigative journalist. 'I must be going.'

'Sorry, I've upset you.' He hastily got to his feet, scraping his chair on the varnished floor. 'I'm always doing that with girls. Saying the wrong thing, I mean.'

'No, not at all.' I tried to reassure him. 'It's been an interesting afternoon. But I must get to Waterloo or I'll miss my train.'

'I'm an idiot. Your reason for asking about Lady Timpson is personal. Of course you don't want to tell some chap you only met an hour ago.'

'You're not an idiot. But you're right. It is something difficult to explain.'

'I hope our paths cross again, Iris. Maybe if you get to know me better, we can continue this conversation. And if you ever want to go dancing, you can always find me in the Foxtrot Club on a Saturday night.' The chatty, eager Percy was back. He waved his hands and tapped his feet again. People were looking at him, but he didn't seem to care.

I smiled. 'I'll bear that in mind.'

I was still smiling when I got on the bus. Father would never allow me to go to a club, but he didn't have to know. Perhaps I could stay with Gran and Aunt Maud and say I was going to a picture house with a friend. Could I sneak out to a dancing club without anyone knowing? Percy was more likely to confide in me in those surroundings, especially if he'd had a few drinks. Besides, it would be fun to go out with an attractive man. There weren't many of those in Walden – except Ben, and he was smitten with Alice.

I got off the bus near Westminster and wandered to the end of the bridge to see if I could find the waterman. He said he'd worked this stretch for over forty years. I cursed myself for not asking his name. I studied the boats near the Houses of Parliament, surprised at how busy the Thames was at this time of the day.

At the end of the bridge, I went down the steps to the spot where Mother had gone in. A familiar sorrow swept over me. What must it have felt like to have sunk into that cold black water? I wanted to walk away but felt mesmerised by the constant fluid movement of the dirty river. I watched the boats pulling into shore and the pedestrians crossing the bridge. My mother's jump, if that's what it had been, must have caused quite a stir that afternoon.

'You back again?'

I turned. It was him, with his scarlet uniform and craggy face.

'Hello. My name's Iris Woodmore.'

'I thought you must be a relation. My name's Raymond Nichols.' He touched his cap.

'Violet Woodmore was my mother.'

'I'm sorry, dear. I wouldn't have run on so if I'd have known.'

'That's all right.'

'It was tragic, what happened.'

'Why do you think she jumped into the water?' I was desperate for any clue as to her state of mind.

'I couldn't see a reason for it. It was a strange thing to do. The river was full of boats and barges. It's a miracle she didn't hit one of them.'

'Are you sure there was no one chasing her?'

'Like I said, the Serjeant-at-Arms didn't come over till after we called him. I couldn't see no one else. There were no police around that day.' He took off his cap and ran his fingers through his sparse grey hair.

'Who else was on the bridge that afternoon?'

'Lots of people. MPs were starting to arrive. Some workmen were putting in these here railings.' He grabbed one of the metal rails that now surrounded this corner of Parliament. 'Shame they didn't get these in earlier, she wouldn't have been able to jump so easily if they had. Then there was this nanny with a group of little 'un's just out of school. Boys in short trousers and girls in gingham dresses running down the steps to look at the boats. You should have heard their screams when she went in.'

I shuddered, imagining the chaos. 'Did she wave or cry out for help?'

'Not that I heard.' He scratched his head. 'She had something in her hands. A pot of some sort?'

'The paint she'd used on the grilles.'

'I thought that must have been what it was.'

'Was anyone with her? Another woman. Or did anyone come looking for her?'

'No. She was on her own.'

I asked a few more questions, but there was nothing more he could tell me.

On the train back, I went over what he'd said. I still couldn't understand my mother's intention. Perhaps it had been a dramatic gesture to get on the front pages of the newspapers – a risky leap into the River Thames in the shadow of the Houses of Parliament to draw attention to the cause. But if that had been the case, why hadn't the WSPU publicised it? And where had Rebecca and Kathleen been? Surely, they wouldn't have just abandoned my mother to her fate. It didn't make sense.

Something had gone very wrong that day – was it possible it had led to Rebecca's death as well as my mother's?

9

'What sort of person did Rebecca Dent seem to you?' I said to the top of Lizzy's head. She'd made me stand on a wooden chair in the kitchen whilst she pinned the hem of my dress.

'I only met her a couple of times.' She paused, pin in hand, to consider. 'I thought she was a sensible young woman. I can't believe she'd run away without a word to anyone. And I'm surprised she went with your mother into the House of Commons.'

'So you think it was Mother who persuaded her to take part in the protest rather than the other way around?' It was something that had been niggling me. My mother had been thirty-eight when she died. Older and supposedly wiser than Rebecca, who'd been twenty-five. But I suspected Mother had been the reckless one.

'Ah.' She realised what she'd said.

'Well, do you?'

'Love, you're only dwelling on this because of what that waterman said. It's a silly story he's made up.' Lizzy took a dim view of Londoners. She'd been employed as our housekeeper when Mother and Father were newly married and living in Elijah's cottage. She'd come with us when we moved to London but had never taken to life in the city. To say she was pleased to be back in Walden was an understatement.

'But do you think it more likely that Mother planned it?'

'You know what your mother could be like. Out of the two, it was probably her idea,' Lizzy conceded. 'But she wouldn't have made anyone do anything they didn't want to do.'

I wasn't so sure. I remembered how I'd been coerced into taking part in Emily Wilding Davison's funeral procession.

'Why are you wearing your best dress to work?' This was Lizzy's attempt to change the subject.

'No trousers, on the boss's orders.'

'I must say I prefer to see you in a skirt. But I'm surprised at Elijah. He's never bothered about your trousers before now.'

'The big boss. Mr Laffaye is coming with us to Crookham Hall today. According to Elijah, "women in trousers offend his sensibilities".'

Lady Timpson had invited press and local dignitaries to an announcement she was making at Blacksmith's Bridge by the curve of the canal that ran through the Crookham estate. There was a rumour she planned to revive the canal navigation.

'You'd have thought he'd seen enough trousers on women during the war to overcome his sensibilities.' She stood back to examine my hemline. 'Men are funny creatures.'

Like many women called on to do manual work, I'd begun wearing trousers and old shirts when I'd helped to clear up bomb-damaged streets. But unlike other women, I hadn't given them up when the war ended. I wore smarter ones nowadays, but they still raised eyebrows in stuffy old Walden.

Elijah had casually asked if I had a frock I could wear for the occasion. He'd been expecting me to object, but I wasn't going to pass up another chance to visit Crookham Hall. I needed to try to get closer to Constance and didn't want to jeopardise this opportunity by arguing over a dress.

* * *

'Is this presentable enough for the boss?'

My pale green, calf-length dress with matching coat was possibly rather modern for Mr Laffaye's tastes, but I wasn't prepared to go as far as to wear a full-length skirt.

Elijah grunted in response. His navy suit was marginally less crumpled than usual. The chauffeur-driven Daimler pulled up, and we climbed in the back, sinking into seats that smelt of expensive leather.

'Miss Woodmore, Mr Whittle, so kind of you to let me join you on this little outing.'

We hadn't been given a choice. I'd taken the telephone call from his secretary, who'd stated: 'Mr Laffaye will pick you up at 2.30 p.m. tomorrow and accompany you to Crookham Hall for Lady Timpson's reception.'

I knew by now that Horace Laffaye chose to give the appearance of being a curious bystander with no inclination to interfere. In truth, he liked to be in control of his surroundings. If anything happened to disrupt the peaceful rhythm of life in Walden, it had his immediate attention.

The cause of his concern today was the fact that Lady Timpson had recently taken ownership of the Basingstoke Canal from the army. The last cargoes of aircraft spares from the Royal Aircraft Factory at Farnborough had travelled from Aldershot to Woolwich Arsenal along the navigation the previous year. Since then, it had been abandoned.

'It's a canny move,' Elijah said.

'Oh, quite the masterstroke.' Horace was immaculately dressed in a pale grey three-piece suit that made Elijah appear even more rumpled than usual.

'But why is it?' I couldn't understand why anyone would want to buy the canal. Like most waterways, traffic had been declining for years as more railway lines crossed the country. Over the past forty years, six different companies had managed the canal navigation. Each one had ended up in the hands of the receivers. 'How is Lady Timpson going to make it work?'

'I doubt that she is, my dear,' Horace said. 'Commercially, it's doomed to failure.'

'She's buying votes,' Elijah explained. 'She's paid the army over the odds for a stretch of canal that's of no further use to them. She's promising to restore the canal for agricultural purposes to support surrounding farms. So now...'

'She has the support of the military and farmers.' Horace finished Elijah's sentence. 'That pretty much covers the entire constituency of our little corner of north-east Hampshire.'

'That's appalling. She's buying herself a seat in Parliament?'

They nodded, smiling at my incredulity. I noticed how in tune they were with each other.

'I'm afraid that's how politics works sometimes,' Horace said. 'This afternoon is Lady Timpson's opportunity to present herself as our saviour.'

'Do you think she'll wear the Star Sapphire?' I asked.

He pursed his lips. 'Now that would be something. But it hasn't been seen since June 1914.'

Elijah raised an eyebrow. 'Are you on the scent of something?'

'Just curious.' Horace gave him a smile. 'It's probably nothing. Lord Timpson may have decided it's safer locked away than being used by his wife for decoration.'

'Wouldn't it have been considered ostentatious to have worn it during wartime?' I remembered what Alice had said.

'That's not a concern that would weigh heavily with Lady Timpson,' Horace replied sardonically. 'However, I take your point. But Constance was presented at Court last year when it was notable by its absence. One would have expected it to have formed part of her attire.'

I didn't know enough about debutantes and 'coming out' balls to comment, but I was intrigued by his observation.

* * *

Lady Timpson was wearing a fitted navy suit, and her only decoration was a single string of pearls. No sign of the Star Sapphire. A large marquee had been erected in a field by Blacksmith's Bridge and filled with trestle tables laden with food. Smartly dressed maids offered trays of drinks to guests who included local dignitaries, members of the military, and representatives of the press.

'The Basingstoke Canal was originally built to provide economical transportation to support agriculture in Hampshire.' She'd allowed her guests time to enjoy her lavish hospitality before starting her speech, but not long enough for anyone to get drunk. 'I intend to return it to its former glory. I'm going to invest in restoring neglected sections of the waterway so it can be used commercially once again.' She turned to Lord Timpson. 'I want to thank my husband for supporting me in this venture. As you know, this section of the canal runs through the estate of Crookham Hall. By building a series of storage sheds alongside this stretch of water, we can offer our farmers the warehouse space they need to be able to transport flour and other produce to London on barges that will return with coal and fertiliser.'

Lord Timpson stood behind his wife, smiling. They made a strange couple. Lady Timpson was a large woman with a full, sensuous mouth, which gave the impression of generosity and warmth. By contrast, her husband was slim with aristocratic features that made him seem cold and aloof. But in conversation, he'd been the friendlier of the two.

I was surprised he'd agreed to allow even a tiny part of his ancestral estate to be given over to a transport business. Why sully the beauty of his magnificent home? I could only imagine his wife had shown her usual forcefulness in the face of his objections.

Lady Timpson droned on, unashamedly emphasising how much personal time and money she'd spent on the project. Most of her guests seemed to be smiling appreciatively, which was bad news for Mrs Siddons.

When the speech ended, I drifted through the crowd, keeping an eye out for Constance. Elijah and Horace were deep in conversation with a uniformed man who looked like he was someone important in the military.

I spotted Constance near Blacksmith's Bridge, talking with her mother. Pretending to examine the canal navigation, I made my way closer. When Lady Timpson went off to speak to one of her guests, I wandered over.

'Iris, join me in a glass of champagne. Let's have a chat.' Constance raised a gloved hand, and a maid appeared with two glasses. 'I was hoping to run into you again. I'm sorry for what my mother said the other day about suffragettes. She's a little old fashioned in her views.'

'I'm used to it.' I raised the delicate glass to my lips. The champagne was cold and delicious.

'For a woman who runs her own business, Mother's strangely unsupportive of women's rights. She's like our old headteacher, I'm afraid.'

'Alice still receives the occasional card from Miss Cotton. But she seems to have lost my address.'

Constance laughed. 'How is Alice? I saw her a few times during the war. Wasn't she part of a women's group that helped poorer families struggling with their menfolk away? I think we donated some clothes to them.'

'She's well. She still works with the Walden Women's Group.'

'Really? I thought they'd disband after the war.'

'They help the families of servicemen who've been unable to find work due to their injuries.' I felt uncomfortable talking about impoverished families whilst sipping expensive champagne in the grounds of a stately home.

'Once this transportation business is up and running, I'd like to be able to offer employment to men like that. I remember how difficult it was for Daniel when he first came back from the trenches. The problem is, I'm not sure it will ever get off the ground.'

Constance had a studious air that didn't detract from her beauty. Her long brown hair was combed into a neat chignon, and although her full-length gown was of a traditional style, it still managed to look modern. My dress didn't feel as fashionable any more.

'Your mother sounded confident,' I replied.

'Mother has her heart set on becoming an MP. She thinks this business will help her achieve that. But business and politics don't mix. I'm afraid Basingstoke Canal Holdings is probably doomed to failure.' She looked panic-stricken, realising what she'd said. Her mother was watching us from the marquee. 'You won't print any of this, will you?'

'Of course not. We're friends,' I reassured her. 'Why does your mother want to become an MP? She's already a successful busi-nesswoman. Why enter politics?'

'I'm not sure myself. I don't think it occurred to her until she heard Mrs Siddons was standing. Then she was obsessed with the idea of becoming the next woman to take a seat in Parliament.'

'Mrs Siddons?'

'They were friends once. And then enemies. Don't ask me why. When Mother heard Mrs Siddons was standing in the by-election, she announced she was standing too. She's been involved with the Conservative Party for some time, but I thought she'd push Father into becoming an MP rather than stand herself.'

'Your father has no interest?' I didn't want to appear too nosy, but I did want to understand how the Timpson family worked.

'Absolutely not. He isn't terribly keen on Mother standing either. Too much hobnobbing for his liking. He'd rather be in his club in London or hunting here. He prefers an easy life.' She glanced back at the marquee and lowered her voice. 'Tell me, why did Mr Whittle ask us about Miss Dent?'

'It's because of something that happened when I went to the House of Commons with Mrs Siddons.' I wasn't exactly sure what I intended to say, but I needed to gain her trust.

'That must have been painful for you.'

'You know about... You know what happened to my mother there?'

'I wanted to write a letter of condolence to you at the time. I wish I had. I was going to send flowers when I heard the funeral was at St Martha's. But Mother wouldn't let me.'

'That was kind of you. I suppose it must have caused quite a scandal.' I remembered little of that day except for the numbness I'd felt standing next to Father as Mother's coffin was lowered into the ground.

She appeared embarrassed. 'You know what it's like in a small town like this.'

'I didn't appreciate it at the time. We went straight back to London.'

'What does this have to do with Rebecca Dent?'

'She was a friend of my mother's. There's something about her you don't know.' I wanted to make her curious. 'I couldn't say anything in front of your parents, especially knowing your mother's opinion of suffragettes.'

'Constance,' Lady Timpson called, right on cue. She glared over at me from the entrance to the marquee.

'I can't tell you here,' I said quickly.

'Come over one day when Mother goes up to London. We can talk then.'

'I'd like that.'

'I'll write and tell you when.' Constance hurried away.

10

'Hello, Iris. I was hoping I might bump into you.'

I turned to find Percy Baverstock dressed in a smart blue suit, sipping a glass of champagne.

'Percy, what are you doing here?'

'Spying.' He gazed appreciatively at the retreating figure of Constance.

'On Constance?' This was taking his pursuit of the fairer sex too far.

'No, of course not. Lovely though she is. You're looking rather splendid too.' He rummaged in his pocket. 'Here's my card, I meant to give it to you the other day. It's got my address on it. Perhaps we could meet sometime.'

'You didn't come all this way to give me this.' I took the card, feeling flattered.

'I'm here to find out what the dreaded Lady T has planned for the canal. It was on our list, you see. The society's, I mean.'

'The list of sites for preservation?'

He nodded. A maid appeared, and he placed our empty glasses

on her tray and took two fresh glasses of champagne, handing one to me.

'We knew it was likely the army would sell the navigation at some stage. But we wanted to maintain the waterway as a nature reserve. Looks like we've lost out to Timpson Foods once again.' He gulped the champagne, evidently determined to enjoy 'the dreaded Lady T's' hospitality.

'How did you find out about today?' I took a more reserved sip.

'I ran into Daniel in town. He invited me to come down here to scout it out.'

'For what?'

'To see if there's anything we can do for the wildlife. He doesn't want his mother building here. He loves this place.'

'I can see why.' The view from where we were standing was of a long curve of water as it wound its way through green meadows and woodland. Early spring flowers provided patches of golden colour. Only the marquee, and the people in it, spoilt the view.

'Stunning, isn't it? We've had our eye on the canal for some time. The waterway provides an ideal habitat for so many species. Otters are thriving here, but they'll soon disappear if it becomes industrialised again.'

'A family of them are living near the bridge.' Daniel appeared alongside his father.

'Hello, Miss Woodmore. How lovely to see you again.' Lord Timpson beamed at me.

'I've never seen this part of the estate before. It's beautiful,' I said. 'So unspoilt.'

'Thank you. Crookham Hall has been in my family for genera-tions. I like to manage it in the tradition of my ancestors.'

'Then why let her build here?' Daniel snapped.

'Sorry, son.' Lord Timpson patted him on the back. 'You know what your mother's like when she's got the bit between her teeth. It may not be as bad as you think.'

Daniel scowled.

'Why don't you show me the holts, old chap?' Percy suggested. This seemed to cheer Daniel up, and the pair set off towards the canal bank.

'What are the holts?' I asked.

'It's where otters live. Daniel's mad about wild creatures, has been since he was a small boy. He's out day and night, studying owls, otters or some such nonsense.'

'No wonder he and Percy get along.' A maid appeared at my side to relieve me of my empty glass. I'd finished the champagne without even noticing. I refused another.

'He spends his whole life outdoors, but he won't shoot. I don't know what I'm going to do with the boy.' Lord Timpson's demeanour was relaxed, but his expression determined. As heir to the Timpson estate, Daniel undoubtedly had expectations to live up to. 'I was hoping to get the chance to speak with you, Miss Woodmore. I wondered why Mr Whittle mentioned Miss Dent the other day. I often think of her, and whenever I run into any of my acquaintances in the police, I raise the matter. But I'm afraid they never tell me anything new.'

'That's kind of you. No one else seems to care about finding her.' I was glad he'd raised the subject. I'd been tempted to but thought it might seem impertinent.

'I care. And so does my family. But I'm afraid too many years have passed for the police to pay much heed now.' He put his hand on my elbow and guided me away from the throng of people. 'Why do you care?'

'She was a friend of my mother's.' I could see Elijah and Horace watching us from a distance. 'What do you think happened to her?'

'At the time, I thought she must have become unhappy working at the hall and decided to leave. My wife can be rather exacting with the staff.' He sighed. 'Crookham Hall used to be such a happy place in my parents' day.'

'Isn't it now?'

'It's become less so. We lost many of our estate workers in the war, and servants are hard to keep.'

'Do you still think she ran away?'

'I'm not so sure now. Six years have passed without a word. I'm more inclined to think something may have happened to her.' He looked grave as he said this.

'All of her belongings were still in her room, weren't they?'

'Yes, they were. At first, I thought that was because she wanted a fresh start. You know, leave behind her uniform and life as a servant. But now I don't know. Was she a good friend of your mother's?'

I nodded, choosing my words carefully. 'I believe Miss Dent was upset by my mother's death. It affected her badly.'

'I see.' His brow cleared. 'I can understand why you want to find out what happened to her.'

To my surprise, he suddenly clasped my hands in his. I squirmed with embarrassment when I saw Elijah and Horace raise their eyebrows. Elijah put his drink down and looked like he might be contemplating a rescue mission.

'I was sorry to hear of the tragic circumstances of your mother's death. Constance told me what happened. Let's make a deal. If I find out anything about Miss Dent, I'll let you know immediately. And if you discover anything, please come and tell me.' His blue eyes were mesmerising, and it was disconcerting to be the focus of such close scrutiny.

'Of course.' I tried not to sound as awkward as I felt. He

beamed, and I breathed a sigh of relief when he released my hands and walked away.

The gathering had begun to disperse, and I made my way to the driveway of the hall, taking a meandering route. I wanted to look at a gothic building I'd spotted near the edge of the gardens. It was decorated with ornate statues of angels and biblical quotations.

Close up, the grey stone sculptures were even more eerie than they'd looked from a distance. I touched the outstretched wing of one of the angels. Despite its coldness, it was extremely lifelike. It looked as if it was about to reach out and embrace me at any moment.

I almost screamed when I felt a hand on my shoulder. Percy leapt back as I swung around and hit him on the chest.

'Steady on, you nearly made me drop my glass.'

'Good grief, Percy. You scared me half to death.'

'Sorry. Sorry. Didn't mean to frighten you.' He went to put his arm around me but thought better of it.

'What is this place?'

'It's the mausoleum. Where the Timpsons house their dead,' he said cheerily.

'Ugh.' I shivered at the thought of a room full of cadavers. 'How horrible.'

'Not pleasant, is it?' He took a swig of champagne. 'Do you want to go to the pictures with me?'

'What?'

'The pictures. On the Strand. We could go dancing afterwards.' He bounded off. 'Drop me a line if you do.'

* * *

'What was all the hand clasping with Lord Timpson about?' Elijah asked as soon as I was seated in the Daimler.

'He asked me about Rebecca Dent.' Now my embarrassment had worn off, I was feeling flattered by Lord Timpson's attention. And amused the incident had aroused such curiosity.

'Did he?' Elijah enquired.

'I didn't bring up the subject,' I said defensively. 'He wanted to know why we were interested in her.'

'What did you tell him?'

'That she'd been friends with my mother.' I was unsure of what Horace knew of my background. 'And that Rebecca had been upset by her death. That's when he held my hands.'

'I've told Mr Laffaye what prompted you to start looking for Rebecca.' Elijah appeared concerned about how I'd react to this. 'I thought he might be able to help.'

Of course. Horace had been living in Walden at the time. And he liked to be informed of everything that went on in the town. 'Do you remember her disappearance, Mr Laffaye?'

'I do. But I'm afraid other events overshadowed the matter. The army had just set up camp at Waldenmere. It did occur to me that a soldier was perhaps responsible for Miss Dent going missing. I spoke to one of my contacts in military intelligence about it at the time. You may have seen us talking to him earlier?'

'The tall man with the moustache?'

'Yes. Captain Finlay Fortesque is an old friend. I'm satisfied he carried out a thorough investigation. Nothing was found to indicate any connection between the army camp and what happened to Miss Dent. I asked him about it again today, but he said nothing new had come to light since we last spoke on the matter.'

I was touched he'd made an effort to try to find Rebecca.

'With so much going on at the time, there was little journalistic interest in a housemaid going missing,' Horace continued. 'Which was a shame. The police didn't have much to go on. Some publicity may have brought something to light.'

'It's not too late. *The Walden Herald* could run a story reminding people about her. You never know, it could prompt someone to remember something?'

'Lord Timpson wasn't the only one to ask about Rebecca,' Elijah said. 'Lady Timpson made it clear to Mr Laffaye and me that she didn't want the matter raised again.'

'Constance was curious to know why we were looking into it too. She's willing to talk to me when her parents are away.'

'Casually mention the Star Sapphire when you see her.' Horace made it sound like a polite request but not one I could decline.

'You don't think Rebecca could have stolen it? You said the sapphire was last seen in June 1914, and she went missing two months later.'

'What would a maid do with a famous sapphire?' Elijah shook his head. 'It's not something you can easily sell. Not without drawing attention to yourself. And the Timpsons would have reported its disappearance.'

'Interesting that young Master Timpson was the only member of the family who didn't raise the subject of Miss Dent this afternoon.' Horace pursed his lips.

'Does that mean he's guilty or innocent?' Elijah asked with a smile.

'That's the question, isn't it?' Horace waved a finger in the air. 'He could be innocent as a lamb. If he has no anxiety over the matter of Miss Dent, he has no reason to query your interest in her. Unlike the other members of his family.'

'Or?' Elijah said indulgently.

'He already knows what happened to her. Hence, he has no curiosity about her disappearance.'

'But surely, if he'd been involved, he'd want to know why we were asking about her?' Elijah countered.

Horace shrugged.

'He would only have been sixteen or seventeen at the time,' I commented. But he'd said he'd liked Rebecca. Could he have been infatuated with her? My father had described her as an attractive woman.

'So why did the other three members of the family each raise the subject?' Elijah pondered.

'Lord Timpson and Constance wanted to help,' I replied. 'But Lady Timpson made it clear she wants us to drop the matter.'

'Hardly surprising given her election campaign,' Elijah retorted.

'But why shouldn't we put something in the paper? What do you think, Mr Laffaye?'

'My editor has made the valid point that if we raise this now, it will look like we're attempting to taint Lady Timpson's reputation.' His hand rested on Elijah's knee. 'We'll have to wait for a more appropriate time after the by-election.'

I knew I'd have to be satisfied with that. 'Is the paper going to remain impartial?' I tried to sound as if I didn't care. 'Or support a candidate?'

'Mr Whittle and I have discussed the issue at some length.' Horace turned to look at his editor.

Would Elijah toe the line to please Horace? I was beginning to realise the two had a closer relationship than I'd supposed.

'And we've decided to support Mrs Siddons,' Elijah said with a slight incline of his head, as though admitting defeat.

'An excellent choice.' I smiled.

'But...' Horace placed the tips of his fingers together.

My elation hovered in mid-air.

'If Lady Timpson were to win, I would not care to publish

anything on Miss Dent's disappearance. It would seem as though we were attacking a newly elected MP because we'd favoured another candidate.'

I looked in vain to Elijah for help.

'I see the dilemma,' he conceded.

My fingers drummed on the leather seat in frustration. I wanted *The Walden Herald* to support Mrs Siddons. But... I'd learnt nothing about Rebecca. An article in the newspaper appealing for information was the next logical step. Without it, I wasn't sure we'd uncover anything new.

And if Lady Timpson were elected, getting anyone to speak out against her would become even harder.

11

When I got home, I was glad to see Father's jacket on the hook and his briefcase on the hallway floor. I wanted to talk to him about Mrs Siddons' campaign. Lady Timpson was taking the lead, and we needed to claw back some support.

'You'll never guess...' The words died on my lips. I entered the drawing room to find Donald Anstey, glass of whisky in hand, seated opposite my father.

'Hello, Miss Woodmore.'

'Oh, hello, Mr Anstey.'

'Donald and I have been discussing his election campaign. I'm going to help him create some literature that will explain the party's statement "Labour and the New Social Order" in simpler terms.'

'Oh.' I was furious but too polite to say anything.

'Where have you been?' Father asked.

'Crookham Hall.'

'Oh yes, what was Lady Timpson's big announcement?'

'She plans to resurrect the canal navigation to help local

farmers transport goods to London.' It was all I could do to sound civil.

'It's been tried and failed too many times.' Father shook his head.

'Buying votes.' Donald Anstey placed his glass on the tray and stood. 'It's what I expected.'

'People will see it for what it is. If we can get Labour's message to the right people, I think we stand a chance.' My father actually slapped him on the back.

They carried on talking out in the hallway whilst I stayed in the drawing room, seething with resentment.

'What about Mrs Siddons?' I demanded when Father returned. 'Don't you think it's important to have more women in Parliament?'

'I do. And if she were standing for the Labour Party, she would have my vote.'

'What about all she did for us when Mother died?'

'I'm grateful to her for helping us then, and I know you're loyal to her because of it. But that shouldn't influence how you vote.'

'I'm not eligible to vote,' I reminded him coldly. 'I intend to support Mrs Siddons with her campaign as I believe she has more to offer than the other candidates.'

'But Donald has a greater understanding of the issues affecting working people. Mrs Siddons comes from a privileged background. I know you're dazzled by her charisma, but that doesn't mean she'll make the most effective politician.'

I swallowed my fury. 'I'm not dazzled by her charisma. I've listened to the policies of all three candidates, and I think Mrs Siddons talks the most sense, especially when it comes to education.'

He sighed and poured himself another drink.

'Oh, and Elijah and Mr Laffaye feel the same. *The Walden*

Herald will be supporting Mrs Siddons.' I made this my parting shot and left the room.

That night, I tossed and turned in bed, still angry. I drifted off to sleep trying to devise a brilliant scheme to ensure Mrs Siddons won the by-election. Instead, I dreamt of dancing with Percy Baverstock on the banks of the Basingstoke Canal.

I was still infuriated when I joined Father at the breakfast table. Lizzy raised her eyebrows at the awkward silence as she handed me a letter from Aunt Maud.

Would you like to come to a meeting on birth control?

it began.

I spluttered into my tea. Why did she feel the need to educate me on this particular subject now? I avoided looking at my father and read on.

Marie Stopes is giving a talk on constructive birth control at the Queen's Hall this Saturday. It's bound to attract some of the old suffragette crowd, and we might come across some of your mother's friends there.

I exhaled in relief. The Queen's Hall had been a favourite venue of the WSPU; I'd been there once with Mother to hear Emmeline Pankhurst address a meeting. It was definitely worth a try.

* * *

Aunt Maud was right. The Queen's Hall was swarming with old-guard suffragettes. I recognised a few faces, but given the size of the crowd, I doubted we'd find Kathleen Hooper. My aunt seemed more confident.

'Stay here whilst I take a look around.' She darted towards a group of women she seemed to know.

I stood at the back of the hall, examining the audience. Most were women, but there were a few men dotted here and there.

'Any luck?' I asked when she reappeared.

'No one's seen Kathleen for years.' Aunt Maud looked disappointed.

'Is there anyone here who can tell us anything?'

'I've found someone who knew your mother and Rebecca. She's going to meet us in the foyer afterwards.'

'What's her name?'

'Ena O'Connor. She must be nearly eighty now. She was a permanent fixture down at Lincoln's Inn House. Everyone's granny. She kept the women going with a constant supply of tea and cake.'

'Tea-urn Ena. I remember Mother mentioning her.' It may not be much, but at least it was a link to the WSPU.

Ena O'Connor was a tiny lady with grey hair scooped up into a bun. Pale, bright blue eyes shone out of a heavily lined face. We joined her on a long wooden bench that ran along the wall of the foyer.

'Look at you. Just like Violet.' She reached up to touch my face.

I wasn't sure how to start this conversation. My aunt took the initiative.

'Iris went to the House of Commons recently. It stirred up some memories, as you can imagine,' Aunt Maud said.

'I'm so sorry for what happened to your mother.'

'I'd like to know more about that day. The day of the protest. Do you know who was with my mother in the House of Commons? Were there many of them?'

She shook her head. People streamed out of the hall, some waving to Ena as they passed.

'Only Mother and Rebecca Dent, then?' I persisted.

'And Kathleen Hooper,' Ena croaked.

'Whose idea was it?'

'Your mother's.'

'Did Rebecca want to take part?'

'As long as it stayed a secret. She wouldn't do anything where she might be recognised. She never handed out pamphlets in the street or went on marches. Usually, she just helped out in the office.'

'But she decided to go with Mother to the House of Commons?'

'Violet told her it would be safe and that all the police would be at the march. The plan was not to draw attention to themselves. They only wanted to paint the grilles and leave the banner dangling over the chamber like a calling card. Violet took the most risk. Rebecca was the lookout.'

'Do you know what went wrong?'

'I'm not sure. Rebecca was supposed to stay in the Members Lobby to watch for anyone coming whilst your mother went up to the Ladies' Gallery. Afterwards, Rebecca was to follow your mother out and take the paint and brush away from her. Then they'd go their separate ways.' Ena stopped to acknowledge more greetings from women leaving the hall. 'Kathleen Hooper was waiting further along the bridge with a horse and cart. Rebecca was to hide the stuff in the back, and Kathleen would drive away, so if Violet or Rebecca were stopped, there'd be nothing incriminating on them.'

'Where were they when Mother fell in the river?' I asked.

'Kathleen was on the bridge with the horse and cart. When Rebecca finally got to her, she didn't have the paint. She told Kathleen she'd got stuck inside and that Violet was being carried off when she came out.'

'I don't understand how Mother was able to get out but Rebecca wasn't.' I was aware the hall was nearly empty, and we'd soon be asked to leave.

'I don't know. We never found out. We didn't see Rebecca after that. Kathleen told us she was too upset.'

'You know that Rebecca went missing not long afterwards?' Aunt Maud said.

'I heard. I often wondered if it was guilt.' Ena blinked back tears. 'Couldn't live with herself after what happened. She blamed herself for Violet's death.'

My chest contracted.

'I used to love being with them all at Lincoln's Inn.' Ena dabbed her eyes. 'But when the war came, and we shut up shop, it was time. There'd been too much suffering.'

Aunt Maud put an arm around her. 'Thank you, Ena. Do you know where we can find Kathleen?'

'I've not heard from her for years. She was in a bad way when she lost her husband, Leonard.'

'If you hear anything of her, could you let me know?'

'I'll ask around. I go to most of the big meetings like this.' She gave us a melancholy smile. 'I'm still a suffragist. I'll die with my boots on.'

* * *

'When did Mother become a suffragette?' I asked after Ena had left. We stayed sitting on the long bench, watching the last few women trickle out of the hall, animatedly discussing the talk.

'It built up over a number of years.' Aunt Maud looked reflective. 'Our father died when Violet was about the same age as you are now. Losing him was a huge shock to her. To all of us. He was the man of the house, and our lives revolved around him. A year later, Violet fell in love with your father. They married within months. She was only twenty-two, and then you came along.'

It was strange to think my mother had married and had a child when she was barely older than me. I couldn't contemplate doing such a thing. My father rarely spoke about those days.

'Violet was happy in Walden. But she started to feel her world was a small one compared to your father's. She'd gone from being a daughter to a wife to a mother without ever considering what she wanted from life.'

'When did she become involved with the WSPU?'

'It was some time in 1911. Your father was away with his work. Violet was feeling lonely in Walden, so you both came to stay with us for a while. We were walking in Hyde Park. You would have been about eleven or twelve at the time. We saw Emmeline and her cronies giving speeches.'

'I remember.' I could picture the women in their sashes shouting from the bandstand. 'Some men were jeering at them. Gran told us to come away, but Mother wouldn't.'

'That's right. She was transfixed. I can still remember the expression on her face.'

'Is that when she joined?'

'No, it wasn't until later. But I suppose that day was an awakening of sorts. She read everything she could about the cause. Then she wrote essays for the suffragette newsletter.'

'And Walden became too small for her?'

'She hadn't been happy with the education you were receiving at Miss Cotton's, but it was all that was available. Your father couldn't have afforded a governess. That's when she began to think about coming back to London.'

'I wish we'd stayed in Walden.' Safe in Elijah's little cottage.

'She'd hoped to find work as a writer. Instead, she got more involved with the cause. Your gran and I were thrilled when you moved to Hither Green. But when Violet's protests landed her in Holloway Prison, we realised it had been a mistake.'

'But you became involved with the suffragettes too?'

'I went to the odd meeting and handed out leaflets. I believed in the cause. I still do. But I suppose I went more to keep Violet out of trouble.'

I'd suspected that was the case.

'I never got involved in the risky stuff,' she continued. 'But I couldn't stop Violet. She felt women should have the vote at any cost. Your father supported her at first. But then he didn't know half of what was going on. Thomas was always so involved with his work, which made it easy for her.'

Father absorbed in his work; Mother driven by the cause – there'd been times I'd felt excluded, like an outsider looking in at them.

'When she was sent to prison, we knew things were getting out of hand. I wish we'd tried harder to...' She faltered.

'I know.' I reached over and took her hand. 'I once asked Mother to stop.'

'What did she say?'

'That she was doing it for me. So I could have a better future. I felt guilty for asking then.' Tears prickled my eyes. 'You're right. She did think women should have the vote at any cost.'

With a heavy heart, I had to accept she may have chosen to pay that cost.

12

I walked with Aunt Maud to Hyde Park Corner underground station but didn't get on the train with her. As I'd expected, she was anxious to get back to Gran.

I'd sent Percy a note, arranging to meet him in Hyde Park at lunchtime. It was a damp grey April day, and I had the park to myself. I was early but wanted time to walk and think before he arrived.

Something had gone wrong that afternoon at Westminster, and I had to face the possibility Mother's protest may have led to Rebecca's death as well as her own. I was beginning to wish I'd taken everyone's advice and ignored what the waterman had said. Should I leave the past alone and stop trying to make sense of that afternoon?

I nearly screamed when someone suddenly grabbed my arm.

'Sorry. Sorry. Sorry. I've done it again. I'm such a nincompoop. But I wasn't sure it was you at first.'

'Percy, you idiot. This is becoming a habit. Do you enjoy scaring me half to death?'

'You're wearing trousers.' He said this as though I might not be aware of the fact.

'Yes, I did know,' I snapped.

'That's why I wasn't sure if it was you. I saw you leaving the Queen's Hall. Was it a good speaker?'

'Marie Stopes.'

'The woman who goes on about er, erm...' He floundered.

'Birth control?'

'That's the thing.' He seemed relieved I'd said the words, so he didn't have to. 'Very enlightened of you. I mean, no, I don't mean. You know what I mean. Shut up, Percy. Do you want to go for lunch?'

'In a minute. I want to talk to you about something first.' I pointed to a bench near the bandstand. 'Do you have time?'

'Of course.' He looked delighted.

'I want to explain why I asked you about Lady Timpson.' We sat on a bench, and I shivered.

'Would you like me to warm your hands?' he offered.

I gave him a stern look.

'No, of course not. Carry on, I'm all ears.'

'I once listened to Emmeline Pankhurst give a speech from that bandstand over there. I was with my mother, aunt and grandmother.'

'That must have been quite the show. I've heard she knew how to rouse the troops.'

'My mother certainly thought so,' I replied, then stopped. What did I know about Percy? He seemed like a decent man, but did I want to share details of my past with him? My doubt must have shown.

'You can trust me, you know.' He stretched out his long limbs and shifted to face me. 'I'm not as daft as I seem, really I'm not.'

I decided to take the risk. I wanted to know more about Lady

Timpson's underhand business deals, and he was the only person who knew the family and the truth behind the land acquisitions. I took the plunge and told him the story of my mother's protest and death. He was silent as I spoke, but seeing his expression change, I was struck again by his ability to switch from chatty and charming to serious and thoughtful in an instant.

'I'm sorry about your mother.' He stood up. 'Shall we walk?'

I nodded. My feet were numb with cold.

'I can understand why you want to find out what happened to Rebecca Dent. But I'm not sure what I'm going to tell you will help you in any way.' He blew on his hands to warm them.

'I want to know more about Lady Timpson and these land acquisitions. It was around the same time. Were you involved with the society back then?' I realised I didn't know how old he was; I'd assumed mid-twenties.

'Yes, I'd flunked my exams the year before. University was out of the question. Father didn't know what to do with me. I was nineteen, and the only thing I'd shown any aptitude for was biology, so he got me a job cataloguing the herbarium at the Natural History Museum. That's when I got involved with the society and became a member.'

'When did the society approach the government for support?'

'It was after a meeting in February 1914. We began communicating with the Board of Agriculture and Fisheries and the Board of Education to see if they'd be willing to support us in any way. We wanted to try to get representatives from the boards onto our council. We made some useful contacts, and one of them gave us a tip-off that there was a plan for the government's Development Commission to reclaim extensive areas of "wasteland" to grow more food.'

'Wasteland?' This didn't sound promising.

'Don't be so sceptical. You've seen that beautiful stretch of the canal at Crookham. On paper, it's a discarded industrialised water-way. But these "wastelands" are exactly the type of places we want to see as nature reserves. Our contact said we should make a list of sites we'd like to see preserved and issue it to the government as quickly as possible. By the summer, we'd identified ninety-eight sites.' His face showed how much he'd enjoyed this project. 'Some glorious places.'

'Who exactly was supposed to buy these sites?'

We stopped by the Serpentine to watch a pair of swans glide through the water.

'The idea was that if the Development Commissioners from the Board of Agriculture and Fisheries purchased any of the sites, they'd retain a small portion of the land to be used as a nature reserve.' He pushed his hair back.

'Was any land used in this way?' I was beginning to realise what had been lost.

'Not a single acre. The list was leaked. Before preliminary negotiations with the board started, someone would tell the landowner that the government planned to claim their land and put it under some sort of protection order. They were persuaded to sell off their wasteland for cultivation and to support livestock. The government couldn't touch the land if it was already being used for food production.'

'So they sold to Timpson Foods?'

'Every time.' He shook his head in disbelief. 'Lady Timpson would show our list to the landowners and tell them the govern-ment was going to force them to hand over their land for free or a paltry sum. Not true, of course. Instead, she put in an offer for the land, lower than its true value and most took her up on it.'

'But how did Lady Timpson get hold of your list?' It crossed my mind that Daniel could have been involved but given his love of nature, it seemed unlikely.

'She paid an MP, who we think was on the Board of Agriculture and Fisheries.'

'How do you know?'

'Donald Anstey told us.'

Donald bloody Anstey. That dratted man again. I sighed in exasperation. 'But how did he know?'

'He said he couldn't reveal his source. He worked for the board at the time and knew lots of people in Westminster.'

'What happened next?'

'Not much. We couldn't prove it. We were fumbling around taking legal advice but didn't have a clue how to fight back. The war was the final nail in the coffin. Food was more important than nature reserves, and Lady Timpson told landowners they'd be helping the war effort as her company would use the land for food production, which was true.' He shrugged. 'Politically, the matter was moved off the agenda and never got put back on again.'

'And Lady Timpson carried on buying up land cheaply and getting even richer?' Anger flared at the thought of her stealing Percy's precious list and using it for her own benefit.

'She did very well out of the war.' He dug his hands in his pockets.

'What about now? Will you try again?'

'We won't be issuing any more lists. We learnt our lesson there. Instead, we're lobbying MPs to introduce a law to make certain sites protected nature reserves. But we could do without Lady Timpson getting elected. She's never going to support us. Anstey's our preferred choice.'

'What about Mrs Siddons?'

'She doesn't know us. We want to try to talk to her as we can't be sure Anstey will get past the post.'

'I can arrange for you to meet her. Can you come to Walden? She's spending most of her time there with the election coming up.' I was even more determined Mrs Siddons should win the by-election. 'I'm sure she can be persuaded to support you. I mean, the society.'

'I'd be delighted to come to Walden.' He beamed. 'Shall we have a picnic at Waldenmere? No, too cold at this time of year, isn't it? I could bring a blanket to keep us warm?'

'There's a meeting at the town hall in a couple of weeks. All of the candidates will be speaking. I'll introduce you to her afterwards.'

'Oh yes, of course. Great fun. I promise to be on my best behaviour.'

I smiled. Then remembered my father and Elijah would be at the meeting.

13

After my trip to London, I wasn't sure how or if I should continue my investigations. Ena's recollections of the protest had made me even more confused about Rebecca. Why hadn't she left the House of Commons with my mother? And what Percy had told me may have given me some insight into Lady Timpson's character, but it hadn't revealed anything else of interest.

Then I received a letter from Constance Timpson inviting me to Crookham Hall on a day when her parents would be in London.

To avoid the expense of a carriage, I decided to walk to Waldenmere and take the lake path up to the canal. By following the towpath of the navigation through to the Crookham estate, I could see the dwellings Donald Anstey had spoken about.

When I reached Blacksmith's Bridge, I crossed to take a closer look. On one side of the bridge were the picturesque pastures and woodland belonging to the Timpsons. On the other side, the bank gave way to patchy grassland, where there was a gathering of about a dozen caravans and shacks. In the distance was the Moffats' farmhouse. It looked derelict. The roof of one of the barns was collapsing, and there was no sign of any livestock.

I had to admit Donald Anstey was right. This was no place to bring up children. I could hear a baby crying inside one of the caravans, and bare-footed toddlers played on the grass. It was a warm April day, but I could see how cold the poorly constructed shacks would be in winter.

A group of young men noticed me; their expressions were far from welcoming. One began to amble towards me. 'What are you doing here?'

I recognised him as Samuel Moffat. His jacket was full of holes, and he looked like he could do with a good meal. This was a young man who'd been awarded a military medal for bravery in the field. I recalled Mrs Siddons' comments about poorly educated young men who'd served their country and were now unemployed and living in poverty. Had Samuel enjoyed better food in the trenches than he was getting now?

'Visiting Crookham Hall.' I stood my ground.

'Well, you're going the wrong way.' He pointed towards his farm. 'That ain't Crookham Hall.' His friends laughed.

'I work for *The Walden Herald*. I've been interviewing some of the candidates standing in the by-election. They've been talking about building housing here.'

'That's all it is. Talk. Same hot air we heard from politicians all through the war,' he growled, to mutterings of agreement from his friends.

'Wouldn't you like to sell this place?' I gestured to the farmhouse. 'It must be hard to make a living.'

'It wouldn't be so bad if the Timpsons paid what's due.'

'What do they owe you?' I couldn't imagine the Timpsons being indebted to the Moffats.

'None of your bloody business.' He moved closer to me. 'And don't go printing any lies in your paper.'

'We don't print lies. If you have a grievance against the Timpsons, we may be able to help you.'

'I don't need your bloody help.'

I decided it was time to leave. I went back over Blacksmith's Bridge and cut away from the towpath into a meadow that was part of the Crookham estate. I didn't think they'd risk following me.

'Hey, you, this is private land.' I saw Daniel Timpson riding towards me.

I'd worn trousers because they were more practical for walking. Now I realised this might have been a mistake. There had been accusations of poaching made about Samuel and his friends, and Daniel might have a gun. I waved in what I hoped was a non-threatening way.

'Miss Woodmore.' He pulled at the reins and came to a halt. 'I'm sorry. I thought you were a poacher.'

'Constance invited me. The easiest way for me to get here was to walk.' I was relieved to see he wasn't armed, then I recalled Lord Timpson saying that Daniel didn't shoot.

'Were Samuel and his cronies bothering you?'

'No. I was just being too nosy for their liking.'

'Sometimes he puts on an act in front of those other ruffians. But he's not a bad lad. We've known each other since we were kids.'

'Why's he so angry?'

'He's had it rough since leaving the army. His twin brother, Isaac, was killed in action, and his parents died of the Spanish influenza towards the end of the war. There's only him and his sister, Hannah, now, and they can't manage that place on their own.'

'Samuel mentioned something about being owed money by your family?' I was curious to see how he would react to this.

'My father used to give old Ned Moffat money to help them

out. But since those shacks have sprung up, Mother's put a stop to it.'

'He made it sound as though there was some sort of arrangement.' Whatever it was, it was callous of Lady Timpson to deprive Samuel and his sister when they were so desperate.

'He's got some ridiculous notion that the farm is an access route to the estate, and we should pay him for using it. It's not true. The council owns Blacksmith's Bridge which used to provide carriage access, but it's a footbridge now, and we don't use it anyway. I suppose it will be a different matter if this business takes off.'

'Their farm's in a terrible state.'

'I'd like to buy it from him. Not that it would be a good investment, it's poor land. I've no idea how old Ned managed to keep it going all those years. But Mother could put her damn warehouses there instead.'

'But what would the Moffats do?'

'I could find work for Samuel on the farm and something for Hannah in the hall. I just need to persuade Mother to stump up the cash.'

When Lady Timpson got to hear of Donald Anstey's plans to build new houses there, she might change her mind about buying the Moffats' land.

'Hop aboard old Marley. I'll ride you to the hall.'

Marley was a huge black stallion, and I wasn't sure hopping aboard was possible. With Daniel's help, I managed to clamber on, though I'm sure I heard a disguised snort of laughter at my ungainly effort.

Once safely seated, I enjoyed the canter across the fields. The landscape was breathtaking and clinging to Daniel, I felt like the heroine of a romantic novel being carried off by her lover. This

fantasy soon wore thin as he began to drone on about the agricultural practices he employed on the estate.

With relief, I part jumped and part fell off Marley when we
reached the hall. 'How interesting. I hadn't realised how much
farming goes on here.'

'Has he been boring you with his views on animal husbandry?'
Constance came out to greet us.

'It was fascinating,' I lied. Far from listening, I'd been
pondering who was better looking, Daniel or Percy. Daniel's dark
lashes and serious expression were appealing. But I was becoming
fond of Percy's open, eager face.

'Are you coming in for tea?' she asked her brother.

'I'll join you briefly.' He was staring at my trousers again.

It felt intimidating to enter the vast green reception room
without Elijah by my side. But Constance and Daniel chatted
easily, and the relaxed atmosphere was in stark contrast to the
stilted family interview. Without Lord and Lady Timpson present,
Crookham Hall was an entirely different place.

'Daniel and I have been talking about Rebecca,' Constance said
in her silvery voice. 'We don't mention her in front of our parents.
Mother's still angry over her being a suffragette.'

'I think she's still alive,' Daniel announced.

'Why are you so certain?' I asked.

'It's just a hunch I have. She was bright, had ideas. I think she
got fed up with being a servant. Who can blame her? I'm not sure
she wants to be found.' A flicker in his eyes made me think he was
trying to convey something without saying it.

'You may be right.' I looked at him closely, but he gave nothing
away.

'I must get back to the stables.' He stood. 'It was lovely to see
you again, Iris. Next time, I'll give you a tour of the whole estate.'

Constance watched him stride from the room. 'I think he's taken a shine to you.'

'I'm sure he was only being polite. He thought I was a poacher when he first saw me.'

She laughed. 'He's not used to girls wearing trousers. We've had a conventional upbringing. And he doesn't socialise much, not since the war.'

'Your mother wants him to go into the family business?'

'She did. In reality, Daniel's better suited to running this place. I'm the one who wants to take over the business.'

'Do you?'

'Yes, despite Miss Cotton's best endeavours, I've managed to acquire some useful skills.'

I laughed. 'I'm not sure I could handle the responsibility. The livelihoods of all those people dependent on you – doesn't that scare you?' Though from my conversation with Daniel, it seemed the Timpsons took for granted the control they had over other people's lives.

'It does. But I think I could improve things. Mother still runs Timpson Foods the way her father ran Hinchcliffe Holdings. I'd make changes, starting by removing all the children from the factories. But something like that takes time. You can't suddenly deprive a family of a wage they need.'

'Wouldn't she welcome another woman following in her footsteps?' Despite my dislike of Lady Timpson, I had a grudging respect for the way she'd become successful in a man's world. But I'd also heard rumours about Timpson Foods' disregard for employee welfare. Success at what cost?

'She's coming around to the idea. She knows how unhappy it would make Daniel to take him away from the farm. Anyway, we're both off the hook for the moment. This election's taking up all of her time. It's stopped her from trying to find me a suitable husband and Daniel a respectable occupation.'

'Can't you do both? Run a business and marry well? She did.' I stopped abruptly. This might imply I thought Lady Timpson had married above her station. 'Sorry, I didn't mean...'

'Don't worry. I know everyone says Father married Mother for her money and she married him for his title. And there's some truth in that. But it's an arrangement that's worked well for both of them. They've had twenty-three happy years together.'

I was taken aback by this candid statement. But it gave me an opportunity to fulfil Horace's request without being too obvious. 'It must be expensive to keep the hall looking so beautiful. I've heard some owners of stately homes have been forced to sell their family heirlooms. At least you have the Star Sapphire to fall back on,' I joked.

She smiled. 'Father's too attached to his family's history to sell it. But what's the point of having something that no one can admire? We're not even allowed to wear it any more.'

'I'd love to see it one day.'

'I sometimes think Father's forgotten where it is. It always used to be on the mantelpiece in his study. We would play with it as children. But I suppose he thought better of it and locked it away.'

It seemed even she hadn't seen the jewel for years.

'At the canal, you said you had something to tell me about Rebecca?' Despite her casual manner, I could tell she was keen to get to the real reason for my visit.

'When I went to the House of Commons, something happened that made me want to find out more about my mother's death.' I wasn't prepared to reveal Mother might have jumped into the Thames. 'That's when I found out Rebecca was with her that day.'

'With your mother? Rebecca broke into the House of Commons?' Constance was astounded.

'She acted as a lookout whilst my mother painted the grilles.'

'I can't believe it. She was such a quiet woman. I'd never have dreamt she could be so daring.' She was shaking her head. 'Are you sure?'

I nodded. 'Did she give any indication that something was wrong before she disappeared?'

'No, nothing. She was simply here one day and gone the next.'

'Did you think someone may have harmed her?'

'Not at first. We just thought she'd run off with a man. She was very pretty. Although it was strange that she didn't take any of her belongings.' Constance paused. 'As the years went by with no word, I did begin to wonder if something may have happened.'

'Do you think she's dead?'

'I'm afraid I do now. Father wrote to one of his contacts in the police. I'm not sure they'd have bothered about her otherwise. I think they would have found her if she was still alive, living in hiding, as Daniel suspects.'

It was what I'd been expecting, but I was dismayed to hear her say it.

'I'm sorry. You were hoping for better news?'

'I wanted to find out more about the House of Commons protest and if there's a link between what happened to my mother and Rebecca's disappearance.' I expected scepticism at this suggestion, but she seemed to consider the idea.

'It shows Rebecca was leading a double life. No one here had a clue what was going on. We never dreamt she was involved with the suffragettes.'

'Do you still have her possessions?'

'Miss Grange, our housekeeper, packed them in a trunk should she ever come back. Would you like to see them?'

'Yes, please.' I had an absurd notion that seeing and touching Rebecca's belongings would give me some insight into her mind.

I followed Constance through the house, up several staircases, glimpsing more vast rooms with high ceilings and tall windows that offered panoramic views of the estate. I wondered what it was like to call this place home. It was a grand palace filled with ornate furniture and precious ornaments. The family coat of arms was displayed under portraits and on shields. Did living here make you oblivious to its beauty? The Timpsons seemed to take their life of privilege for granted. But what if you were a servant? Did you enjoy working amongst this splendour? Or was there a darker side to being part of the Timpson empire?

Even the box room was a grand affair. I'd expected a dusty, windowless attic. Instead, it was light and airy, thanks to a domed atrium in the ceiling. In one corner of the room sat a large black trunk. Next to it was a wooden table that had seen better days.

'I often used to sit with Rebecca at this sewing table when it was in the nursery.' Constance touched its tarnished surface. 'Her embroidery was exquisite. She taught me to sew, but I never had her gift.'

'She taught me, as well. I once helped her embroider sashes for the suffragettes, but I could never achieve her tiny, precise stitching.'

'She kept so much a secret from us.' Constance opened the trunk. 'Do you know what you're looking for?'

'No, not really.' I hadn't a clue what I hoped to find. 'I'm probably wasting your time.'

'Don't worry, I'll leave you to it. Take as long as you like. Come and find me in the reception room when you've finished.'

I was grateful to her for leaving me alone. For some reason, I wanted to do this by myself.

I opened the trunk and began to take out Rebecca's possessions. One by one, I carefully placed each item on the table. Out of habit, I made a detailed list:

*Bloomers, chemises, corsets, corset covers and petticoats –
none new but all clean and carefully repaired.*

Two full-skirted grey dresses with stiff white collars.

Three white starched aprons.

Two white starched caps.

A winter dress and a few summer dresses.

A pair of frayed calfskin gloves.

A box of hairpins.

Hair ribbons.

*A matching hairbrush and mirror decorated with tiny pink roses
on a white background.*

A nearly empty jar of Ponds cold cream.

A box of powder, one of rouge, and a powder puff.

*A paste and glass brooch of a bouquet of flowers tied with a
ribbon.*

A book on vegetarian cookery.

A timetable showing trains from Walden to Waterloo.

A copy of Votes for Women *newspaper dated February 1914.*

A silk postcard with the word Friendship *embroidered on the
front. Handwritten on the back are the words* Or love? *and the
initial* D.

It wasn't much to show for a life. I picked up the postcard. The
words were written in dark blue ink in a precise, almost square
type of handwriting. There were few curves to the letters but lots
of sharp lines. Was D the mysterious boyfriend? The one Rebecca
didn't talk about? I slipped the card into my pocket. No one would
miss it, and it was the only clue I had.

14

I was placing the clothes back in the trunk when it occurred to me that there were no shoes or boots amongst the items. Or coats. Hope flared. Perhaps Rebecca had run away after all.

I left the box room and was on my way downstairs when I spotted a green baize door, which I guessed would take me through to the servants' quarters. No one was around, so I gave it a gentle push. The hinges moved silently, and in one step, I left the grandeur of the main house, with its ornate furniture and luxurious drapes, for a dark corridor with white painted walls. There were no decorations except for a row of bells with labels underneath.

I stood for a moment, wondering what to do next. I had no idea of the layout of the house. All I knew was that if I worked my way downwards on this side of the door, I'd eventually land up in the kitchens.

I walked along the corridor and found it led into yet another corridor, lined with doors on either side. One of them opened, and a maid appeared. She jumped at the sight of me.

'Who are you?' she demanded.

'Iris Woodmore. I'm visiting Constance. Miss Timpson, I mean. I took a wrong turning.'

'You're a long way from the reception room.' She eyed me with distrust.

'I was in the box room. Miss Timpson allowed me to look through a trunk.'

'Oh, yes. Rebecca's things.' She looked slightly appeased by this. 'Miss Grange did say you were up there.'

'Her room must have been along here? Rebecca's?' I had no idea if this was true or not.

'It's my room now. I'm Head Housemaid.' She had a youthful, fresh face, slightly plump, with freckles across her cheeks.

'Did you know Rebecca?' I doubted she'd remember her.

'A bit.'

'You must have been quite young.'

'I was fourteen when I went into service. I was a laundry maid when I started here. Then I got moved into the house. Rebecca had to train me.' She still regarded me with suspicion. 'Why are you looking for her?'

'She was a friend of my mother's. I've only just found out she's missing.'

'Didn't your mother tell you?'

'My mother died shortly before Rebecca disappeared.'

'I'm sorry, miss.'

'What's your name?' Her frostiness had thawed slightly, and I decided to take advantage of her sympathy.

'Olive Evans.'

'I hope you don't mind me asking, but did you like Rebecca?' It was an odd question, but her answer could be revealing.

'I didn't really know her. She kept herself to herself, but she was kind to me. Some of the others thought she was a bit stuck up, but she wasn't. She read books and spoke better than us. But she didn't think she was better than us.'

'Did she seem upset when you last saw her? Or unhappy?'

'She wasn't upset. But she wasn't happy either. I don't think she'd been happy for a long time.'

'What makes you say that?'

'She didn't fit in. She didn't want to fit in. I think she wanted to be somewhere else. Do something else.'

'You think she ran away, then?'

She shrugged but scrutinised my face.

'What is it?' I could tell she was tempted to say more.

She looked up and down the corridor and beckoned me into the room she'd come out of. It was simply furnished with a single bed pushed up against the wall, a slim wardrobe, and a chest of drawers with a washbasin on top. The scent of rose water hung in the air.

Olive lifted the corner of a patterned rectangular rug lying next to the bed and removed a small section of floorboard.

I knelt beside her. For a wild moment, it crossed my mind she'd found the Star Sapphire. But when I peered into the small square cavity, it was empty.

'What did you find?'

'Nothing.'

'Oh.' I sat back on my heels.

'But something must have been hidden here. Look, it's lined with fabric.' She pointed. 'So Rebecca must have taken whatever it was.'

I saw what she meant. Nothing had been left behind in her private hiding place. But had the sapphire once been there?

'There's another thing.' Olive's eyes were bright, and her gestures animated. She'd obviously given this some thought and was eager to share her findings. 'They said none of her possessions were gone, but that's not true. She had a small gold locket. I never saw it around her neck here at the hall. But I saw her once at the railway station when she got off the train from London. She was wearing it then. But it wasn't there when I helped Miss Grange pack up her belongings.'

'Do you know where she got it?' I stood, contemplating the sparsely furnished room.

Olive replaced the board and moved the rug over it. When she rose, I could see she was blushing.

'Do you think it was given to her by a boyfriend?' I asked.

'Maybe.' Again, she looked as if she was wrestling with herself over whether to tell me something.

'Do you know anyone with the initial D?' I tried. 'A member of staff, perhaps?'

'The postcard, you mean? I couldn't figure that one out. It's not from any of the staff. It could have been Daniel. He did moon after her a bit. But I can't see him sending a postcard like that.'

I couldn't help thinking Olive was a girl after my own heart. A natural detective. Or nosy parker, as Elijah preferred to call it.

'Who do you think gave her the locket?' I asked.

'One night, I got up late. I thought I heard a noise coming from her room and opened my door. My room was further up the corridor then, nearer to the backstairs.'

'What did you see?'

'Lord Timpson was walking along the corridor. I can't be sure, but I think he must have come from this room.'

'You think he and Rebecca had...' I tried to think of an appropriate phrase. 'Been together?'

She nodded.

I didn't know much about places like Crookham Hall, but I guessed it would be highly irregular for Lord Timpson to venture into this part of the house.

'You won't tell anyone I told you, will you?' She brushed down her skirt and straightened her apron.

I shook my head. 'Do you like working here?'

'It's considered one of the finest houses in Hampshire.' Her expression told me she knew this wasn't what I'd meant.

'Do the family treat you well?'

'I like my room. And the food's good.' She hesitated. 'Sometimes Lady Timpson can be difficult to please. But Lord Timpson's always nice. That's why I was so shocked when I saw him that night.'

'One more question. Have you ever seen the Star Sapphire?'

She laughed. 'Just once. It's quite spectacular. Dark blue with this white light.'

'When was that?'

'Lady Timpson wore it at the last big garden party we had before the war.' Olive considered further. 'That would have been in June 1914, I think. I've never seen it since then.'

I was tempted to ask if she knew where it was kept but decided this might make me sound like a potential jewel thief.

'I've got to get downstairs now.' She opened the door and checked it was clear before we went out into the corridor.

I was about to thank her when a shrill voice interrupted us.

'Olive, what's going on?' A primly dressed woman emerged from a door at the end of the corridor.

'Miss Woodmore was lost, Miss Grange. I was taking her to Miss Constance.' Olive's innocent expression looked well-rehearsed.

'Sorry, I must have come through the wrong door.' I tried to appear confused.

'I'll take you downstairs. Olive, get to the kitchen.'

'Thank you, Olive. I'm sorry to have disturbed you,' I said to her retreating figure.

'That's alright, miss.' She gave me a broad wink.

I smiled and sprinted after Miss Grange, who was heading at speed towards the door to the main house. 'I was wondering about Miss Dent's coats and shoes,' I said to her back. 'There don't seem to be any in the trunk.'

'I gave them to one of the undermaids. There was a shortage during the war. It seemed a shame to let them go to waste.'

That glimmer of hope died. She pushed open the green baize door and ushered me through.

'Did you know Miss Dent well?' I asked.

'Not well.' She paused to look at me. She seemed happier now I was back on the right side of the door. 'I don't think anyone knew her well. But she was a diligent employee. I had high hopes for her.'

'What hopes?'

'I planned to train her to take over from me when I retire. It would have been a huge step up for her. But she showed little interest.'

After what I'd learnt about Rebecca, this didn't surprise me.

'She said, "A servant is a servant no matter what the title." This was just after she'd been promoted to Head Housemaid and given her own room.' Miss Grange shook her head in disbelief.

I followed her down to the wisteria-papered reception room, where Constance was seated at a desk by the window. I hoped Miss Grange wouldn't feel the need to mention where she'd found me.

'I came across Miss Woodmore in the servants' quarters with Olive,' she announced. I resisted the urge to poke my tongue out at her.

I gave a helpless shrug. 'Went through the wrong door.'

Constance raised her shapely eyebrows, her expression doubtful. After Miss Grange left, she asked, 'Did you find anything?' Her tone wasn't as warm as it had been earlier.

I shook my head. 'I'm not sure I really expected to. But it was kind of you to let me see her things.'

'My parents have the car in London, but I've arranged for one of our carriages to take you home.'

I replied that I was happy to walk, but she insisted. I suspected she wanted to make sure I left the estate without snooping any further.

As the carriage rolled away from the hall, I looked out at the acres of land. Had this vast estate somehow swallowed Rebecca up? Or had she escaped? I was grateful to Constance for her openness, but part of me still felt vexed by the Timpsons. Who had mourned Rebecca? She hadn't any family. Constance and Daniel had expressed a fondness for her, but she was just another servant to them. A new head housemaid had been trained, and life had gone on as usual.

I took the postcard out of my pocket. D, whoever they were, had cared for Rebecca. Friendship. Or love? That was the question.

Two people in the family had the initial D – Daniel and Delphina. I couldn't imagine either one of them writing such a message. Daniel had been sixteen at the time. It was conceivable he'd developed feelings for Rebecca but unlikely he was the mysterious boyfriend she would meet in London. He would have been away at school in Winchester. But it was possible.

What about Delphina? Would Lady Timpson risk everything for a love affair with another woman? I couldn't see it. If it became known, the scandal would be too great. She'd end up losing her family and her business. But again, it was possible.

And had Rebecca reciprocated her admirer's feelings? Or had she been in love with Lord Timpson? If their affair, if that's what it was, had soured, it would have given her a reason to run away. It would also have given Lady Timpson a reason to hate her.

I was confused as to what Rebecca had wanted from life. She'd clearly hoped for change. Against her better judgement, she'd taken part in a risky protest. She'd probably wanted to leave Crookham Hall. But why disappear off the face of the earth when she could have just handed in her notice?

Although I'd learnt more about Rebecca, I still didn't have a clue where she was. Would the mystery only be solved if her body was discovered?

As the carriage turned, I caught a glimpse of the strange mausoleum in the distance. What better place to make a body disappear than to hide it amongst other bodies. But it wasn't a place I'd care to search.

15

'Here they are in all their glory.' Elijah placed photos of the three candidates in a row on his desk. All had provided us with their own pictures rather than sit for our photographer.

Mrs Siddons and Lady Timpson had opted for professional portraits. Still styling herself on Lady Astor, in her full-length shot Lady Timpson was sporting a tricorn hat and neatly fitted suit. She'd adopted a serious, meditative expression.

Mrs Siddons had gone for a head-and-shoulders portrait. She wore a velvet cap, drop earrings and a dress with a low neckline. She gave a *Mona Lisa*-like half-smile, as though she were planning to seduce the electorate.

By contrast, Mr Anstey had provided a snapshot of himself standing on a wooden box in the street, addressing a group of workers holding placards saying 'Restore Trade Union Rights'.

'God help us.' Elijah shook his head with a grin.

I had to smile. What would voters make of this diverse choice?

'Drop these off downstairs on your way out.' He handed them to me. 'Along with this.'

He'd finally approved the article I'd written on Mrs Siddons.

We could begin our campaign. But I knew that by aligning the newspaper with her, Mr Laffaye would refuse to publish an appeal for information on Rebecca should Lady Timpson win.

After I'd finished with the typesetter, I went to the lake and found Alice painting at Heron Bay. I told her about my visit to Crookham Hall and my encounter with Daniel Timpson and his stallion, Marley.

She laughed. 'How romantic. It was probably just as well you were wearing trousers. I wouldn't have attempted to climb on that horse.'

'How well do you know Daniel?' I was thinking of the postcard signed 'D'. 'Has he ever written to you?'

Her smile vanished. 'You sound like my mother.' She looked at her wristwatch and began to pack up her paints and easel. 'She's been encouraging me to pursue my friendship with Constance. What she really means is, try to get to know Daniel better. What a match that would be.'

I'd rarely heard Alice sound so bitter. 'I didn't mean that,' I stammered. 'It never occurred to me.'

'Ignore me. I'm being too sensitive. I know you don't think about such things. I wish I didn't have to.'

She was right. My family was unlikely to try to talk me into a marriage against my will. Well, Gran might. But it wasn't something I had to be concerned about. Alice, on the other hand, had good cause to worry.

'Why do you want to know if Daniel has written to me?' She took my arm as we walked.

'I want to see his handwriting.' I explained about the postcard I'd found.

'You think he may have had a relationship with Rebecca?'

'He could have been infatuated with her.'

'It's possible, I suppose. Socially, he's a little awkward with girls.

I remember Constance asking me to dance with him. She said he's a different person when he's out on the farm. But in the ballroom, he's a wallflower. She had to fill his dance card for him.' Alice pushed her long red hair back over her shoulders.

I pictured her dancing with Daniel. They would have made a striking couple.

'When was he away fighting?' I asked.

'He got a commission when he was eighteen and did a stint at Mill Ponds before being sent to France. That would have been 1916, I think.' She frowned, trying to remember. 'I didn't see much of him after that. Oh, apart from one dance. He was home on leave and even more withdrawn than he had been before.'

Of course he would get a commission. Straight to officer if you were the son of a lord.

'I wonder why Constance invited you to the hall,' Alice mused.

'Curiosity. I get the impression she wants to be the first to know if I find out anything.'

'To protect someone?'

'More to protect the family name and business. It's clear she intends to take over Timpson Foods one day. You should have seen the look she gave me when she found out I'd been snooping in the servants' quarters.'

She laughed. 'She does have a quiet determination. I wouldn't like to get on the wrong side of her.'

'Me neither. She's one of those people who always seems to know exactly how to behave and what to say. I wish I could be that poised.'

'And I thought you didn't care what people thought of you.' She gave me an affectionate nudge. 'I've always admired that about you.'

'I'm not that thick-skinned. I know people in Walden think I'm a bit odd.' I touched my cropped hair.

'Not odd.' She squeezed my arm. 'A little modern for our conventional town, perhaps.'

'That's what Constance said, in her way. But I don't think she's as conventional as she makes out. When I mentioned Donald Anstey's plan to build houses in place of the shacks and caravans, she wasn't as appalled as I'd expected. I thought she'd hate the idea of anything spoiling the landscape of their beloved ancestral home.' As I spoke, I realised I admired Constance.

Alice considered this. 'I don't think she loves the estate in the same way Daniel does. She wants to escape and make her mark in the world. I get the impression she feels trapped being Lord and Lady Timpson's daughter.'

'Her mother wants to find her a wealthy husband.' We were back to the uncomfortable subject of marriage.

'Poor Constance,' she said with feeling. 'Why can't she be allowed to choose her own husband?'

'She won't be short of admirers. Percy thinks she's splendid.' I smiled, thinking of his absurd chatter.

'I'd like to meet this Percy. He sounds funny.' Alice gave me a sideways glance. 'He obviously hasn't been put off by your unconventional appearance.'

'He's asked me to the pictures. And to one of those modern dance clubs in Soho.'

'Will you go?' She looked thrilled at the idea.

'Maybe.' I realised for the first time how much I wanted to see Percy again. 'Would you like to go out with Ben?'

'There's no chance of that.' She glanced at her wristwatch. 'I have to get home. Father doesn't like it if I stay out too long.'

I stood under the old jetty and watched her climb the slope to Sand Hills Hall. To a stranger, Alice Thackeray would appear to be a young woman blessed with good fortune. Beautiful, intelligent, kind-hearted and from a wealthy family. But since returning to

Walden, I'd come to realise how much her father ruled her life. She had little say in any decisions he made on her behalf, and I worried for her future.

I walked back past Grebe House and noticed Mrs Siddons' carriage was on the driveway. She was yet to be persuaded of the value of a motor car.

I knocked on the door, and her housekeeper showed me into the drawing room, where Mrs Siddons was writing letters.

'We've gone to press with my article.'

'Excellent. Pass on my thanks to Mr Whittle. I'll send a note to Mr Laffaye. *The Walden Herald*'s support could make all the difference.' She gestured to the sofa. 'Now sit down and tell me what else you've been up to.'

I sank into the red velvet cushions and recounted my visit to Crookham Hall. 'Has Lady Timpson ever mentioned Rebecca Dent to you?'

She shook her head. 'We've not been in contact for years. We occasionally run into each other at functions but rarely speak. I did once have a long conversation with Constance at a luncheon party. An astute young lady. I was impressed with her knowledge of industry.'

'She'd like to see children removed from their factories.'

'Good. My father took a stand on this many years ago. It made him highly unpopular at the time, but since then most factory owners have followed suit. Timpson Foods is still in the dark ages in many ways.' Her sapphire drop earrings swayed as she spoke.

'Have you ever seen the Star Sapphire?' I asked.

'No. And believe me, I'd like to.' She laughed. 'It's supposed to be incredible. A white six-rayed star on a deep blue stone. I'm surprised Delphina hasn't worn it during the campaign to get one up on me. I can't compete with anything like that.'

This was true. By wearing the sapphire in public, Lady

Timpson would be certain to generate newspaper attention and outdo one of her opponents. Why had she resisted the temptation?

'How did you meet her?' I was curious about Lady Timpson's background.

'Her father and my father weren't exactly friends, but they moved in the same business circles. Delphina and I were of a similar age and met socially at parties and dances.'

Mrs Siddons' father had been a well-known businessman and philanthropist who'd made a fortune in the textile industry and set up dozens of charitable institutions.

'Was this in York?'

'Yes, we lived in the city, and Delphina would often travel over from Barnsley to stay with us. We became friends.' She smiled. 'We squabbled a lot, but we laughed a lot too.'

'When did you fall out with her?' I could imagine these two strong-willed women coming to blows.

'Much later on. I was married and living in London with my husband. I expressed certain reservations when Delphina told me she planned to marry Tobias.'

'What reservations?'

She hesitated. 'It was a marriage of convenience. I wasn't sure that's what she wanted.'

I told her what Olive Evans had said about seeing Lord Timpson possibly coming from Rebecca's room.

'It doesn't surprise me.' She toyed with the sapphire ring on her finger.

'If Lady Timpson found out about it, how would she react?'

'She wouldn't.' She gave a dismissive wave of her hand. 'It's probably not the only cross she's had to bear. As I say, it was a marriage of convenience. Delphina was in love with his title.'

Constance had said as much, but it made for a strange relationship.

I changed tack. 'Did you hear about Timpson Foods buying parcels of land from under the nose of the Society for the Promotion of Nature Reserves?'

She smiled. 'Does this have something to do with the young man you want me to meet? He sounds like an interesting chap.'

'It was Elijah who put me on to it,' I countered. I knew she was fishing for information on Percy.

'I heard the rumours at the time. Something like that is typical of Delphina. Why are you interested in it?'

'Because it was around the same time as Rebecca's disappearance. And Lady Timpson has a reputation for being ruthless.'

She shook her head. 'It's true she was determined to succeed when she took over her father's business. She was always seeking his approval, and when he died, she felt it was her duty to continue his work.' She looked thoughtful. 'I wouldn't describe her as ruthless, though.'

But I got the impression something had occurred to her about Delphina that she wasn't willing to share with me.

16

'Iris,' a breathless voice called.

Percy bounded up the steps of Walden Town Hall two at a time. 'I ran from the railway station. Didn't want to miss any of the action.' He bent over double to gather his breath, taking advantage of this position to view the hemline of my dress. 'Jolly nice legs.'

My father and Elijah had made their way up the steps at a more sedate pace. But they reached us in time to hear these words.

'Percy,' I said loudly before he could say anything else. 'Let me introduce you to my father, Thomas Woodmore. And my boss, Elijah Whittle, Editor of *The Walden Herald*.'

'Ahhh.' Percy straightened up. 'Good to meet you, sirs. Percy Baverstock.'

'Of the Society for the Promotion of Nature Reserves, I presume?' Elijah gave me a wry smile.

'That's me.' Percy beamed. 'Looking forward to meeting Mrs Siddons this afternoon. Want to try to win her over. I plan to avoid the dreaded Lady T, though.'

There was a gentle cough from Lady Timpson, who was standing at the side of the steps with Daniel.

'Ahhh. Sorry. I mean, hello there.' Percy breathed. 'What ho, Daniel, old man.'

I couldn't help but admire the ease with which he floundered from one blunder to another.

'Hello, Percy,' Daniel said with a grin.

'We must go in now.' Lady Timpson glared, and we all shuffled to one side to let them pass. Daniel pulled a face at Percy and followed his mother.

'Shall we go in before I make an idiot of myself again?' Percy asked.

'I think that would be a good idea,' I replied.

Inside the hall, I went in search of Mrs Siddons.

Leaving Percy with my father and Elijah was risky, but I was intrigued to see how 'Delphina' and 'Sybil' would greet each other.

'How nice to see you again.' Lady Timpson was kissing the air around Mrs Siddons' cheek.

'Delphina, you're looking well.' Mrs Siddons returned the air kiss.

Wafts of expensive perfume competed with each other.

'Thank you, I think politics suits me.' Lady Timpson straightened the jacket of her fitted grey two-piece.

'More than business?' Mrs Siddons enquired.

'Fortunately, I have the stamina for both.'

I exchanged an amused glance with Constance, who was standing behind her mother. Lord Timpson was at his wife's side.

'You remember my old friend, Sybil, don't you, darling?' Lady Timpson gripped his arm.

'Of course.' Lord Timpson smiled warmly. 'Delighted to see you again. You must come and visit us at Crookham Hall sometime. Once all this election business is over.'

Lady Timpson stiffened at this suggestion – a hint of tension creased her brow.

'May the best woman win and all that. No hard feelings after the results are declared,' Lord Timpson continued. 'After all, it's only politics.'

'Quite right.' Mrs Siddons gave him her most gracious smile. 'We should all learn to forgive and forget.' A flicker passed between her and Lady Timpson as she said this.

'There's nothing to forgive.' For once, Lady Timpson sounded sincere.

As usual, Mrs Siddons' face gave nothing away.

A thought occurred to me. Before her marriage, could Mrs Siddons have once set her cap at Tobias Timpson? Perhaps rivalry over him had played a part in their falling out.

The two women made their way onto the stage whilst Constance, Lord Timpson and I went to find seats in the hall.

Lord Timpson placed his hand on my shoulder. 'Any news on our missing friend?'

I shook my head.

'Never mind. Perhaps no news is good news.'

I wasn't sure this was true. He'd called Rebecca a friend. Perhaps that's what she'd been to him. A friend. A lover. Or both? I thought of the words on the postcard. Friendship or love? Could they have had pet names for each other? A secret code between master and servant. Was Lord Timpson 'D'?

I sat down next to Percy as Lady Timpson took to the stage. Her speech was basically a repetition of the one she'd given at Blacksmith's Bridge. But this time, her audience hadn't been on the receiving end of her lavish hospitality beforehand. Nor were they local dignitaries. The working-class folk of Walden made up the majority of the crowd in the hall, and they seemed sceptical about her plans for the canal.

Mrs Siddons was next and gave a speech that was broader in its range, focusing particularly on education and housing. She received a warmer but still muted response. Although both women were dressed more sombrely than usual, even in their 'political suits', they were more expensively clothed than anyone else in the room.

'I think we've heard enough from the ladies for one afternoon,' announced Councillor William Mansbridge, who was hosting the proceedings. 'It's time to listen to what a man has to say.'

Sniggers from around the hall greeted this comment, and I caught a few mutterings about women taking men's jobs.

'Stupid man,' I whispered.

'Patronising nincompoop,' Percy replied loudly just as the applause died down. The audience turned to look at him, and Councillor Mansbridge glared in our direction.

I snorted with laughter. My father raised his eyebrows at me while Elijah regarded us with amusement.

Donald Anstey took to the stage, his expression as worn as his suit. But I had to admit, he looked more comfortable in this venue than his opponents. The town hall had the neglected feel of so many other municipal buildings since the war, and his appearance matched the surroundings.

He droned on about the Labour Party for a while, and I heard a few stifled yawns. As I'd anticipated, his ponderous way of talking was lulling the audience into a bored stupor.

But when he began to describe his plans for building a housing estate near Crookham Hall, he came to life. And so did the audience.

The look of disgust on Lady Timpson's face was a sight to behold. Even Lord Timpson's good-natured expression faltered. By contrast, Constance seemed to be hanging on Donald's every word.

He finished to loud applause, and to my annoyance, my father was clapping and nodding in agreement. I hoped the rest of the audience were only applauding because they'd enjoyed seeing Lady Timpson's horrified expression.

The hall emptied quickly, and with some trepidation, I took Percy to meet Mrs Siddons.

I needn't have worried that he would fail to impress. When it came to his work, Percy was knowledgeable and committed. He succinctly explained the society's objectives and why they were seeking legislation to create nature reserves. Mrs Siddons had been enthusiastic in her offer of support.

I felt absurdly pleased with him and agreed to his suggestion of a stroll around Waldenmere before he caught his train back to London. The weather was perfect, showing the lake at its best. Sunshine with the odd puff of white cloud reflected on the water. Birdsong filled the air, otherwise, all was quiet.

'It's beautiful.' Percy linked his arm through mine. 'You're lucky to have this on your doorstep.'

'It's the best thing about Walden.'

'Is it why you moved back?'

'My father thought we'd be happier here.'

'Are you?'

I shrugged. 'I'm not sure. I don't know where I want to be. I miss London. But I love being near Waldenmere – I find it soothing.'

'I can see why. I enjoy walking in the parks in London, but they're nothing compared to this.' He took a deep breath, as though inhaling as much of the scene as he could. 'I should like to live here.'

'There aren't any dancing clubs in Walden.' I smiled, thinking him a strange mix, a city boy with a love of nature.

'That's true. I do love dancing. What do you do of an evening?' His face wrinkled in concern at the lack of dancing opportunities.

'Not much. But I have some good friends here.' I gestured towards Heron Bay. 'Two of them are over there.'

Alice was painting in her usual spot while Ben perched on a log, watching her. We strolled over, and I introduced Percy.

'That's so life like.' Percy inspected the picture. 'You're very good.'

Alice blushed. 'It helps to have such glorious scenery to paint.'

'I can see why it's called Heron Bay.' Percy squinted at an island of tall fir trees close to the shore. 'I can see fourteen nests.'

'Isn't it early for chicks?' I asked.

'Herons lay their eggs in February or March and incubate for around twenty-five days. They'll be hatching now. Look, see that male? His throat's full of fish to feed his young. I wish I'd brought my field glasses.' He raised his hand to shield his eyes from the sun. 'It's so quiet and peaceful compared to London. I bet nothing bad ever happens here. Does the local bobby sit in the pub drinking stout and playing dominoes all day?'

Alice giggled.

'I sometimes tear myself away to go on my rounds,' Ben said drily.

'Ben's our local police constable,' I explained.

'Ahh, sorry, old man. Didn't realise you were a Peeler. Nothing but admiration for you chaps.' Percy lent towards him confidingly. 'Always been most obliging when I've had one too many lemonades and forgotten where I live.'

'Indeed,' Ben said with a smile.

Alice laughed again.

'I once spent the night in Marylebone Police Station with some fascinating ladies...'

'Time to catch your train, Percy,' I interrupted.

'Is it? Of course, yes, must go. I hope we meet again.' He looked at Alice when he said this.

I took his arm and dragged him away.

'She's jolly pretty,' he commented as soon as we were out of earshot. 'That policeman chap certainly thinks so.'

'I just hope her father doesn't catch them together.'

'Surely he can't disapprove of a policeman? I'd have thought any father would be delighted to have an upright citizen like that for his daughter instead of some idiot like me.'

'Alice is from a distinguished family, the daughter of a Colonel. Ben is the son of the local blacksmith.'

'Oh, the good old British class system. Thankfully, I've got parents who don't give a jot. They'd welcome any girl willing to have me with open arms. But so far, there haven't been any takers.'

I chuckled.

'What's your father like?' Percy asked.

'A bit of a socialist.'

'Probably wants you to marry some chap like Anstey.'

I shuddered at the thought. 'I have no intention of marrying anyone,' I declared. 'Not if I'm supposed to become the property of my husband.'

'Yes, chattels and all that rot. I'm in no rush to enter into the state of matrimony either. Too many pretty girls to dance with. Daniel's sister, Constance, is a complete stunner, isn't she?'

'Percy, is there any girl you don't like?'

He considered this. 'I am quite keen on the fairer sex. But after being stuck in an army camp and the trenches for years, I feel I've spent quite enough time with my own sex.'

'It must have been rough.' I knew better than to ask how rough. Few men liked to talk about their wartime experiences, and I'd learnt to curb my tongue on that particular subject.

'I'm one of the lucky ones. For whatever reason, I came back in one piece.' His expression became serious. 'Lost some great pals. I feel it would be wrong to squander my good fortune. It's my duty to live for them.'

'I can understand that.' Having seen so many lives lost, I couldn't blame Percy for wanting to enjoy his.

'Does that mean you'll come dancing with me?' He skipped ahead and turned to block my path.

'Maybe one of these days when I'm feeling daring.' I pushed him to one side and carried on walking.

'You mean one of these days when you've had a row with your father and want to rebel?' He returned to my side.

I laughed. 'You're more astute than you look.'

He pulled a face. 'I'll take that as a compliment, I think.'

We stopped outside the railway station.

'Any news on Rebecca?' A sudden switch from playful to serious again.

I told him about my trip to Crookham Hall. 'Constance thinks she's probably dead.'

'She may be right. It's been a long time with no word. Don't look so forlorn.' He kissed me lightly on the cheek before I could protest. 'You've come back to Walden to be happy. And you deserve to be happy.'

With that, he bounded off towards the station.

* * *

I opened the front door quietly. I'd spent longer with Percy than I'd intended. I paused in the hallway, listening for voices. If Elijah was in the drawing room with my father, I could tiptoe upstairs to my room without them noticing. If Father were alone, he'd start asking me questions.

'Your father's not back yet.' Lizzy appeared from the kitchen, startling me.

'He must have gone for a drink with Elijah. Or he's having another meeting with Donald Anstey,' I said with irritation.

'No, Mr Anstey was here a while ago looking for him. He left those documents for your father to read.' She gestured to a folder on the hall table before returning to the kitchen.

I was halfway up the stairs when I glanced down and something caught my eye.

A handwritten note was clipped to the front of the folder. It was signed 'D'.

I went up to my room and rummaged in the drawer of my old wooden desk. I found Rebecca's mysterious postcard and took it downstairs.

On the hall table, I placed the postcard and Donald Anstey's note side by side. The handwriting appeared to be identical – precise letters written in sharp lines with no curves – and the same shade of dark blue ink had been used on both. Could Donald Anstey be Rebecca Dent's secret boyfriend?

17

'So, what does young Mr Baverstock want with you?' Elijah stood over my desk.

'To go dancing with him in a club in Soho.'

He sniggered. 'Have you mentioned this to your father?'

'No. I thought I'd go and stay with Gran and Aunt Maud. I could sneak out at night in my short dress, meet Percy, get drunk and then sneak back without them knowing.'

'Hmmm,' was all he said.

'I'm joking.'

'I know.' He ambled towards his den. 'Perhaps I wish you weren't.'

'What do you mean?' I said to his retreating figure.

He turned to stand in the doorway. 'Why aren't you a silly girl?'

'Would you want me to be?' We'd had bizarre conversations before but usually brandy had been involved.

He contemplated me. 'No. But sometimes I think you ought to be.'

'Why?'

'I'm not sure.' He shrugged. 'I don't know what girls are supposed to be like. But perhaps you grew up too soon.'

'There's not a lot I can do about that now. I think you'll find a whole generation has grown up too soon.'

'That's true. Mind you, young Percy seems daft enough.'

'He's not as daft as he looks,' I retorted. 'Well, he is at times.'

I followed him into his den and placed Rebecca's postcard on his desk. Beside it, I put the note from Donald Anstey that I'd sneakily retrieved from the wastepaper basket in my father's study.

'What's this?' He inspected them as he lit a cigarette.

'It's a postcard sent to Rebecca. It was amongst her possessions at Crookham Hall. This is a note Donald Anstey left for my father yesterday.'

Elijah examined them closely, then let out a low whistle. 'It does look like the same hand,' he admitted. 'It's quite distinctive.'

'I want to ask him about her. I could make up some reason to call at his cottage. Tell him I'd like to write a piece on his housing project.'

'No.' He leant back in his chair. 'I'm not saying Anstey's done anything wrong, but I don't think you should tackle him alone. We'll talk to him together.'

'When shall we go? What shall we say?' I dropped into the chair in front of his desk.

'Slow down. We're not going anywhere. Anstey's supposed to be stopping by to collect his photograph. It's the only copy he has. We'll wait for him to show up here. It'll be better than turning up at his home and asking him personal questions about his love life.'

I had to swallow my impatience. I could see the sense in this. 'Do you think they were seeing each other?'

'Was he taking her dancing in Soho?' Elijah puffed on his cigarette. 'Can't see it somehow.'

He wasn't going to let me forget Percy and his dance clubs for a while. 'He probably took her on a romantic evening out to a trade union rally,' I said.

'You may joke,' he waved his cigarette in the air, 'but if they were courting, it could well have been politics that brought them together.'

He had a point. My parents had met at a political meeting.

* * *

We had to wait two long days before Donald Anstey made an appearance.

'Hello,' he called from the door of the outer office.

I signalled to Elijah in his den. He reached into his drawer for the appeal page we'd mocked-up and placed it at the centre of his desk. The headline read:

Crookham Hall Maid Still Missing After Six Years.

'Mr Anstey, you've come for your photograph.' Elijah pushed the photo across his desk, so it sat next to the mock-up.

Donald Anstey went to pick it up and then stopped. His hand hovered in mid-air; his eyes glued to the headline.

'Rebecca Dent?' He was suddenly alert. 'Has there been a development in the case?'

'No.' Elijah pushed the mock-up to one side as if it were of no interest. 'We're preparing an appeal for information. We won't be publishing this until after the by-election.'

'Why now?' He managed to force his gaze away from the headline to focus on Elijah.

'I'm surprised you're aware of the case.' I watched him from the doorway. 'You mentioned you'd only lived in Walden for about a year.'

'I read about it at the time.'

'Really?' Elijah said. 'The case didn't receive much newspaper coverage. That's why we want to appeal for information now.'

Donald was silent.

Elijah slid the mock-up back across his desk. 'If we remind people, someone might come forward with new information for the police.'

'The police aren't interested.' His eyes stayed fixed on the tiny photograph of Rebecca under the headline.

'Why do you say that?' I asked.

'Just the impression I got.'

I expected him to say more, but he was silent.

I grew impatient. 'Rebecca Dent was a friend of my mother's.'

He nodded, seemingly aware of this. Another silence followed.

'When I found out Rebecca was with my mother at the House of Commons, I wanted to speak to her. That's when I discovered she was missing. I've been trying to learn all I can about her disappearance.'

Donald didn't seem surprised that Rebecca was involved in the protest. But he still didn't say anything.

I looked at Elijah in exasperation. He gave a slight nod. We'd given him every opportunity to tell us about his relationship with Rebecca. And judging by his reaction, there had been one.

'I have something to show you.' I placed Rebecca's postcard on the desk.

'What's this?' He picked up the card and turned it over.

'Constance Timpson allowed me to go through Rebecca's possessions. This was amongst them. I recognised your handwriting from the note you wrote to my father.'

Donald's face crumpled. He slumped down into a chair, looking defeated. But he still didn't say anything.

'The message would indicate you were on fairly intimate terms with Miss Dent?' Elijah pressed.

'I loved her.' He buried his head in his hands.

I wasn't sure if he was crying, and I didn't care. At last, he'd shown some emotion. 'How did you come to know her?'

Donald raised his head. 'She had a friend, Kathleen Hooper. Kathleen's husband, Leonard, was a member of the Labour Party. The Hoopers brought her along to a talk I was giving. She stood out from the crowd with her long blonde hair. Leonard introduced us, and I fell for her at once.'

'You used to meet with her on a Friday?'

He didn't ask how I knew this. 'It was her day off. She would come up to town to get her hair done and then meet me from work. I finished early on a Friday.' He was smiling. 'Those were the happiest days of my life.'

'You knew she was a suffragette?'

He nodded. 'I also campaigned for suffrage. But I became concerned by some of the WSPU's activities. Rebecca told me she was thinking of leaving them and joining a less militant organisation.'

Again, I had that niggling worry of how much influence my strong-willed mother had exerted over the younger woman.

'Did she want to leave her job too?'

'She wasn't happy at Crookham Hall. She wanted to move away and start afresh as a seamstress. I planned to help her, but I didn't have much money. We began to save what we could.'

'When did you last see Rebecca?'

'In July 1914. I told her I'd be away for a few weeks, staying with my family in Scotland. I knew war was inevitable. If it was declared, I felt it was my duty to enlist right away; my work at the board was hardly vital. But I wanted to see my parents before I did.' He paused, his face haggard. 'I never saw Rebecca again.' His expression showed the bewilderment he evidently still felt.

'Is Rebecca the reason you moved to Walden?' I asked.

He nodded. 'I couldn't do much to find her during the war. I was away fighting for over four years. As soon as I returned to England, I came here.'

'Have you discovered anything since you've been in Walden?'

'Not much. But I think the Timpsons are hiding something.'

'Why?' I wondered if he suspected an affair.

Elijah shook his head slightly. He'd advised me not to mention Olive Evans' suspicion that Lord Timpson had been in Rebecca's room.

'I don't know. Anything I say now will look as though I'm trying to discredit an opponent.' A spark of anger lit his weary face. 'But one of the family is involved, I'm sure of it. Daniel was smitten with her.'

'Did she tell you this?' I asked.

He nodded. 'She was kind to the boy, but she had to be firm with him. He was just out of school. Lady Timpson noticed, and it made things awkward for Rebecca.'

This gave both Daniel and Lady Timpson a motive for wanting Rebecca out of the way. Daniel could have become angry at her rejection. Or discovered she was having a relationship with his father. It was also possible Lady Timpson had taken action to solve the problem.

'Why didn't you go to the police after she went missing?' I couldn't understand why he hadn't revealed their relationship at the time. He seemed to have genuinely cared for Rebecca.

'I had no reason to. There was nothing I could tell them.' His tone was defensive.

It was an inadequate response, and I was about to say so, but

Elijah gave another warning shake of his head. We'd pushed Anstey far enough for the time being.

But why had he hidden his involvement with Rebecca? And had he really been in Scotland at the time of her disappearance, or was he giving himself an alibi? If he'd discovered she was secretly seeing Lord Timpson, he could have reacted violently. By his own admission, he'd been in love with her.

* * *

'I'm going to call in at the Station House on my way home and tell Ben about Donald's relationship with Rebecca.'

Elijah grunted in reply. His head drooped, his chin nearly resting on his chest. I picked up my jacket and bag and left him to doze.

But when I reached the high street, a horse-drawn black Maria sped past, followed by Ben and PC Sid King on their bicycles, pedalling furiously. I set off in the direction of the town hall.

The high street was livelier than usual, with people chatting outside shops, enjoying the April sunshine. Something had definitely happened to rouse Walden from its usual slumber.

Inside the town hall, members of the Walden Women's Group were standing behind long trestle tables, sorting through piles of clothes and dividing them into cardboard boxes. The room was buzzing with animated conversation.

I spotted Alice at a table towards the back of the hall with Mrs Gilbert and a couple of other ladies.

'What's going on?' I asked. 'I've just seen Ben and Sid following a black Maria. Where are they heading?'

'Crookham Hall.' Alice placed a baby's blanket into a box labelled 'Carter family'.

'Why, what's happened?' I immediately thought of Rebecca. Had a body been found?

'Ben wouldn't say.' She pushed the box across the table. 'This is everything on the Carters' list, Mrs Gilbert.'

'There's been an incident,' said an elderly lady in a theatrical whisper. I recognised her as Miss Briggs, who lived on the same road as me.

'Someone saw the doctor at Blacksmith's Bridge,' a red-faced woman added. 'I wouldn't be surprised if it's got something to do with those folks living in the shacks.'

Miss Briggs agreed, waving a lavender-scented handkerchief under her nose as if she could smell the shacks from here. She began an indignant conversation with the red-faced woman about the disgraceful way some people lived.

'We'll find out soon enough,' Mrs Gilbert said with a frown.

I realised I'd caused yet another interruption to an already eventful afternoon.

'Do you think someone at the hall came across a poacher?' Alice said quietly.

'That's what I was thinking,' I replied.

After my visit to Crookham Hall, I'd asked my father what would happen if a poacher did get shot.

'It depends how serious it is. If they're just wounded and one of the Timpsons did the shooting, the magistrate will probably let them off,' he'd replied in disgust. 'Anstey's right to prioritise the problem. It's a disaster waiting to happen. These people have families to feed. You can't expect them not to go looking for food.'

I hadn't been able to argue.

* * *

'You've heard the gossip then?' Elijah called from his den when I turned up early for work the following morning.

I didn't bother to pretend my appearance at this hour was due to anything other than pure nosiness. I dropped my bag on my desk and hurried into his office.

'I saw the police heading to Crookham Hall yesterday after I left here. What have you heard?'

'Lord Timpson is dead.'

18

I gasped. His expression told me he was serious.

'Dead? How?'

'I don't know yet. I received a note from Ben Gilbert first thing. He wants to talk to me this morning.'

'Why? Do you know something about it?'

He shook his head. 'Ben and I have an agreement. Or to be more accurate, he acts on orders from Superintendent Cobbe. Ben gives me certain information about a crime if the superintendent thinks some publicity might help.'

'It's a crime, then?'

'That's the impression I'm getting.'

'Poor Constance and Daniel.'

'And Lady Timpson,' he reminded me.

'Yes, I suppose so.' But despite what Constance had said, I wasn't convinced Delphina Timpson had cared for her husband. 'Shall I take notes for you when Ben comes in?'

He snorted. 'You'll probably listen at the door if I say no.'

'I will not,' I lied.

'Make some coffee and I'll let you sit in.' He yawned. 'I'm sure Ben could do with a cup. He's probably been up half the night.'

I hurried to the outer office and put the water on to boil.

* * *

Ben sank into the seat in front of Elijah's desk and took the coffee from me. He was unshaven, his usual air of efficiency diminished by tiredness.

'What's happened?' I sat down next to him.

Elijah coughed, giving me a sardonic smile.

'Sorry.' I was supposed to let him ask the questions. I picked up my pencil and notebook and tried to look efficient.

'Lord Timpson was found floating in the canal at Blacksmith's Bridge. It appears he suffered a head injury and drowned.'

I inhaled sharply.

'Bloody hell.' Elijah dropped his cigarette.

'A shotgun was found in the water. But there are no wounds to suggest Lord Timpson had been shot. A Home Office pathologist is coming from London later today to examine his body.'

'Had the gun been fired?' Elijah asked.

'A ballistics expert is checking it over.'

'When was Lord Timpson last seen?' I frowned, this wasn't looking good for Samuel Moffat and his pals.

'He went out riding with Lady Timpson after breakfast yesterday morning. She returned first. This wasn't unusual. On the occasions they rode together, Lord Timpson generally stayed out longer than his wife. She left him at around ten o'clock.' Ben checked his notebook. 'At one o'clock, the family sat down to luncheon. That's when they realised he wasn't back. Daniel went to look for him and found his father's body in the canal by Black-smith's Bridge.'

'What do you think happened?' I asked. 'Could it have been a poacher?'

'We're looking into it.' Ben sounded cautious. 'It's possible he challenged someone and they retaliated.'

'Did he have any valuables on him?' Elijah asked.

'His family said he would have had a pocket watch, cigarette case and lighter. We can't find them, but they could be in the water. We're searching the canal. His horse is a valuable beast, yet it was still there. Daniel spotted it – that's how he came to find his father.'

'Could Lord Timpson simply have lost his footing? Or fallen from his horse?' I asked.

'We've examined the scene. It doesn't seem likely. But we'll wait to hear what the pathologist says.' Ben rubbed his eyes and yawned.

Elijah picked up his pen. 'I take it Superintendent Cobbe wants to appeal for information?'

Ben nodded. 'He asked if you could report that Lord Timpson was involved in a tragic accident at Blacksmith's Bridge. He wants you to mention the precise location and ask anyone who was in that area in the last couple of days to contact Walden Station House.'

Elijah nodded, scratching his chin. 'Unofficially, what are your thoughts on this?'

'I don't think it was an accident.' Ben leant forward. 'Judging by the marks on the ground, a scuffle took place. It could have been an altercation with one of the men from the shacks on the other side of the canal. Or...' He trailed off.

'What?'

'It's possible it could have been an employee, or former employee, with a grudge.'

'Anyone in particular?'

Ben shook his head. 'It's just a general line of enquiry.'

'Why is it?' My thoughts raced to Rebecca. 'Why should someone have a grudge?'

'Nothing specific. Some of the servants we interviewed at Crookham Hall commented that the Timpsons were demanding to work for. A few years ago, there was a maid who took her own life. And before that, Rebecca Dent went missing.'

'Lord Timpson seemed a decent enough chap, though,' Elijah commented.

'Perhaps he had a habit of seducing maids,' I remarked.

'The complaints tended to be about Lady Timpson rather than the rest of the family. As I say, it's just something that came up during our enquiries.'

I poured him more coffee. 'Could there be a connection between Rebecca's disappearance and Lord Timpson's death?'

'Possibly. But unless we know what that connection is, there's not much we can do.'

I was silent. A terrible thought occurred to me. By trying to find Rebecca, had I put others in danger? Was it possible that Lord Timpson had discovered something about her? Then been killed before he could tell anyone?

* * *

Over the following weeks, the police continued to question everyone at Crookham Hall and on the Moffats' land. Despite the appeal in *The Walden Herald*, no new information emerged. Lord Timpson had been seen at Blacksmith's Bridge in the days prior to his death by some of his estate workers, but they hadn't noticed anyone with him.

The pathologist wasn't certain but suspected the head injury had caused Lord Timpson to fall into the canal and drown. No gunshot wounds had been found on the body.

Walden was rife with gossip, and this only intensified as time went by and no arrests were made. With nothing new to report, we had to focus on the by-election. But this was of secondary interest to our readers, although there was speculation that Lady Timpson would stand down.

'I'm going to the Station House to see if anything's happened.'

Elijah looked up from the note he was reading. 'Be back by two. We've been summoned. Mr Laffaye would like us to pay him a visit.'

'Why?'

'He'll explain when we get there.'

A bleary-eyed Ben opened the door to the Station House.

'Any news?'

He shook his head. I followed him into the tiny kitchen, wrinkling my nose at the stack of unwashed dishes in the sink. He shared the house with PC Sid King, and the pair of them only cleaned up when they knew Ben's mother was due to call in with their laundry.

'I've been thinking about Rebecca. Donald Anstey said he was in Scotland when she went missing.'

'And?' Ben looked wary.

'Is there any way you can check his alibi?' I wondered if I should try to ingratiate myself by offering to do the washing-up. I inspected the sink and decided against it.

'Only by questioning his parents. And I wouldn't get permission.' He placed a kettle on the stove.

I changed tack to something else that had been bothering me. 'This is going to sound macabre, but I've been thinking about the mausoleum.'

'Mausoleum?' He rubbed his unshaven chin. His expression was still not encouraging.

'At Crookham Hall.'

'I see what you mean.' He looked more interested. 'A body hidden amongst bodies?'

'Yes. No one would think to look there.'

'Superintendent Cobbe did.'

'Did he?'

He went into the office and rifled through a messy heap of papers on the desk.

'The Super let me read his notes from the original investigation into Rebecca's disappearance.' He scanned the pages. 'Here it is. The hall and all its outbuildings were searched.'

'But did that include the mausoleum?'

'The general manager had keys to all of the outbuildings except the mausoleum. Lord Timpson was the only one with a key. The Super insisted the mausoleum be opened up.' He wrinkled his nose. 'Pity the poor bugger who got that job.'

I nodded in agreement. I'd quickly dismissed the idea of somehow trying to gain access and take a look myself.

'Lord Timpson accompanied the officer to the mausoleum.' Ben read from the notes. 'He stood by whilst a search was made and then locked it up again afterwards.'

'What did they find?'

'Nothing. Except what was supposed to be there.'

I was disappointed but relieved at the same time. I hadn't wanted that gothic tomb to have been Rebecca's final resting place. 'The grounds were searched too?'

'Not by the police. The estate's too large and there wasn't the manpower. Lord Timpson organised a search; he had his estate workers out for hours. They didn't find anything out of the ordinary.'

I frowned. 'I can't help wondering if Lord Timpson did come across something incriminating to do with Rebecca.'

'We'll never know.' He showed me to the door. 'I'll see you at two o'clock.'

I looked at him in surprise.

He grinned. 'I've been summoned by Mr Laffaye too.'

* * *

That afternoon, Elijah and I strolled down to Heron Bay Lodge. Tall trees obscured much of the house from public view, and I was looking forward to finally seeing beyond the gates.

Elijah fished a key from his pocket, unlocked a small side gate and escorted me through. I lingered to take in the splendour of the gardens. The lawns looked like they'd been trimmed with a pair of nail scissors. Flowering shrubs and herbs in lilacs and purples had blossomed in the early May sunshine, and the borders were a mesmerising haze of colour.

Ben was already seated on the high veranda that dominated the front of the house. He'd loosened his collar, evidently hot and uncomfortable in his police tunic.

A smartly dressed young man greeted Elijah and ushered us through a reception room and up some stairs. Horace waited for the young man to return with a tray of glasses and a jug of lemonade before getting down to business.

'So kind of you all to join me.' He paused to sip his drink. 'It's been weeks since Lord Timpson's death, and I'm concerned at the lack of progress being made in the case. I contacted Superintendent Cobbe, and he's been most helpful in allowing PC Gilbert to come here to discuss the matter with us.'

Elijah smiled at this. I guessed Horace had somehow made it worth the superintendent's while.

'I'm about to give PC Gilbert a file that contains information on Lord Timpson's financial affairs, which may or may not have a bearing on the case.' Horace's hand rested on a bulging manila folder.

I was beginning to understand how he operated. He'd instructed his network of contacts to do some digging on Lord Timpson. He was now using their findings as leverage with the superintendent to gain access to the enquiry.

'I've managed to acquire Lord Timpson's financial records. They show he was in considerable debt. He owed a substantial amount of money to gambling clubs.' Horace coughed. 'And other establishments of a dubious nature, shall we say.'

I wasn't entirely sure what he meant by this. I assumed he was referring to brothels but wasn't about to ask. Being at this meeting was making me feel grown-up, and I didn't want to spoil the illusion. However, I was shocked by these revelations. They certainly didn't fit in with the image I'd formed of Lord Timpson.

'Do you think he could have taken his own life because of his debts?' Elijah asked.

'No,' Ben said. 'The head wound wasn't self-inflicted. It could have been the result of a fall. But the evidence would suggest something happened at the scene to make him fall.'

'Besides,' Horace added, 'his wife is not in any debt. Quite the contrary, she's an extremely wealthy woman. His records show that in recent years, she's been bailing him out of his financial predicaments. She owns Timpson Foods, which in turn finances Crookham Hall.'

'But if she controls their finances, how was he able to accrue such large debts before she began bailing him out?' Elijah asked.

Horace smiled at him. 'That's the interesting part. Up until six years ago, he'd used the Star Sapphire as collateral. But records show the last time he did this was in July 1914.'

'Shortly before Rebecca went missing.' It couldn't be a coincidence.

19

'If Rebecca Dent had stolen the Star Sapphire, wouldn't he have reported it?' Ben finished his lemonade.

Horace enlightened him. 'If he did, his financial affairs would have come crashing down. He couldn't afford to let his creditors know he didn't have it.'

'But why would she take it?' Elijah shook his head. 'She wouldn't be able to sell it without drawing attention to herself.'

'True. My contacts have checked, and there have been no rumours of it making an appearance on the market, legally or otherwise. It could still be safely locked away at Crookham Hall.' Horace ran his finger around the side of his glass. 'As his debts increased, Lord Timpson may simply have decided he didn't want to risk losing it and sought financial support from his wife instead.'

'But if it had been stolen, it would explain why he was so keen to find Rebecca.' I thought he'd cared about her, but it could have been concern over his sapphire. 'When I spoke to Constance, it was clear she hasn't seen it for many years. Neither has their Head Housemaid, Olive Evans.'

It dawned on me that Horace had probably asked me to accompany Elijah because of my friendship, albeit slight, with Constance and Daniel. He was looking for inside information on the family.

'It would also explain why he allowed Lady Timpson to use the estate for her canal business.' I wanted to prove my worth. 'He wasn't enthusiastic about the plans, and Daniel hates the idea.'

'She bails him out in exchange for getting her own way?' Ben suggested.

'That would make sense,' Horace agreed.

'But perhaps she was getting tired of bailing him out. Any hint of scandal could scupper her chances of becoming an MP,' I offered.

Ben nodded. 'And she was the last person to see him alive.'

'Why does she want to become an MP?' Elijah pondered.

'To try to influence labour laws?' Horace suggested. 'Or am I being too cynical?'

'You're probably right.' Elijah took a swig of lemonade and grimaced. This wasn't his usual tipple.

It was true the introduction of new legislation on pay and conditions in factories could have a significant impact on Timpson Foods. But there was also the matter of the strange rivalry with Mrs Siddons. Constance had thought it was this that had prompted her mother to stand. I wasn't about to mention my theory that the two women had rowed over Lord Timpson. My friendship with Mrs Siddons was too valuable for that.

'But why would she risk killing him if she was already getting her own way?' Ben said.

'True.' Horace sighed.

'What about the employee with a grudge?' I asked Ben. 'You mentioned a maid who died by suicide. When was that?'

'In 1916. It was Lydia Moffat, younger sister of Samuel and Hannah Moffat. She was fifteen and had been working as a laundry maid at the hall.'

No wonder Samuel was angry. 'Have you spoken to the Moffats?'

'Samuel didn't have much to say. He'd enlisted and was in France when it happened. Hannah told me Lydia was scared because their parents were frail. They'd been struggling to cope on the farm without their brothers. Isaac, Samuel's twin, had been killed a month before.'

'The war was a frightening time for many young people,' Horace observed.

He was a strange man, I thought. Compassionate but at the same time controlling.

'Perhaps Samuel held the Timpsons responsible for Lydia's death?' I suggested. 'And he seems to think they owe him money for using his land as an access route to the estate.'

'We'll try speaking to him again. But he and his pals are closing ranks. We know they've probably been poaching on the estate at night, and they're reluctant to talk.'

'Is that your main line of enquiry?' Horace asked.

Ben nodded. 'A poaching or trespassing incident that went wrong. We think it was unlikely to be deliberate. More an unfortunate encounter. The person probably didn't mean to kill.'

'But in broad daylight?' Elijah queried.

'That's the problem,' Ben conceded. 'Samuel and his cronies generally don't risk venturing over the bridge during the day.'

'What about the shotgun?' I asked. 'Do you know where it came from?'

Ben shook his head. 'No one has reported a gun missing.'

'Could Lord Timpson have been threatened by his creditors?' Elijah suggested. 'And they acted on those threats?'

'I'll discuss it with Superintendent Cobbe when I deliver this.' Ben tapped the manila folder. 'It's worth looking into.'

'Could he have been killed because he found out something

about Rebecca?' I had to mention my fear. 'Donald Anstey said Daniel Timpson was infatuated with her. And Olive Evans thinks she saw Lord Timpson coming from her room.'

'Mr Anstey should have come forward at the time and told the police he was seeing Miss Dent.' Ben was clearly unimpressed by Donald's behaviour.

'He's convinced the Timpsons know what happened to her,' I said.

'The boyfriend is more likely to be the killer.' Ben wiped his brow with a handkerchief. 'He could just be trying to shift the blame.'

'You think she's dead?' I wished I knew one way or the other.

'I don't know.' He shrugged. 'But it's been six years and no trace of her. If she is dead, it's likely she was killed at the time of her disappearance.'

'When Donald Anstey was in Scotland with his parents,' Elijah reminded me.

'We've only got his word for that. Did you ask Superintendent Cobbe if you could check?' I said to Ben.

'The answer was no. I'm sorry. But after all this time, it's unlikely we're going to find out what happened to her. Unless a body suddenly materialises.'

* * *

Ben and I walked back into town together. Elijah had been persuaded to stay and enjoy a small nip of Horace's specially imported French brandy. I didn't expect to see him again that day.

'What do you think Horace hoped to gain from that meeting?' I wasn't sure we'd made any progress.

'An afternoon's entertainment?'

I laughed. 'He does make you feel as though you're a pawn in his game of chess.'

'He certainly does,' Ben replied with feeling.

'Does he interfere often?'

'Not often. But he always knows what's going on in town. And he has the ear of people in high places.' He waved the manila file.

'I'm beginning to realise how wide his network of contacts is.'

'He usually just wants to help. But it can be unnerving. It's not only Superintendent Cobbe I answer to.'

'Do you think his information will help?'

'It's given us an insight into Lord Timpson's character. But I'm not sure what his creditors would gain by harming him. Not if they knew Lady Timpson was likely to bail him out.'

'What do you make of Lady Timpson?' I could imagine her reaction to police questioning.

'A difficult nut to crack. Her account of where and when she left her husband during their ride that morning is a bit hazy. If we press her, she says she's a busy woman and can't possibly remember every detail.'

'Will you question her again?'

'No, the superintendent says not. There's nothing to suggest she was involved. He wants us to concentrate on other leads.'

I felt that Lady Timpson was being let off too easily. But then again, how plausible was it that she'd attack her husband in broad daylight?

I'd written a letter of condolence to Constance and Daniel and was tempted to visit but decided that might be trespassing on our slight friendship too much.

Then, to our surprise, Elijah received a telephone call from Lady Timpson's secretary asking us to visit Crookham Hall. She informed him that her Ladyship would send a carriage.

Once again, we were shown into the green wisteria-papered

reception room that was becoming familiar. Constance was seated next to her mother, but there was no sign of Daniel.

Lady Timpson rose to greet us, and Elijah and I spotted it at the same time.

He managed to suppress any sign of surprise, but I gasped.

'Is–is that...?' I stammered.

Around her neck was an amazing deep blue stone. A white six-rayed star seemed to burst from its surface.

20

'The Star Sapphire? Yes.' Lady Timpson touched it lightly with her fingers as though it were her private talisman. 'I felt I should wear it in honour of my late husband.'

Elijah and I sat down, our eyes fixed on the stone. It was mesmerising. I noticed Constance kept peeking at it too.

'I wanted to thank you for your kind article regarding my husband's death.' Lady Timpson paused. 'And to ask for a favour.'

Elijah inclined his head for her to continue. He would be desperate to tell Horace about this.

'I've decided to stop campaigning.' She looked pale, and her hands shook as she took a sip of tea.

'Does that mean you're standing down as a candidate?' My attention was momentarily diverted from the sapphire. Mrs Siddons would have it in the bag if there was only Donald Anstey to contend with.

'No. I've come this far. I'd be letting my family and supporters down if I withdrew at this late stage. But it wouldn't be appropriate to continue campaigning given my tragic circumstances. I'd be grateful if you could let your readers know.' Lady Timpson lacked her usual vigour, and there was even a touch of fragility about her.

'Certainly,' Elijah replied.

'Of course, what the other candidates choose to do is their affair,' she added, her implication clear.

'Mother. I'm not sure we can expect Mrs Siddons or Mr Anstey to bring their campaigns to a halt.' Constance shot me an apologetic look.

'Whether they think it appropriate to continue is for their consciences to decide,' Lady Timpson murmured.

It was a shrewd move, designed to put her opponents in an awkward position. I could imagine Mrs Siddons' reaction. Delphina Timpson may be weakened, but she wasn't going down without a fight. And she might gain some sympathy votes.

'Has anyone come forward with any information following the publication of your article?' Her hand went back to her chest as if checking the sapphire was still there.

'Not that I'm aware of,' Elijah replied. 'Superintendent Cobbe hasn't informed us of any new developments.'

'I was afraid that would be the case. Blacksmith's Bridge is rather remote. And, of course, it's private land. Not many people pass that way.'

'PC Gilbert mentioned your husband had been seen there in the days prior to his death. Have you any idea what he might have been doing there?' Elijah asked.

'I can only imagine it was something to do with Basingstoke Canal Holdings. He was full of ideas about the new venture.'

Constance frowned at this. Lord Timpson had shown no enthusiasm for his estate being used to accommodate a freight business. She plainly thought it unlikely this had been the reason for her father's visits to the canal.

I'd hoped for a private word with Constance, but with Lady

Timpson clinging to her, there was no opportunity. I gave her a sympathetic smile as we left – and took a last, lingering look at the Star Sapphire. Elijah did the same. I guessed he was storing up every detail to share with Horace.

We went out into the courtyard, where the carriage was waiting, but the horses were still at the trough. Elijah lit a cigarette and told the groom not to rush.

Enclosed by three sides of the hall, I appreciated how vast the building was – and how many people worked there. Grooms, farmworkers, kitchen and house staff bustled around us, keeping the machine that was Crookham Hall well oiled. This wouldn't have made it easy for Rebecca to have left the servants' quarters without being seen.

I heard a whispered, 'Miss Woodmore', and saw Olive Evans peeking out from behind two massive milk churns. She beckoned me to join her in her hiding place.

'You work for the newspaper, don't you?' She stared at me with round eyes. Her face was flushed, and the scent of her rose water perfume mingled with the smell of fresh milk.

'Yes, *The Walden Herald*.'

'Can I tell you something privately that won't go in the paper?'

'Of course. But you should tell the police if you know anything about Lord Timpson's death.'

'It's not that.' She pushed her hands into the pockets of her apron. 'It's just that I overheard Daniel and his father rowing about Rebecca Dent. I thought you'd want to know. You seemed so keen to find her.'

'What did they say?'

'I couldn't hear. Daniel raised his voice a few times, and Lord Timpson told him to shut up. But I definitely heard Daniel say her name.'

'When was this?'

'The day before Lord Timpson's accident.'

'Did you tell the police?'

She shook her head. 'Daniel's a gentle sort. I don't think he had anything to do with what happened.'

I thought for a moment. 'Olive, I'm going to mention what you've told me to PC Gilbert. He's a friend of mine. He won't say anything unless it turns out to be important. But he might want to talk to you. I'll ask him to be discreet and speak to you privately. Would that be alright?'

She readily agreed, obviously not averse to the thought of a private meeting with Ben. 'PC Gilbert interviewed us. He was nice.'

'I must go.' From between the milk churns, I could see Elijah looking puzzled by my disappearance. 'Thank you for telling me.'

Checking no one was around, I emerged whilst Elijah's back was turned, taking delight in confusing him even more.

'Where have you been?' He climbed up into the carriage.

I waited until we'd moved off and couldn't be heard above the horses' hooves before I told him what Olive had said. 'What do you make of it?'

He scratched his head. 'A strange end to an already strange afternoon.'

It had been an odd interview. 'I think Daniel knows something or suspects something about Rebecca. Perhaps it involves his mother. But he couldn't speak to her, so went to his father instead?'

'Possibly. She's a strange woman, Delphina Timpson.' He reached for his cigarettes. 'I can't make her out.'

'Why wear the Star Sapphire now? She touched it like it was a good luck charm rather than a priceless family heirloom.' But I was relieved to know Rebecca hadn't stolen it. And it showed Lord Timpson had been genuinely concerned for her, not his sapphire.

'It can't be a coincidence she gets to wear the jewel now her husband's dead.'

'You think he stopped her from wearing it before?'

'Yes, I do. It's his family's legacy, not hers.'

Aside from the astonishing reappearance of the sapphire, there was something else about Lady Timpson's reaction that jarred. But I couldn't put my finger on precisely what it was. 'Do you think she's involved in his death?'

'Not directly. But she knows something.'

'When you say not directly, you mean she may have got someone else to do her dirty work for her?' I wanted Elijah to make sense of it all, but he seemed as bewildered as I felt.

'Maybe.' He stared out of the window at the hall. 'There's something not right about that place.'

'What happens now?'

'I'm afraid that nothing is going to happen now.' He gestured towards the estate. 'Anything hidden out there is likely to stay hidden.'

'And Lady Timpson's not the sort of woman to admit to anything.' I sat back and listened to the sound of the hooves on the gravel drive. I didn't want to look at those vast acres of woodland.

But it turned out that Elijah was wrong. Some of Lady Timpson's secrets were about to be uncovered.

21

'We've arrested Lady Timpson on suspicion of murdering her husband.'

I gaped at Ben. I'd arrived in the office to find him slumped in Elijah's den, gulping coffee.

'Why?' I demanded.

'We questioned Samuel Moffat again. He admitted to being near Blacksmith's Bridge on the morning of Lord Timpson's death. He saw Lord and Lady Timpson ride towards the bridge and dismount.'

'And then what?'

'He scarpered before they saw him.'

'Why didn't he tell you this before?' From Elijah's expression, he was still reeling from this news.

'He was scared. He thought if we knew he was there, we'd assume he had something to do with Lord Timpson's death.'

Elijah tapped his pen on his blotter. 'But what about the shotgun you found in the canal?'

'Samuel swears he never saw a shotgun.'

'Could it have been concealed on one of the horses?' I asked.

'The groom says not. He helped both Lord and Lady Timpson mount and is certain neither had a shotgun. It wouldn't have been easy to conceal.' He yawned. 'Have you got any more coffee?'

I went to reheat some.

'But what did Lady Timpson do?' I stood by the door, keeping one eye on the stove.

'Only she can tell us that. And so far, she's not talking.' Ben raised a hand in a helpless gesture.

'Which looks suspicious.' Elijah rummaged around for his cigarettes. 'But would she really hit him over the head and push him into the water? That's a pretty risky way to kill someone.'

'You said the other day she knew more than she was letting on.' I poured the coffee and put a cup in front of Ben.

'Yes. But not that she killed him herself.' Elijah waved his cigarette at me. 'Why take that risk? Would she really lure him there, bash him over the head with a handy rock and push him in the canal? That would take some strength. And where does the shotgun fit in? It doesn't make sense to me.'

'But she lied about not going to Blacksmith's Bridge with him,' Ben argued. 'She told us she left him at around ten o'clock when they reached the meadows to the south of the canal. She said he must have ridden on to the canal afterwards. But Samuel Moffat saw her there at around ten fifteen.'

'He could be lying. He could have attacked Lord Timpson himself.' I breathed in the coffee and cigarette fumes, trying to get my brain to work.

'He could.' Ben sipped his coffee. 'But Lady Timpson's not denying what he said.'

'What does Superintendent Cobbe make of this?' Elijah stubbed out his cigarette and picked up his pen.

'He was reluctant to take her into custody. But she left us with no choice. We've been questioning her at Crookham Hall, and she won't talk.'

'I can't make her out.' Elijah leant back in his chair.

'Nor can we,' Ben said in exasperation.

'Maybe she murdered Rebecca too?'

'How?' Elijah countered. 'It can't be easy for a well-known figure like Lady Timpson to dispose of a body.'

'She could have arranged for someone to do it for her.'

'But then we're back to the question of why kill her husband herself if she had other means at her disposal? If she paid someone to kill Rebecca and got away with it, she'd almost certainly do the same thing again. Not ride to the canal with her husband and do it herself.' Elijah shook his head, clearly yet to be convinced of Lady Timpson's guilt. 'What happens now?'

'We can't keep it a secret that we have her in custody. The staff saw us taking her away. We want you to break the story. But sympathetically. No doubt the London papers will print all sorts of rubbish. Here's what Superintendent Cobbe would like you to publish.' Ben pulled out a crumpled sheet of paper. 'He's happy for you to quote him directly.'

At last, we had something other than the by-election to put on the front page.

'What's he hoping to achieve by this?' Elijah scanned the sheet of paper.

'We need people to give us information. This case isn't solved. If Lady Timpson doesn't talk, we'll have no choice but to charge her. But we need more to get a conviction.'

Elijah read what the superintendent had written and nodded.

After Ben left the office, he got up and plucked his jacket off the hatstand.

'Where are you going?' I thought he'd start drafting the article immediately.

'To see Horace. I need to tell him in person what's going on.' He had a definite spring in his step.

'Can I use the telephone?' I asked.

'Why?' He regarded me suspiciously.

'I'd like to speak to Constance.'

'Alright. But don't go to the hall on your own.' He paused, his hand resting on the doorknob. 'I know you're concerned about her. But we still don't know what's going on there.'

Half an hour later, I was speeding to Crookham Hall. When I'd finally managed to get through on the telephone, Constance had begged me to come over and sent their chauffeur to pick me up. Even though I was distracted by events, I still enjoyed the experience of being driven fast in a motor car.

When I got to the hall, Constance was seated in the reception room, dabbing her eyes with a handkerchief. 'I can't take it in.'

It was Daniel who took charge. He put an arm around her shoulder. 'They've got it all wrong. Mother will be home soon.'

'Daniel's right,' I said. But I wasn't convinced. 'How can I help?'

'Could you talk to Mrs Siddons for us? We know she's your friend.' Daniel frowned. 'When they took Mother away in that horrible black van, she said something about asking Sybil to come and see her.'

'Mrs Siddons?' I had no idea why Lady Timpson would want to see her rival at a time like this. 'I'll go straight to Grebe House when I leave here.'

'Our car will take you,' Daniel said. 'They may charge Mother today. If they do, they'll move her to a prison. Do you think Mrs Siddons would go to such a place?'

'She's visited women's prisons before.' This didn't answer his question, but I wasn't sure how Mrs Siddons was going to react to this.

'But would she be willing to go and see Mother if she was in one?' Constance asked.

'I think so.' I tried to reassure them. 'When my mother died, it was horrible. We didn't know what to do. But she took charge and sorted everything out for us. I'm sure she'll do the same for you.'

They looked relieved.

'We feel so helpless.' Constance had lost her usual poise, and there was a hint of desperation in her voice. 'Please tell her how grateful we'd be. We'll do anything she advises.'

'I will.' I paused. 'Do you know why your mother denied going to Blacksmith's Bridge that morning? The fact that she was seen there is all the police seem to have against her.'

'She must have forgotten,' Constance replied quickly. 'She was distressed. It's not surprising she didn't remember where she last saw Father.'

Daniel said nothing, his face showing doubt and confusion.

* * *

I left Crookham Hall and went straight to Grebe House. To my relief, Mrs Siddons was at home.

'Why do you think Lady Timpson wants to see you? Do you think she did it?' My feelings were running high. By contrast, despite her initial shock at hearing of the arrest, Mrs Siddons was her usual serene self.

'It's possible.' She inclined her head.

'But why?' The only motive I could think of was that Lord Timpson had found out something about his wife, and it could be linked to Rebecca.

'I'd rather not say until I speak to Delphina.' She considered the emerald ring on her outstretched hand. 'I've decided to reduce some of my campaign activities.'

'You won't stand down, will you?' If Lady Timpson was forced to withdraw, Mrs Siddons would be the favourite. But this wasn't how I'd expected us to win the election.

'No. I still plan to go out and meet people in the constituency. I want to hear the problems they feel strongly about. But it would be inappropriate to hold any prominent public events.'

I gripped one of the soft cream cushions. 'Do you think Lady Timpson could have been involved with Rebecca's disappearance?'

'I can't see why she would be.'

'But you said you thought she might have murdered her husband?' I was confused and conflicted. On the one hand, I hoped Lady Timpson was innocent for her children's sake. On the other hand, she might be the only person who could shed some light on the mystery of Rebecca.

'No, that's not what I said.' Mrs Siddons was annoyingly calm. 'We'll talk again when I come back from seeing Delphina.'

'Will you ask her about Rebecca?'

'I can't make any promises.'

22

I sat at the kitchen table, clumsily spreading marmalade on a slice of toast.

'You look tired.' Lizzy took a cloth from the sink and wiped a splodge from the table. 'What are you worrying about? The Timpsons?'

'Partly. And Rebecca. And Mother.'

'You never could let things go.' Lizzy stroked my hair. 'You mustn't keep harking back to your mother's death. It was a terrible tragedy. There's nothing more to say.'

A ring on the doorbell saved me from replying. To my mind, there was still plenty to say. I had so many unanswered questions about that day at Westminster.

Lizzy returned to the kitchen. 'It's Donald Anstey.'

'What does he want?' I hadn't seen him since the postcard confrontation.

'To see your father. I told him he was out. Mr Anstey asked if you were in.'

'I don't want to speak to him.' I wasn't interested in discussing politics with Donald. Or had he come to see Father about me? He may have resented the way Elijah and I had forced him to talk about Rebecca.

'I told him you were having breakfast. He's waiting for you in the drawing room.'

I groaned.

'Wash your hands and go and speak to him, for goodness sake.' She flapped a tea towel at me.

I got to my feet and did as I was told.

Donald Anstey was seated in one of the leather armchairs. He stood as I entered the room.

'Miss Woodmore. I'm sorry to disturb your breakfast. I was hoping to speak to your father.' He was dressed formally in a suit, as though on an important errand.

'He left early for London. I'm not sure what time he'll be back.'

Donald nodded and sat down again. It was clear he wasn't going to leave, so I sat in the chair opposite.

'I'm going to see the police. I should have spoken to them before about my relationship with Rebecca.' He left the familiar long pause before continuing. 'There's something I should tell them. But as it concerns your mother, I wanted to talk with you and your father first.'

I looked at him expectantly. Another long pause. My irritation rose. 'Well, what is it?' It came out rather more harshly than I'd intended, but I was in no mood for his drawn-out silences.

'I knew Rebecca was with your mother at the House of Commons that day. She told me about it afterwards.'

'What did she say? Did she tell you how my mother ended up in the river?' I'd guessed from his reaction in Elijah's office that he was aware of Rebecca's role in the protest. Was he going to reveal something new about Mother's death?

'No, she didn't know. She was still inside when it happened.' He looked at me with a mournful expression as if he knew this would disappoint me.

My frustration rose as my expectations fell. I took a deep breath. 'Why was she still inside? Why didn't she leave with my mother?'

During the expected pause whilst he seemed to consider what to say next, I had to clasp my hands together to stop myself drumming on the arm of the chair. Or punching him. I wished he'd just blurt everything out instead of being so cautious.

He cleared his throat. 'The plan was for them to leave separately and to meet by the river. But Rebecca got delayed.'

'Delayed?' How could she get delayed inside an empty House of Commons? It didn't make sense. 'Did someone see her?'

'No, but she saw someone. Her employer.' He paused and placed his fingers together. 'Lady Timpson came into the Members' Lobby with a man. Rebecca hid behind a screen. She couldn't leave her hiding place without them seeing her.'

'Who was with Lady Timpson?' At last, this was getting interesting.

'Rebecca didn't know his name. But from what she overheard, it was clear he was an MP. This MP had got hold of a list of sites the Society for the Promotion of Nature Reserves had put forward for preservation. He gave it to Lady Timpson, telling her he could help her buy some of the land for a low price.'

'Why would he do this?' For money, if what he'd told Percy was true.

'It was clear from their conversation that Lady Timpson was to pay him a fee in return.'

'When did Rebecca tell you this?' The protest had been on the twenty-first of May, and Rebecca had gone missing on the thirteenth of August.

'A few weeks after it happened, sometime in June. She was

upset by your mother's death. She kept saying how guilty she felt. She couldn't leave her hiding place until after Lady Timpson and the MP had left. Then she found she couldn't get out the way she'd come in, via a door into Speaker's Court. The door had been locked. By the time she got out, your mother was being carried off.'

'Why haven't you spoken about this before?'

'Because Rebecca didn't want me to. I tried to persuade her to tell someone. She agreed I could tip off the Society for the Promotion of Nature Reserves. Let them know what was happening to their list. It was clear Timpson Foods was exploiting farmers and landowners. And that an MP was taking advantage of his position to help her.' He shook his head in anger. 'I wanted to take her to the House of Commons with me to see if she could identify him.'

'But she wouldn't go?' Poor Rebecca. What a mess she'd got caught up in.

He shook his head. 'She was too upset. And I think she was scared of Lady Timpson.'

'Why didn't you go to the police after Rebecca went missing?'

'Because I didn't want to get her into trouble. She was involved in an illegal activity when she overheard that conversation.' He looked anguished. 'I was afraid Rebecca would show up, and they'd arrest her because of what I'd told them.'

I could see his dilemma. 'But you're going to the police now?'

He nodded.

'Because of Lady Timpson's arrest?'

'It's made me wonder...' He trailed off.

'Wonder what?' I wanted to hear everything he had to say. Was I right to be afraid that searching for Rebecca may have led to someone else's death?

'Perhaps Lord Timpson discovered something about his wife. Something she couldn't risk coming out.' He shrugged. 'It sounds far-fetched, I know.'

'You think she had Rebecca killed? Then her husband found out – and now he's dead too.'

'It's a theory,' Donald admitted. 'Maybe a ridiculous one. But I owe it to Rebecca to tell the police what I know.'

* * *

That evening at dinner, I told Father what Donald Anstey had said.

'I wish your mother had never dreamt up that silly scheme. Maybe she'd still be here now, and so would Rebecca.' He pushed his plate away, not bothering to finish his meal.

'Do you think Rebecca's dead?' My appetite had vanished too.

'It's likely. Anstey's right to go to the police with what he knows.'

'You think Lady Timpson killed her?'

'I don't know what to think. I never liked the woman, but I wouldn't have imagined her capable of anything like murder. However, she does have the means to arrange someone to do her dirty work for her.' He sighed and rubbed his face. 'It's in the hands of the police now. There's nothing we can do.'

My father was the most rational of men. If he thought it plausible Lady Timpson was involved in murder, it couldn't be dismissed as fantasy.

'I still don't understand how Mother ended up in the river.'

He leant over and took my hand. 'It was a ghastly, horrible accident. I wish it hadn't happened. I wish your mother was still with us. But we have to carry on without her. I don't want you to fret over this. We came back to Walden to be happy.'

I squeezed his hand and gave him a weak smile. But I wasn't sure Walden was where I belonged. For some reason, I'd imagined that finding out about the past would help me figure out the future. But maybe I was deluding myself. Perhaps I would always feel out of place wherever I was.

When I received a message from Mrs Siddons, I hurried to Grebe House, hoping for answers.

'What did Lady Timpson have to say?'

Mrs Siddons was her usual unhurried self. She finished pouring tea and sat back in her upright armchair. 'It was an accident. Delphina was defending herself against her husband. He tried to kill her.'

23

'Do you believe that?' I said incredulously. I allowed myself to sink into the depths of her sofa.

Mrs Siddons gave a sad smile, as if anticipating my reaction. 'Yes, I believe Delphina was telling the truth. I just pray to God a jury will believe her.' It was clear she feared they wouldn't.

'Defending herself against what exactly?' I couldn't imagine Lord Timpson threatening anyone. He was far too mild-mannered and polite.

'Tobias planned to kill her. He produced a shotgun and was about to fire when her horse reared up and startled him.' She took a sip of tea. 'The gun went off as Delphina pushed him away, and he ended up in the canal. She got back on her horse and rode away. She says she believed he would climb out of the water, but he must have struck his head as he fell.'

I stared at her in disbelief. 'Why would he try to kill her? It doesn't make sense.'

'For money. She held the purse strings. And she'd told him she wouldn't pay off any more of his gambling debts. She was trying to force him to stop. Any scandal would prevent her from becoming an MP.'

'But how did he think he could get away with it?' It was an incredible story. Lord Timpson wasn't the sort of person to go around waving a shotgun at his wife because he wanted money.

'Delphina thinks he intended to shoot her and blame it on a poacher.' Mrs Siddons spoke as if the whole thing made perfect sense. 'She believes he planned to say there was a confrontation, and she was shot in the commotion.'

'But that's nonsense. He wasn't that sort of man.'

'Do you think you know what sort of man he was?' she said mildly.

'He was kind on the few occasions I met him. He was the only one that bothered about Rebecca.' I felt she was patronising me. 'Everyone I've spoken to thought he was a charming man.'

'He was certainly a charming man.' Her eyes were steel. 'But he wasn't a good one.'

'Constance and Daniel adored him.' I couldn't understand why Mrs Siddons believed this story. She wasn't a gullible woman. She hadn't even been on friendly terms with Lady Timpson.

'That's the problem. Delphina shielded them from the truth. But if she's to defend herself, she's going to have to tell them what he was really like.'

'What was he like?' Did Mrs Siddons really think he was a calculating murderer who'd fooled everyone? Or was his memory being destroyed for selfish reasons? I knew which I believed.

'He was a controlling, manipulative man who bullied her.'

'That wasn't how it seemed to me.' I'd always trusted Mrs Siddons' judgement, but in this case, I thought she was being deceived.

'You think she was the bully in their relationship?'

Again, I was riled by her patronising manner. 'No. Yes, I mean. She was the more forceful of the two.'

'I'm afraid no one knows the true state of any marriage except the two people in it. Not even their children. The public perception is often a far cry from what goes on behind closed doors.'

'Lady Timpson is a bossy, domineering woman. Not some timid wallflower.'

'Delphina is a strong-willed woman,' Mrs Siddons acknowledged. 'But in many ways, she's a fragile and naïve one. She didn't want to admit to herself what a mistake she'd made in marrying Tobias. And she can't bear the thought of her children knowing what he was like. But if she's to offer a defence, she'll have to testify in court that he used to hit her.'

I inhaled sharply. 'He hit her?'

'Frequently at the start of their marriage. Less so in recent years.'

I shook my head. 'I can't believe that. Did he hurt Constance or Daniel?'

'She says not. She says he was a loving father. She'd always hoped to shield them from the truth. But now she must be persuaded to tell the police everything.' She looked apprehensive. 'If she doesn't, she'll hang.'

I was silent, absorbing her words. I wasn't sure what I believed, but the thought of Lady Timpson being executed was horrific.

'I've advised her to write a letter to Daniel and Constance telling them everything,' she said. 'Once she's done that, I'm going to visit them and try to help them come to terms with what's happened. I'd like you to come with me.'

'They loved their father. I'm not sure they'll believe her.' Or was I wrong? Had they suspected something wasn't right with their parents' marriage? Constance had given no indication of it.

'If they don't, they'll be sending their mother to the gallows.' Mrs Siddons rested her heavily ringed fingers in her lap.

'What do you mean?' I felt this was becoming a gruesome farce.

'If Daniel and Constance turn against her, Delphina has said she won't offer up a defence. She'll stand trial but won't give evidence. If that happens, a jury is likely to convict her.'

I felt a heavy weight descend as I sank further into the cushions. Everything had been flipped on its head. And my shock was nothing compared to how Constance and Daniel were going to feel.

'Why did Lady Timpson ask you to go and see her?' This had been at the back of my mind throughout our conversation. 'I mean, why you? I know you were once friends, but...'

'To tell me I was right,' Mrs Siddons replied.

'Right? Right about what?' As perceptive as she was, she can't have predicted Lord Timpson would one day decide to murder his wife.

'Tobias Timpson was the cause of our row all those years ago.'

'Had you at one time wanted to marry him?'

'Me?' she spluttered, for once losing her poise. 'Good grief, no. I never had any designs on him. I only met him after I was married.'

'Then why did you fall out?'

'My husband had heard things about Tobias. How he liked to drink, gamble and womanise. How he used his fists against women.'

'You told Lady Timpson this?'

'We were friends. When she said she planned to marry Tobias, I had to tell her what I knew of his character.'

'She didn't believe you?' By all accounts, Delphina Hinchcliffe had set her heart on gaining a title. I could imagine her reaction.

'She didn't want to believe me. She said I was jealous because she was marrying a lord. I told her not to be such a fool.'

'What happened then?' No one likes being called a fool, least of all the future Lady Timpson.

'They married.' Mrs Siddons waved her hand in a final gesture. 'And our friendship came to an end.'

'You never heard anything to suggest she regretted marrying him?'

'Quite the contrary. She went out of her way to show the world that theirs was a happy and loving marriage. Whenever our paths crossed, she would put on a great display of affection. I was glad to be proved wrong. But I had my doubts.'

'That must have been a heavy burden for her to carry alone.' I was voicing my thoughts aloud. Did I now believe Delphina Timpson's story? I had to admit, my sympathies were starting to shift. But was I right to give credence to this new version of events?

'I hate to think how she's suffered. I want to help her now. I've found her a decent barrister. Philip Johnson is an old friend of mine.'

'I'm afraid there's something that may not help her defence.' I told her about Donald Anstey's visit and the conversation Rebecca overheard in the House of Commons.

She sighed. 'When it comes to Delphina, this doesn't surprise me.'

'Donald Anstey has gone to the police. He suspects she may have had something to do with Rebecca's disappearance. What if Lady Timpson found out her conversation had been overheard?'

'Delphina could easily have talked her way out of that one. She wouldn't have needed to resort to violence.'

'What about Lord Timpson?' I was beginning to see him in a different light, although part of me still resisted this version of his character. 'Could he have hurt Rebecca?'

Mrs Siddons placed her hand under her chin. 'When you told me about his possible relationship with her, it did make me wonder.'

'What should we do?'

'First, we need to speak to Daniel and Constance. Without them, there'll be no defence. Will you come with me?'

I nodded. Crookham Hall still held the answer to so many questions. But I felt uncomfortable at the thought of being present when they were subjected to this violent exposure of their parent's lives.

* * *

'You've received your mother's letter?' Mrs Siddons asked.

'We appreciate all you've done,' Constance replied coolly.

'Have you written back?'

'Not yet. You'll appreciate there's a lot for us to think about.'

I perched on the edge of the green sofa, focusing on the contents of my teacup. I had no idea if Lady Timpson was telling the truth or not. She'd convinced Mrs Siddons. But wouldn't Daniel and Constance have known if their father had been violent? By their expressions, this had come as a complete shock to them.

'Why didn't she tell us what was going on?' Daniel's brow was creased with anxiety.

'Because she felt ashamed. She wanted to protect you,' Mrs Siddons replied.

'Why should she feel ashamed?' he demanded. 'It wasn't her fault. It was his.'

While Constance was stiff and unyielding, Daniel seemed more inclined to believe his mother.

'She felt that it was her fault. She didn't want to admit it, not to anyone,' Mrs Siddons said. 'She preferred people to think their union was a happy one. And I think she once loved him.'

'Yes, I believe she did.' Constance grasped at this crumb of consolation. 'We knew it was a marriage of convenience. But there was mutual affection between them.'

'No, there wasn't.' Daniel's words crushed his sister's conviction. 'He loved us. But he never loved her.'

'Do you believe your mother?' Mrs Siddons asked him.

I'd expected Daniel to defend his father and Constance to support her mother. Instead, it was the other way around.

He ran his fingers through his hair. He looked again towards Constance, but she was unrelenting. 'I don't know what to believe.'

'You understand that she won't offer a defence if you don't support her?' Mrs Siddons pressed. 'That will put her in a very dangerous position.'

Constance said nothing.

Daniel balled his hands into fists. 'I'm going to write to her. Tell her I support her.'

'You believe Father was a murderer?' Constance wasn't going to concede. I could see Lady Timpson's self-possession and control in her.

'We can't let Mother go to the gallows, Con.'

His sister turned away.

24

I heard nothing more from Mrs Siddons or the Timpsons over the next week. They seemed to have reached a stalemate. The thought of what this could mean for Lady Timpson dominated my thoughts. As expected, she'd withdrawn from the by-election, and Councillor William Mansbridge had taken her place as the Conservative candidate.

I was diverted from my preoccupation by a letter from my aunt. I'd rather have read it in private, but Lizzy placed it on the breakfast table in front of me. My father watched as I scanned the pages. Aunt Maud had received a letter from Kathleen Hooper. She said Kathleen hadn't given her home address but could be contacted via a dress shop called Hartnell's Boutique in Covent Garden. My aunt had arranged to meet her at the Lyons Corner House on the Strand on Saturday.

'Would it be alright if I went to stay with Gran and Aunt Maud this weekend?' I hoped Father wouldn't ask too many questions. I hadn't told him about our search for Kathleen.

'Of course. Any particular reason? Are they well?'

'I think Aunt Maud would like some company other than

Gran's.' I felt him scrutinising me.

'This doesn't have anything to do with that Percy fellow, does it?' Father sipped his tea, trying to appear unconcerned.

I almost laughed. I hadn't been expecting that. 'No, it doesn't.'

'You can tell me if you plan to see him.' He put down his tea. 'I won't be cross. As long as I know where you are, I won't mind.'

I was pretty sure he would mind if he thought I was going to a dancing club in Soho.

'I haven't made plans to see him.'

But now he'd put the idea in my head, I decided to write to Percy.

* * *

'It's strange she doesn't give her home address. Why do you think she wants to speak to us now?'

It was good to be out of Walden. Talk in the town was of nothing but the Timpsons, and this gave me the opportunity to focus on Mother again.

'She says she's only just found out I've been looking for her.' Aunt Maud frowned. 'I suspect the real reason is the Timpson case. She must have read about it in the newspapers. If Rebecca told her what she overheard, she might want to try to find out what we know. And what's likely to come out at the trial.'

We'd arrived early to ensure we could get a table in the Corner House. My aunt watched the door, and it wasn't long before Kathleen appeared. I judged her to be in her mid-thirties. She had fine blonde hair piled untidily on top of her head. The brow of her pretty face was furrowed, and there was tension in her eyes. Her shoulders seemed to droop with fatigue.

'You were twelve or thirteen when I saw you last. You look like your mother.'

'I was sorry to hear about Leonard.' Aunt Maud patted the chair for her to sit down. 'How have you managed?'

Kathleen's lips trembled. I listened as she confided her struggles to my aunt, her loneliness plain. A tiny fraction of her tension seemed to lift as she spoke.

'It's good to chat with someone.' She twisted the napkin between her fingers. 'Ena said you were looking for me, but I wasn't sure why.'

'We wanted to talk to you about the day of Violet's accident.'

'I'm sorry for what happened.' She glanced at me from under pale lashes. 'Why are you asking about it now?'

She seemed wary, and it made me wonder when she'd seen Ena. I got the impression she'd taken her time before contacting us.

'Because of something I found out recently.' I told her what the waterman had said. 'You were at the House of Commons that day, weren't you? You and Rebecca Dent?'

'Not so loud,' she whispered. 'That's Mrs Hartnell over there. She runs the dress shop I work for. I don't want her to hear.'

A smartly dressed lady was sitting by the window. Kathleen gave a polite wave, and the woman waved back.

'Yes, we were there.' She stopped talking as our tea and cakes arrived. Once the waitress had gone, Kathleen turned to me. 'Seeing the Timpson case in the papers has made me think about Rebecca and what happened. She was so upset. Rebecca, I mean. She felt responsible for your mother's death.'

'Why?' I asked.

'Because she didn't meet your mother with the canister when she was supposed to.' She took out a handkerchief. 'We were all desperately sorry for what happened to Violet.'

'The canister?' I hadn't heard anything about a canister before.

'For the acid.' Kathleen clearly thought this was something we were aware of.

'What acid?' Aunt Maud looked alarmed.

'The acid Violet used to paint the metal grilles. It was dangerous stuff.'

My heart began to beat a little faster. At last, I was learning something new. I'd always assumed Mother had used paint.

'They had a large jar of acid in a metal canister,' Kathleen explained. 'Once they were inside, Violet took the jar out of the canister and went up to the gallery. She had a brush hidden in the pocket of her skirt. She painted the metal grilles with the acid to turn them green.'

'Where was Rebecca?' I asked.

'She was the lookout. She stayed downstairs in the Members' Lobby to make sure no one else went up to the gallery. When Violet left through Speaker's Court, Rebecca was supposed to follow her out with the canister, Violet would drop the jar and brush into it, and they'd go their separate ways. I was waiting with a horse and cart at the foot of Westminster Bridge so Rebecca could hide everything in the back under the tarpaulin. I'd drive off with it, then if anyone stopped Violet or Rebecca, there'd be nothing incriminating on them.'

'But Rebecca didn't follow my mother out. She was still hiding in the Members' Lobby, listening to Lady Timpson's conversation, wasn't she?'

Kathleen's head shot up. 'How do you know that?'

'Donald Anstey.'

'Oh.' Lines of tension reappeared across her forehead.

'He lives in Walden now. He moved there to try to find out what happened to Rebecca.'

'I read he was standing in the by-election.'

'You knew he and Rebecca had been seeing one another?'

Kathleen nodded. 'My husband and I introduced them.'

'Was she in love with him?'

'He was good to her. But when he disappeared up to Scotland, she felt abandoned.'

I thought abandoned a strange word to use. I still wondered why Donald Anstey had gone to Scotland. He said it was to tell his parents he planned to enlist, but war hadn't even been declared then. I wanted to get back to the subject of my mother, so I pushed the thought to the back of my mind.

'Mother was stuck on Speaker's Green with a jar of acid?'

'We thought the Serjeant-at-Arms must have seen her, and she panicked because she still had the acid. It was terribly toxic. She might have been dizzy. We were worried about her inhaling it in the Ladies' Gallery; it was such a pokey little space. She probably couldn't wait to get out into the fresh air.'

'But the waterman said the Serjeant didn't appear until after she'd gone into the river.'

'The acid may have started to leak. It was supposed to go back into the canister that Rebecca had. Violet was wearing protective gloves. But if anyone else had come into contact with it, they could have been badly burnt. Maybe she jumped to stop it spilling?'

I made a strange noise, a combined sob and exclamation. Aunt Maud and Kathleen looked at me with concern. A rush of emotion overcame me as I realised the truth.

'Mother was trapped.' My words were uneven. I pictured the corner of Westminster where she'd jumped. 'She couldn't get up to the bridge as the children were running down the steps. She jumped to stop them from running into her and spilling acid over themselves.' The mad, impulsive jump suddenly made sense.

People at nearby tables had stopped talking and were watching us. I lowered my voice.

'I went to talk to the waterman again. He told me a nanny was coming down the steps with a group of a dozen young children who wanted to look at the boats. Small boys in short trousers and little girls in gingham dresses, all running towards Mother. She probably tried to get back into the Commons, but the door had been locked, which is why Rebecca couldn't get out.'

'Why didn't she throw the jar in the river?' Aunt Maud whispered.

'Because the jetty was full of barges, and she was too far above them. The acid would have rained down on the men in the boats. The waterman said she was clutching a pot. She must have kept her hand over the top of the jar when she jumped. I think she just wanted to sink it in the water.' For the first time, I could visualise the sequence of events. 'She probably thought she'd be able to scramble out and say she fell or something like that.'

My aunt nodded slowly, as if imagining the scene. Kathleen was nodding too. 'It would make sense. Violet always abided by that rule.'

'What rule?' I asked.

'The suffragette rule never to hurt any human life but your own. We made a pledge. You could damage property or yourself, but no other,' Kathleen explained. 'In all her activities, your mother never physically hurt another person.'

Tears rolled down my face. I tried to steady my breathing.

'I'm sorry your mother didn't make it.' Kathleen reached out to pat my arm.

I wiped my eyes, and Aunt Maud filled our cups. We drank in silence and soon the people at nearby tables lost interest and returned to their conversations.

After a while, Kathleen spoke. 'What did Donald Anstey tell you?'

I briefly recounted what he'd said.

'Is he going to tell the police?'

'He already has.' Seeing her distress, I realised the repercussions this could have. Three people carried out a criminal act in Westminster that day. Kathleen was the only one left who could be held accountable.

'I'll go and see him when I get back to Walden; find out exactly what he said.'

'Have the police been to see your father about it?' she asked.

I shook my head. 'I don't think they're planning to investigate it now.'

She looked relieved. 'Will they question Lady Timpson about bribing an MP?'

'Possibly. The police are still trying to build a case against her.' But I wasn't sure this would give them much ammunition.

'It's all wrong.' Kathleen clenched a screwed-up napkin.

'Do you think she's innocent? Despite what the newspapers are saying?' I'd been shocked by some of the lurid headlines. Lady Timpson was sure to hang if everyone in the country believed what was being written. I was curious to hear the opinion of someone whose only knowledge of the case was what they'd read in the papers. I was too involved to have an unbiased opinion.

'She shouldn't hang,' was all Kathleen said. It wasn't really an answer.

'They could decide to charge Lady Timpson with Rebecca's murder too. The prosecution might say she had a motive for wanting her dead if Rebecca had tried to blackmail her.' This wasn't true, but I wanted to see how Kathleen would react.

'Has Lady Timpson said she was blackmailed?' Her alarm was tangible.

I was touching a nerve.

'No, she hasn't,' I admitted. I noticed a flicker of relief in her eyes. 'What do you think happened to Rebecca?'

'I don't know. But I don't think Lady Timpson had anything to do with it.'

25

'How did it go?'

Percy was waiting for me on a bench in Trafalgar Square. It was a sunny June afternoon, and he was wearing a white shirt with the top button undone. His hair was more wayward than usual, but his dishevelled appearance made him even more attractive. I averted my eyes from the top of his chest and told him of our conversation with Kathleen.

He took my hand. 'Your mother was quite a woman.'

'That's one way to put it.' I let him entwine his fingers with mine. 'At least I know now she didn't mean for her life to end that way.'

'From what you've told me, she was fragile already,' he said gently. 'I think she showed great courage to do what she did.'

'So do I.' The weight I'd been carrying for so long seemed to get lighter.

'Come on.' He switched to excitable Percy, pulling me up and linking his arm through mine. 'Let's go and see what's showing at the cinemas on the Strand.'

Arm in arm, we strolled along the busy street, chatting and

stopping to look at the posters outside the picture palaces. It had been a long time since I'd felt so young and carefree.

It was clear Percy had his heart set on seeing the new Douglas Fairbanks film. I agreed as long as we could watch all the news-reels beforehand.

'Most girls want to see Mary Pickford. But you want to watch Pathé News,' he complained. 'I bet your friend, Alice, likes Mary Pickford. She looks a bit like her.'

I smiled but experienced a pang of sadness. Alice would love to go to the pictures, but her father wouldn't allow it. At least I could tell her that Percy thought she looked like a film star.

He insisted on buying me a box of chocolates and then proceeded to eat most of them during the film. This amused me as much as his frequent changes of expression. He seemed to be living every swashbuckling moment alongside Douglas Fairbanks.

We emerged to find that it was just as warm outside as it had been inside the theatre. The air was filled with the smell of exhaust fumes and manure.

'Have you seen much of Constance?' He took my hand as we crossed Waterloo Bridge.

'I've been over to Crookham Hall a couple of times. Have you seen Daniel?'

'He came to stay at my flat for a bit. That's unusual for him. He's not fond of the city. But he needed to get away from the hall to clear his head.'

'He's told you what his mother's claiming?'

He nodded.

'He seemed to believe her more than Constance did,' I said. 'That surprised me.'

'Probably because his father used to hit him, whereas Constance was the adored daughter.'

'Lord Timpson hit Daniel?'

He stopped and leant against the bridge. 'We sat up talking one night. We'd had too much whisky, and he blurted it out. I don't think it was a regular thing. His father would sometimes lash out, telling Daniel he needed to grow up, be tougher, that sort of thing.'

'Good grief.' I gazed over to the dome of St Paul's Cathedral.

'Daniel's a gentle soul. He prefers the company of animals. He hated being an officer, but he didn't have a choice. He can't stand violence, and I think that's why people try to push him around. The boys at school, the soldiers under his command and his parents all seem to think he's a soft touch.'

'It explains why he's sympathetic towards his mother.' I pulled on Percy's hand. It was getting late, and I'd promised my aunt I'd be back in time for cocoa.

'Are they definitely going to prosecute her?' His fingers caressed mine as we strolled towards the station.

'Ben thinks it's likely.'

He sighed. 'What an awful mess.'

'Do you believe Lady Timpson's story?'

'Truthfully? I've no idea what to think. I didn't know what to say to Daniel. And you know me, not usually short on words.' He gave a self-deprecating smile.

'That's how I feel. How can I support Constance when I don't know what to believe?' I gave a helpless shrug.

'You can still be a shoulder to cry on.' He put his arm around my waist and pulled me closer.

'Percy,' I warned, breathing in his citrus cologne.

'I know, I know.' He nuzzled my hair. 'You just want to be friends.'

I kissed him on the cheek and pulled away, even though I would have preferred to have stayed where I was.

* * *

'This is what comes of bringing women into politics.' Colonel Thackeray waved a newspaper at me. He limped into his study and slammed the door before I could reply. I wasn't sure how he'd come to the conclusion that women becoming MPs had led to Lord Timpson's death.

'Sorry,' Alice murmured.

I smiled. A visit to Sand Hills Hall always meant braving Colonel Thackeray's unpredictable temper.

I knew Alice's situation well enough not to question her father's behaviour. The Colonel had lost a couple of fingers in a grenade attack. The blast had also caused inner ear damage, which had left him with a sense of imbalance, though he refused to use a stick. But his physical injuries were the least of his problems. He'd always been a stern man, but since the war, he'd become reclusive and aggressive. His wife, Florence, bore the brunt of his anger. The only person who could calm him was Alice.

'I feel so sorry for Constance and Daniel.' When she'd heard I was visiting Crookham Hall with Mrs Siddons, she'd asked if I would deliver a letter to Constance. 'I'd like to go and see them, but Father won't let me.'

Like the rest of Walden, Alice's parents had been quick to assume Lady Timpson's guilt. At least there would be no further pressure on Alice to get to know Daniel Timpson.

'Do you believe her? Lady Timpson, I mean.'

'I just don't know.' I'd told her privately what I'd learnt from Mrs Siddons.

I followed her through to a small writing room. She sat at the desk, placed a sheet of ivory writing paper onto the blotter and scribbled the date below the Sand Hills Hall letterhead. As she wrote, I realised Alice felt some kind of affinity with Constance and Daniel.

She paused, pen hovering over the paper. 'He seemed such a nice man.'

If this went to trial, I could imagine those words being uttered countless times.

From his study, I could hear the colonel shouting. I'd often wondered if Colonel Thackeray was violent towards his wife, and, heaven forbid, Alice. But she was fiercely protective of her father, and if I broached the subject, she shut me out. So, like everyone else, I accepted that Colonel Thackeray had a temper because of his wartime experiences. Was that how it had been for the Timpsons? Had Lord Timpson's brutality to his wife just been accepted?

I thought of Mrs Siddons' comment about not knowing what went on behind closed doors. Had Lady Timpson loved her husband? If not, why had she put up with his abuse? She was a rich woman: she had choices. Alice loved her father dearly, but she was a young woman with no money and very few choices.

* * *

'Alice asked me to give you this.' I handed Constance the letter. 'She wanted to call on you, but...'

'Her parents thought it unwise?'

'Something like that.' How the tables had turned. Lady Timpson had stopped Constance from sending flowers after my mother had died, not wishing her daughter to be associated with anything disreputable. Now the Timpsons were tainted by a much bigger scandal.

'Tell her not to worry. I appreciate her friendship. And yours.'

'We've been to see Mother.' Daniel stood by the mantelpiece.

'How's she coping?' Mrs Siddons patted the sofa, and he sat down next to her.

'She's lost weight,' he said. 'And she seems confused.'

'You've told her you'll support her?'

'Yes. We said we'll be there for her at the trial.'

Constance nodded but didn't look as sure as her brother. 'We wanted to thank you for the article in *The Walden Herald*. So different from the rubbish they're putting in the London newspapers. Please pass on our gratitude to Mr Whittle.'

'It's disgusting what some of the papers are printing. Complete lies. It shouldn't be allowed.' Daniel started to pour coffee but spilt most of it in the saucer.

'Will you and Mr Whittle be attending the trial?' Constance asked.

I nodded, embarrassed by the admission. But Horace Laffaye would expect us to report every detail. Unless there was an unexpected acquittal, it was going to be a gruelling ordeal.

'Is there anything you can think of that might help your mother's case?' Mrs Siddons took the coffee pot from Daniel and finished pouring.

'We've spoken to all the staff,' Constance said. 'The ones who've stayed in our employ.'

Daniel stood and went over to the window. 'I can't blame them for leaving. They have their futures to think about. Financially, we don't know how we're going to be left.'

'A few of them heard Mother and Father arguing about money,' Constance continued. 'Mother was angry at how much Father was spending at gambling clubs. They were reluctant to tell the police. They all adored Father. He was charming to them, and they were loyal to him.'

'Which is why some of them have left,' Daniel said. 'They think Mother must be guilty.'

'Was your father ever violent towards you?' Mrs Siddons said it gently, but the question caused Constance's nostrils to flare.

'Of course not,' she said instantly.

We waited for Daniel to speak. Mrs Siddons looked at him and nodded slightly.

'Sometimes he'd strike me. When I wouldn't do as he wanted.' He pushed his hands into his pockets.

'Daniel,' Constance exclaimed. 'Is that true?'

'Of course it's true,' he snapped.

'Why did your father get angry with you?' Mrs Siddons asked.

'He told me I was too weak. He wanted me to be more like him.'

'Perhaps he meant you were too soft with the animals at times. On the farm. And because you won't hunt.' Despite supporting her mother, Constance seemed no closer to accepting the accusations made about her father.

'Could Daniel give evidence?' I asked, incurring a hostile look from her.

'I think it unlikely Philip Johnson would put him on the stand,' Mrs Siddons replied. 'Sadly, a man hitting his son wouldn't be considered unreasonable. Just a way of toughening him up.'

'That's what he thought. He wanted me to be stronger.' Daniel studied the pattern on the oriental rug. 'You know, with women. He said I'd never produce an heir at this rate.'

Constance's face flushed. 'I'm sure he was only joking.'

'It was a painful joke.' Daniel touched his cheek.

I felt like wrapping my arms around him. For someone as gentle as Daniel, it must have been mentally as well as physically distressing to receive a blow from your father.

* * *

The following day, Ben poked his head around the door of the office.

'Come in. You can have the last of the coffee if you want?'

'Yes, please.' He sank into the nearest chair.

Elijah came out of his den and sat on my desk. 'Any news?'

'Lady Timpson's talking. She's offering up a defence at last.'

I guessed this was because of the visit from her children.

'And?' Elijah demanded.

'She paints a damning picture of her husband.'

'What do you make of her story?' I asked.

'I don't know.' Ben took the coffee. 'Her description of Lord Timpson doesn't bear any resemblance to the man I knew. Not that I had much to do with him, but when I did, he was always pleasant. Most people say the same.'

'Men can act differently behind closed doors.' Elijah echoed Mrs Siddons' words. 'Is there anything to corroborate her version of events?'

'One shot was missing from the shotgun found in the canal.'

'Which tallies with what Lady Timpson is claiming,' Elijah said. 'That he threatened her with a shotgun, it went off when her horse reared and she pushed him back.'

'Maybe. When or how the shotgun came to be in the canal is uncertain, but it hadn't been there for long.'

'You say the groom is positive neither one had a gun on them when they left the stables?' Elijah shifted his weight on my desk. I hastily removed a sheaf of paper before he sat on the draft of the next edition.

'He'll swear to it in court. He helped them mount. He says it's not possible either one of them could have hidden a shotgun on their person or the horses.'

'So where did Timpson get the shotgun from?' Elijah asked. I noticed he seemed to be inclined to believe Delphina Timpson's version of events.

'Lady Timpson said her husband must have taken it from somewhere near the bridge. She had her back to him whilst she was trying to tie up her horse. When she turned, he was pointing it at her.'

'He must have concealed it near the bridge earlier.' Elijah stroked his chin. 'You said that he'd been seen in the area in the days before his death.'

Ben nodded. 'The case is going to trial, but we need more evidence. We want you to publish another appeal.'

'Saying what?' Elijah reached for his pen.

'We need to know anything that went on at Blacksmith's Bridge in the weeks before the murder. Specifically, we're looking for anyone carrying a shotgun or trying to conceal something.'

Elijah nodded, and Ben got up to leave.

'Did Donald Anstey come to see you?' I asked.

'He did,' Ben replied. 'I'm not sure it changes anything.'

'It put Rebecca in a dangerous position.' It also gave her a reason to run away.

'Only if someone knew she'd overheard the conversation.'

'Lord or Lady Timpson could have found out,' I said.

'But there's nothing to suggest they did,' Ben countered.

Elijah stopped scribbling to refill his pen. 'How will it affect Lady Timpson's chances if a jury hears about her bribing a corrupt politician?'

'It's unlikely to be given in evidence at the trial. It's too insubstantial,' Ben said. 'We don't even know who the MP was.'

'What about the fact that Lord Timpson was seen coming from Rebecca's bedroom?' I asked.

'Again, it's too insubstantial. Olive Evans thought that was where he'd come from, but there's nothing to substantiate it.'

'When is the trial?'

'We have no choice but to put it forward for the midsummer assizes. It's likely to be held in Winchester in July. The superintendent would like more time, but he can't hold her indefinitely.

That's why he wants the appeal for information to go in the next edition.'

Only a matter of weeks before Lady Timpson would have to stand in front of judge and jury. If found guilty, the sentence was death.

26

I folded the last of the manifesto pamphlets. It was the final week of campaigning, but it felt like the heart had gone out of the by-election. All the town talked about was the Timpson case.

Councillor Mansbridge, who'd taken Lady Timpson's place, wasn't popular. The race was between Mrs Siddons and Donald Anstey.

Mrs Siddons' supporters had decided to make one last push. We were going to deliver pamphlets to all the houses in the area, giving voters a final reminder of her pledges before they went to the polling stations.

It was a pleasant Sunday afternoon, perfect for a walk. I planned to call on Donald Anstey but decided to deliver the pamphlets first. I could hardly turn up at his cottage promoting the opposition.

But as I strolled by the lake, I saw him standing once again on the jetty near the railway station. There were no flowers this time; he was just staring into the water. I hesitated. I didn't want to disturb him, but he looked up as I approached, so I joined him.

'Rebecca loved Waldenmere. She often used to talk about it. I only got to see the lake after she'd gone. I wish I could have been here with her.'

'Is that why you bring flowers? Sweet violets because she was a suffragette?'

He nodded. 'I feel a strong connection to her when I'm here. Her spirit. She loved being a suffragette. It gave her a sense of purpose. Of independence. She believed that one day women would have control over their own destinies. I wish that could have been true for her.'

'I'm sorry.' I told him about my meeting with Kathleen Hooper.

'Don't worry. I didn't mention Mrs Hooper's name to the police. I felt there was no need. I got the impression they weren't interested in pursuing old suffragette cases at this time,' he said. 'Unfortunately, they weren't particularly interested in investigating Rebecca's disappearance either.'

'I know. I've spoken to PC Gilbert. He said without any new information, Superintendent Cobbe would be reluctant to look into the case again. You said you last saw Rebecca in July 1914. What did you do?' I was still curious to know why he'd suddenly gone to Scotland.

'We walked around Hyde Park, talking. We listened to the band play for a while.'

'How did she seem?'

'Distant. As though she was thinking of other things. I asked her if there was something wrong. She told me she was fine.' He paused. 'I was afraid I was losing her.'

'Then why did you go to Scotland?' I blurted out.

He gave me a long look, and I thought I'd offended him with the question. Then he took a small square box from his trouser pocket and handed it to me.

I opened it. Inside was an old-fashioned diamond and emerald ring.

'It was my grandmother's. She left it to me. I went to see my parents to get it. I told them I was planning to ask Rebecca to marry me. I never got the chance to propose, so I bring it here and tell her how much I loved her.'

'I'm sorry.' I returned the box.

'I was thirty. I thought it about time I settled down. I wanted to provide for Rebecca, have children with her. But when I got back, she was gone. Then we were at war, and I ended up in France. Funny how your life can change so quickly.' He rotated the ring in his fingers. 'Sometimes I think I should just throw this in the lake and walk away. Leave Walden.'

Defeat and despair showed in every line on his face. If he was innocent of involvement in Rebecca's disappearance, I could understand why he looked so world-weary. All his dreams had been shattered in the space of a few weeks. And he still didn't know why.

* * *

Later that week, the three candidates stood on the platform in Aldershot Town Hall, waiting for the results to be announced. Donald Anstey had the look of a man who'd already lost.

Mrs Siddons, on the other hand, was on fine form. Dressed in a midnight blue silk gown with perfectly coiffed hair, she had the demeanour of a woman who expected victory. William Mansbridge's scowl suggested he'd never wanted to take part in the election in the first place.

Tension built as the officer read the results. I held my breath.

'Mr Donald Anstey, Labour, 6,315 votes. Mr William Mansbridge, Conservative, 2,816 votes. Mrs Sybil Siddons, Liberal, 9,131 votes.'

We'd done it. We'd finally made progress. This was what my mother had fought for.

'I hereby declare Mrs Sybil Siddons Member of Parliament for Aldershot.'

Loud cheers echoed around the hall. I felt a smug satisfaction at my father's look of disappointment. I also took a certain amount of pleasure in seeing Colonel Thackeray's disgust. He limped out of the hall, muttering something inaudible.

Mrs Siddons swept from the stage and began to hug her supporters. Donald Anstey came over to offer his congratulations.

'Mr Anstey, I've been thinking about your ideas for replacing the slum dwellings over at Crookham with proper housing. Your plan has merits.' A few people turned their heads at Mrs Siddons' words. 'I wonder if you'd care to work with me on the project?'

Donald appeared surprised but pleased. 'Certainly. This is a matter that outweighs party politics. I'd be happy to help.'

Although I could understand why my father had supported him, a part of me still felt it was a betrayal of Mother. This is what the suffragettes had fought for, a say in the parliamentary process.

Since meeting with Kathleen, my anger towards my mother had started to diminish. I couldn't deny I still felt resentment at losing her, but I now had a sense of pride in her commitment. And a new determination to continue her work in my own way.

To my surprise, I received an invitation from Mrs Siddons asking me to join her and Donald Anstey on a visit to the Moffats' farm-house. I accepted, glad to put my elation following her victory into practical action.

'I want to get started immediately,' she announced. Donald was already seated in her carriage. 'I know there's going to be some local opposition to this development, which is why I want you to come along. I'd like you to write an article on the conditions these people face. Try to gain sympathy for them from the outset.'

Donald nodded in agreement but didn't say anything. His weariness seemed to have settled on him like a permanent cloud.

The winding track that led to the Moffats' farmhouse was badly in need of repair. We lurched forward every time the carriage hit a pothole. It was a relief to jump out and finish the journey on foot.

Donald and I trailed behind Mrs Siddons as she swept past the farmhouse and over the grassland towards the caravans and shacks. In the distance, I could see Blacksmith's Bridge and beyond it, the pastures of the Crookham estate.

At the sound of our carriage, a group of men had gathered, fronted by Samuel Moffat. They viewed us with suspicion that bordered on aggression. Donald went over to explain the purpose of our visit.

Meanwhile, Mrs Siddons introduced herself to a group of women sitting with their children around an open wood fire. Although she'd dispensed with her usual jewellery, she was still overdressed for the occasion. But the women appeared fascinated by her silk gown, and in typical Mrs Siddons style, she began to win them over.

Elijah had warned me not to take notes as it could arouse hostility. Instead, I stood in the background, listening to the dual conversations taking place. Despite, or perhaps because of, their differences, Mrs Siddons and Donald Anstey worked well together. Each was slowly beginning to elicit slight nods of agreement from their listeners.

Donald was pointing to the farmland owned by the Moffats. Samuel jerked his head and indicated for us to follow him to the farmhouse. The outbuildings were in a terrible state. One barn was only partially standing, and it looked as if no attempt had been made to repair it. However, there had been some improvements since I last saw the place. Chickens were pecking the ground in a newly mended coop.

A young woman of about twenty poked her head around the door of the farmhouse and regarded us with large hazel eyes. She had tanned skin and long caramel coloured hair tied back from her face.

'Make some tea, Hannah,' Samuel called. 'These people want to talk to us about buying this place.'

After seeing how neglected the outside of the house was, I'd expected the inside to be in a similar state. But the kitchen was clean and well organised. Loaves of fresh bread rested on the sideboard alongside a basket of eggs. The sweet smell of baking filled the air.

Mrs Siddons, Donald Anstey and Samuel Moffat sat around the kitchen table. There were only three chairs, so I stood with Hannah Moffat by the stove.

'You've bought some new chickens, I see?'

'Samuel got them.' She shot her brother a look of disgust.

I wondered where Samuel had got the money to buy a brood of hens. Hannah's disapproving expression suggested he may have stolen them.

Mrs Siddons described how a new housing estate could be built if the council bought the farm and its surrounding land and merged it with the wasteland it already owned. Samuel was nodding, but I could tell by the tautness of Hannah's face that she was less keen.

'Where are we supposed to live if we sell this place?' She slammed the brown teapot down onto the wooden table.

'We're going to make sure the new houses are affordable to rent and buy.' Mrs Siddons tried to reassure her. 'I'd make sure you're given priority. You won't be homeless.'

'But we won't have jobs if we don't have the farm.'

'We can't make the farm pay,' Samuel said in a tired voice. This was a conversation they'd obviously had before.

'Pa said we'd always have this place.'

My heart ached for her. She'd lost her mother, father, a brother and sister, and now she was about to lose the only home she'd ever known.

'Pa's not here any more. And I don't know how he ever made this place pay. It can't be done.' Samuel pulled at her sleeve with grubby fingers. 'We'd have the money to leave here. Start fresh somewhere new.'

I wondered how the Moffats had managed to survive there for so long. Daniel had said the land was poor.

'I could ask Miss Constance if there's anything going in the hall. I heard some of their servants have left...' She trailed off.

'There's no more money to be had from the Timpsons,' Samuel muttered.

'Things are a little unsettled at the hall at present.' Mrs Siddons spoke gently. 'Perhaps once the trial is over, something can be arranged.'

'What will happen if she's found guilty?' Hannah asked.

'Then Daniel and Constance may be forced to sell Crookham Hall,' Mrs Siddons said.

'I meant to Lady Timpson,' Hannah replied.

27

The trial opened on the ninth of July 1920 at Hampshire Assizes in the Great Hall, Winchester.

Outside the court, reporters had gathered, shoving one another to take photographs of Daniel and Constance. Mrs Siddons put a protective arm around Constance and led her up the steps. I followed them, aware that beside me Daniel was being jostled, but unable to offer him much protection as he stumbled in the chaos.

Suddenly a tall figure appeared. He swept the photographers aside, slapped Daniel on the back and shepherded him up the steps with one easy movement. The doors closed behind us, silencing the noise from the street.

'Percy,' Daniel said in surprise.

'Hello, old chap. Thought you could do with the Baverstock shoulders in that scrum.' Percy grinned at us, pushing his unruly hair from his face.

'How kind of you to come,' Constance said.

'Wanted to offer you my support. You may not want me here. Just say the word, and I'll go. But if I can be of any assistance, I'm at your disposal.' He gave a slight bow.

It constantly surprised me how the same person could be as thoughtful and sensitive as he was idiotic and tactless.

'That's decent of you,' Daniel said. 'I could do with another fellow around right now.'

'Come on then, let's go and find ourselves a cup of tea.' Percy slapped him on the back again.

'Here's Philip,' Mrs Siddons said.

Philip Johnson, KC, was tall and broad. He looked more like a rugby player than a lawyer. He led us up a flight of stairs.

'How's Mother?' Constance asked.

'Frightened,' he said over his shoulder. 'She's worried about how you and Daniel will to react to some of the evidence that I'll present.'

'Would she rather we weren't here?' Daniel asked.

'Probably. But it's vital that you are present. The jury needs to see you're supporting your mother and haven't turned against her.'

The Great Hall, built on the remnants of Winchester Castle, had stained-glass windows and medieval aisled halls. It was like walking into a cathedral rather than a courtroom.

We all stood as Judge Radden entered. He was a tall, thin man with a haggard face.

'He looks severe,' I whispered to Elijah.

'Actually, he has a reputation for being lenient. But he won't stand for any playacting.'

We were seated in the public gallery. Elijah was on one side of me and Mrs Siddons on the other. Next to her sat Constance, then Daniel and Percy.

The jury of twelve men took their seats.

'Still no women,' I whispered to Elijah. I found it infuriating that despite a change in the law the previous year, a woman was yet to serve as a juror.

He sucked in his breath. 'Shame Johnson couldn't have got just one included. It might make a difference in a case like this.'

Judge Radden addressed the court, emphasising to the jurors the need to ignore outside comment on the case. 'You must disregard any newspaper articles you have read or gossip you have heard regarding this trial. You should only discuss proceedings amongst yourselves and not with anyone else. People around you may offer you their opinions – you must ignore their views. It is your duty to listen carefully to the evidence presented in this courtroom and base your decision solely on that evidence.'

Once the judge had finished, the clerk got to his feet.

'Will the prisoner stand.'

Lady Timpson rose stiffly as if each movement caused her pain. She'd lost weight, and her face looked pinched. It must have been unbearable to swap the luxury of Crookham Hall for a prison cell.

'Lady Timpson. You have been charged with the wilful murder of Lord Tobias Timpson on the fifteenth of April of this year. How do you plead?'

'Not guilty.' Her voice was weak and hoarse. A murmur went around the courtroom.

'You may be seated.'

Sir Nigel Bostock, KC, rose. He appeared as broad as he was tall. The buttons of his waistcoat strained against the force of his bulk. Outlining the case for the Crown, he presented Lady Timpson as a strong, calculating woman who'd murdered her husband because he was squandering her money and derailing her election campaign. He claimed she'd pushed or struck Lord Timpson, rendering him unconscious, aware that he would drown in the canal. The courtroom was airless, and by the time he'd finished, beads of sweat were glistening on his brow.

Philip Johnson, KC, opened his address. 'My learned friend has labelled my client as a cold-blooded killer.' He paused to look at Lady Timpson. The jury followed suit. The pathetic figure in the dock didn't look like the ferocious harridan described by the counsel for the prosecution. 'Nothing could be further from the truth. Members of the jury, what I'm going to tell you will shock you at times. You may be astonished to learn that my client was a victim of her husband's violence long before his attempt on her life. She was the subject of abuse and cruelty throughout her marriage to Lord Tobias Timpson. She put up with physical beatings and harsh verbal treatment from a man who believed it was his right to treat women as he wished. However, she took great pains to hide this abuse from the world and, more importantly, her children.'

He paused, this time to turn to Sir Nigel.

'My learned colleague will try to persuade you that my client lured her husband to a remote spot on the estate of his ancestral home, Crookham Hall, and murdered him there with her bare hands. This is sheer fiction. It doesn't make sense. My client isn't a strong woman, and her husband was a fit and healthy man. Would she really attempt to kill him in such a crude manner? The truth is – it was Lady Timpson who was in danger. It was her life that was under threat. She was the one who was lured to this secluded spot and threatened with a shotgun by her husband.'

Daniel and Constance winced at this statement.

'You're going to hear testimony that will leave you in no doubt as to what sort of a man Lord Timpson was and why he was driven to take such desperate action. He owed a significant amount of money to his creditors. And the only person who could save him was his wife. Her money had kept him solvent throughout their marriage and saved him from bankruptcy. If it hadn't been for my client, Crookham Hall would have been sold years ago to pay his creditors. The only reason Lord Timpson was able to keep his ancestral home and enjoy his privileged life was because his wife paid for it. But he resented that fact. He wanted to take back control, which is why he wanted her dead.'

* * *

PC Ben Gilbert was the first witness to be called by the Crown. He was asked to explain what had led to the arrest of Lady Timpson.

'We had an eye-witness placing Lady Timpson at the scene of the crime.'

'This contradicted the prisoner's previous statement?' Sir Nigel said.

'Yes. Previously she had told us that she'd parted company with Lord Timpson at around ten o'clock that morning after riding through the meadows to the south of the canal. She said she presumed he must have ridden on to the canal after she'd left him.'

'It was then that you decided to take Lady Timpson in for questioning?'

'That's correct.'

'Did Lady Timpson answer your questions?'

'No, initially she did not. I believe she wanted to correspond with her children before she told us what went on that morning.'

'After she did this, what was her new version of events?'

'She told us that her husband had asked her to ride with him to Blacksmith's Bridge that morning. When they got there, she was attempting to tie up her horse when he produced a shotgun. Her horse was not yet tethered, and it reared up in fright. It was then that she pushed Lord Timpson away, and he fell into the canal.' Ben stood like a soldier on parade, his shoulders back and eyes fixed on one point.

'Did you find any evidence to support this story?'

'We did a thorough search of the area. We found prints of hooves from two different horses. But nothing to indicate what had occurred. Later, when we searched the canal, we found a shotgun.'

'Who did that shotgun belong to?'

'The ownership of the shotgun is unknown.'

'Is there any evidence to suggest the gun belonged to Lord Timpson?'

'No guns are missing from the estate's collection according to the estate manager. The Timpsons' groom is also positive neither Lord nor Lady Timpson had a shotgun in their possession when they left for their ride that morning.'

'When you questioned Lady Timpson, did you ask her about her relationship with her husband?'

'I did, yes.'

'Did she tell you it was a happy marriage?'

'She did at first.'

'At first? She changed her story?' Sir Nigel said in mock surprise.

'That's correct. When we initially questioned Lady Timpson, she told us her relationship with her husband had been a kind and loving one.'

'Kind and loving. She used those words?' Sir Nigel repeated.

'Yes, she did.'

I didn't know how much experience Ben had of being questioned in court. I was certain he'd never been called to give evidence in a famous murder trial before, but he seemed unperturbed by the questioning.

'But later this description changed?'

'Yes. Later she told us that he had been a violent man and had subjected her to abuse during the course of their marriage.' Ben recited these facts without emotion.

'Did you find any evidence to corroborate this version of events?'

'A few of the staff at Crookham Hall said they'd overheard arguments between Lord and Lady Timpson.'

'Were these arguments violent?'

'No, they were described as heated.'

'What were these arguments about?'

'Money. On each occasion, Lady Timpson seemed to be accusing her husband of running up debts in various London clubs.'

'Did you investigate this further?'

'We obtained details of Lord Timpson's financial affairs.' Ben gave no indication these details had been obtained by means other than police investigation. I noticed Superintendent Cobbe watching him from the back of the courtroom.

'And what did they reveal?' Sir Nigel asked.

'That he owed over ten thousand pounds to his creditors.'

There were audible gasps from around the courtroom.

Sir Nigel raised his eyebrows. 'It's understandable Lady Timpson took her husband to task. That's a significant amount of money. Could you tell us how Lord Timpson came to acquire these debts?'

'Most were to gambling clubs, and there were some outstanding bills from other establishments,' Ben replied.

'Thank you, PC Gilbert. No further questions.' Sir Nigel sat down.

I remembered Horace Laffaye's coy phrase, 'establishments of a dubious nature'. I was surprised Sir Nigel didn't ask Ben to elaborate.

Philip Johnson got to his feet. 'PC Gilbert, could you tell us how the shotgun came to be in the water?'

'I wouldn't like to speculate. It's possible it was discarded by an unknown person and has nothing to do with this case.'

'Was the shotgun in good condition? Did it look old or new to you?'

'It was new.'

'Was it loaded?'

'Yes.'

'Had it been fired?'

'Just once.'

'Let me recap. It was a new shotgun, fully loaded. One shot had been fired from it, and you found it in the Basingstoke Canal, near the vicinity of Blacksmith's Bridge. Is that correct?'

'Yes.' Ben nodded.

'Lady Timpson told you that her husband confronted her with a shotgun, it fired as her horse reared up, and she pushed him away. He then fell backwards into the canal.'

'Yes.'

'Doesn't that tell you how the shotgun came to be in the canal near Blacksmith's Bridge?' Philip Johnson smiled.

'This is more like it,' Percy whispered.

'We have no evidence to corroborate her story or any way of knowing how the shotgun came to be in the water.' Ben would not be drawn. 'There have been reports of poachers in that area. The gun could have belonged to one of them.'

'Who reported these poachers?'

'Lord Timpson mentioned it on a few occasions.'

'Did he want you to track them down?'

Ben shook his head. 'Poaching has always gone on in the woods around Crookham Hall. It would be impossible for us to keep an eye on the place all the time.'

'In truth, these poachers had only ever stolen the odd pheasant from the outskirts of the estate. But perhaps Lord Timpson needed them to be blamed for something more serious?' He said this to the jury before turning back to Ben. 'I find it difficult to believe that a poacher would have thrown away a new shotgun so readily. But let us move on. You say that Lord Timpson owed money to gambling clubs and other establishments. Could you enlighten us as to what those other establishments were?'

'It appears that Lord Timpson frequented some exclusive salons, which upon further investigation, were found to be high-class brothels.' Ben's gaze was still fixed firmly ahead.

'Was Lord Timpson a regular visitor to these "exclusive salons"?'

'Yes. He had known some of the salon owners for many decades.'

'He was on good terms with these owners?'

'No, I wouldn't say good terms.'

'Why not? Surely a man of Lord Timpson's standing would be a highly sought-after client?'

'The owners made two complaints about the deceased. One was his tardiness in settling his account.'

'And the other?' Philip Johnson put weight on these words to signal what was to come.

'He was sometimes violent towards the women, the prostitutes he was with.'

'In what way violent?'

'He had been known to punch or slap them.'

'I see. Can you tell us what type of injuries they sustained?'

'Mainly bruises, sometimes a black eye or a cut lip.'

'Thank you for your time, PC Gilbert. That will be all.'

Ben stepped down from the stand. He'd given an impeccable performance, showing no emotion throughout and left the court without looking at anyone. The judge decided to adjourn for lunch at this point.

Sitting in the public gallery with Daniel and Constance, listening to these revelations had been uncomfortable, to say the least. I found myself avoiding their eyes as we shuffled along the benches and out of the courtroom.

28

When we returned, Samuel Moffat took the stand. He looked smarter than when I'd last seen him. He was wearing a corduroy jacket that looked new, and he'd had his hair cut. His testimony was brief. He confirmed he'd been in the vicinity of Blacksmith's Bridge at a quarter past ten that morning when he'd seen Lord and Lady Timpson riding together, and they'd appeared to be about to dismount.

'How did Lord and Lady Timpson seem to you? Were they riding side by side? Did they exchange any words?' Philip Johnson asked.

'Lord Timpson was riding ahead of Lady Timpson. They didn't say anything to each other. They just seemed normal.' Unlike Ben, Samuel didn't know where to look. His eyes darted between Philip Johnson, the judge and the jurors.

'Did you see a shotgun either on their persons or anywhere near the bridge?'

'No, sir.'

'You ran away when you saw them coming, is that correct?'

Samuel nodded. 'I'd been trying to catch fish. I was on my side of the canal, but I didn't want them accusing me of poaching, so I scarpered.'

'You didn't witness what happened next?' Philip Johnson enquired.

'No, sir,' Samuel mumbled. 'I went back to the farmhouse.'

'Did you hear a gunshot as you walked to your farm?'

Samuel looked uncertain. 'I'm not sure.'

'You don't know if you heard a gun being fired or not?'

'No, sir. I might have done, but I didn't take no notice. There are always guns going off in the woods.'

Philip Johnson looked exasperated and said he had no further questions.

Sir Nigel indicated he had no desire to cross-examine the witness. It was clear Samuel had little to offer.

The judge decided to call a short break before we heard from the most significant witness of the day. Philip Johnson was going to put Lady Timpson on the stand.

Outside the courtroom, Percy leant on the curved rail of the staircase. 'I think the prosecution's case is weak. I'd say Sir Nigel's got his work cut out.'

'I agree it's weak.' Elijah took his cigarette case from his pocket. 'But I suspect he plans to strengthen it by his cross-examination of Lady Timpson.'

'I'm curious to see what impression she'll make on the stand,' I said.

'A lot will rest on that.' Elijah took a deep drag of his cigarette. 'If the jury doesn't warm to her...' He left the sentence unfinished.

* * *

It was painful to watch Lady Timpson walk slowly to the witness stand. She looked frail and frightened. Gone was the formal political suit. Instead, she wore a demure dress of plain green linen. Philip Johnson smiled at her encouragingly.

Once she'd taken the oath, he rose. 'Lady Timpson, were you afraid of your husband?'

'Yes, I was.'

'Why?'

'Because he was a brutal man.'

'Did he ever strike you?'

'Many times, over the years.' She appeared subdued, almost resigned to her fate.

'With his fists?'

'Yes, usually he would punch or slap me.' It was almost a whisper.

The judge leant forward in his seat. 'Lady Timpson, could I ask you to speak up? It is imperative the jury is able to hear every word you say.'

'I'm sorry,' she said louder. 'Yes, he would often punch or slap me.'

'Did he ever hit you with an implement?'

'Just once. Shortly after our marriage.' She took a sip of water.

'May I ask what that implement was?' Philip Johnson asked.

She avoided looking at her children. 'It was his belt. He removed it from his trousers and used it to beat me across my back and buttocks.'

A collective gasp from the court. I could feel Constance shudder. All colour had drained from Daniel's face. He put his arm around his sister, and she buried her head in his shoulder.

'What were you wearing at this time?'

'I was wearing a silk nightdress. He pulled this up so he could strike my bare skin.' She raised her head as she said this. 'He said he wanted to make it clear who was in charge. He told me I was socially inferior to him and that I should know my place. He said he wished he'd never married me, but he had no choice if he were to keep Crookham Hall.'

'Did your husband ever force you to have sexual intercourse with him against your will?'

'Objection.' Sir Nigel got to his feet. 'A man has conjugal rights. He is perfectly entitled to have intercourse with his wife, whether she likes it or not.'

'Legally, Sir Nigel, you are correct,' Judge Radden agreed. 'The crime of rape does not exist within a marriage. However, I am going to allow Mr Johnson to ask his question.'

Sir Nigel gave the judge a curt nod and sat down again.

'Thank you m'lord.' Philip Johnson inclined his head towards the judge. He turned back to Lady Timpson. 'I will ask again. Did your husband ever force you to have sexual intercourse against your will?'

An eerie silence fell in the courtroom.

'Yes.' It was little more than a whisper.

Judge Radden leant forward. 'Would you like to take a break, Lady Timpson?'

'I'd rather continue,' she said resolutely.

I didn't blame her. In her position, I'd want to get this over with as quickly as possible. She was a proud woman. Sometimes an arrogant woman. To stand in court and reveal the humiliations she'd been subjected to over the years was clearly taking every ounce of strength she had.

'When was this?' Philip Johnson glanced at the jurors. They were staring at Lady Timpson with rapt expressions.

'On many occasions during the first few years of our marriage.'

'And these beatings, did they occur regularly?'

'Yes, during those early years. But they became less frequent as time went on.'

'Why was that?' Philip Johnson's eyes seemed to be willing her to keep going.

'He showed me a little more respect as the children got older. He loved them.' She looked up at them and almost managed a smile. 'He didn't want them to find out, and I gradually began to regain some control. Tobias had sizeable gambling debts, and I held the purse strings. All our money came from the business, which my father had entitled to me. My husband couldn't touch it. We came to an unspoken agreement.'

'What was that agreement?'

'We avoided each other as much as possible. We slept in separate rooms. But we put on a united front for the sake of appearances. And because of our children. We both loved our children.'

'You've told us your husband used to assault you regularly. The prosecution would say this gave you a powerful motive for wanting him dead.'

'The beatings had stopped. We rarely spent time alone together. We didn't like each other, but we had settled into the relationship we'd fabricated. At one time, I'd begun to think Tobias had mended his ways.' She took a deep breath. 'But I couldn't have been more wrong.'

'Indeed, you could not. My learned colleague will ask you to recount the events of the fifteenth of April. However, I have just one question. Do you believe your husband intended to kill you that morning?'

'I have no doubt his plan was to shoot me dead and claim we were set upon by poachers.'

'Thank you, Lady Timpson. I can see you're distressed.' Philip Johnson gave her a polite nod. 'I have no further questions for you.'

'If she's lying, she's a damned good actress,' Elijah whispered to me.

29

Judge Radden decided it was too late for Sir Nigel to begin his cross-examination and called a halt to proceedings. Lady Timpson's ordeal in the witness box would continue the following day.

Elijah and I took the train back to Walden and strolled around the lake. I left him at Heron Bay Lodge – I knew he was keen to talk to Horace.

I wandered beside Grebe Stream, going over the evidence we'd heard. My thoughts strayed back to the comment Ben had made about a maid taking her own life. It had been Samuel and Hannah Moffat's younger sister, Lydia. Given what we now knew about Lord Timpson's behaviour, I wondered if there was a connection.

On impulse, I decided to take the footpath up to the canal. When I got there, I kept walking until I reached Blacksmith's Bridge.

At the scene of the crime, there was nothing to indicate anything unusual had ever taken place there. In fact, there was something uplifting about the expanse of open countryside. I thought of Lady Timpson confined to a tiny prison cell, anticipating the questions she'd be subjected to by Sir Nigel.

Walking over the bridge was like stepping between two worlds. Behind me was the splendour of the Crookham estate. What lay ahead was the squalor of the shacks.

The smell of wood smoke and cooking food filled the air. Families were sitting outside their makeshift homes, enjoying the warmth of the July evening. A few watched me as I passed but didn't say anything. I nodded, but they gave no sign of recognising me from my visit with Donald Anstey and Mrs Siddons.

I knocked on the door of the red-brick farmhouse. Paint was peeling from the window frames, and a broken pane of glass had been covered with a wooden board.

Hannah Moffat opened the door and peered at me with large hazel eyes. 'Can I help you?'

'My name is Iris Woodmore. Do you remember me? I came here with Mrs Siddons and Mr Anstey.'

She nodded.

'Could I talk to you for a moment?' I wondered where Samuel was.

'What about?' She checked to see if anyone else was in the farmyard.

'I won't stay long,' I promised.

Hannah opened the door, and we went through to the kitchen. She seemed mesmerised by my appearance, inspecting first my hair and then my clothes.

'I was in court today for Lady Timpson's trial. Do you know what she's claiming?'

'I've heard the gossip and seen the headlines in the newspapers when I go into town.' She gestured for me to sit down. I could see how curious she was.

'Today she told the court that her husband used to punch and slap her.'

She gasped.

'She said he'd once beaten her across the back and buttocks with a belt.'

'He was a bastard.' Hannah bit her lip.

'Was he? You believe Lady Timpson is telling the truth?'

She didn't answer immediately, then she said, 'Did they believe her? In the courtroom, did they believe her?' Her eyes searched my face.

'I think so.' I added truthfully, 'It's difficult to tell.'

'What will happen if they don't?'

'She'll hang. Unless other witnesses come forward to say Lord Timpson was violent to them.' I paused. 'Your younger sister, Lydia, used to work at Crookham Hall as a maid, didn't she?'

She nodded, biting her lip again.

'Hannah.' I reached out my hand to hers. 'Did Lydia kill herself because of something Lord Timpson did?'

She gave a loud sob.

I pulled my chair closer and put my arm around her. 'I know it's painful, but can you tell me what happened?'

She hiccupped, wiping her face with a teacloth. 'Lydia was walking home from the hall one evening when Lord Timpson came riding up. She was pleased when he got off his horse and talked to her. She liked him; thought he was lovely. But then he got rough.' She lowered her eyes in embarrassment.

'What do you mean by rough?'

'He wanted to kiss her. That scared her. She said she had to go home. She tried to run away. But he pushed her to the ground and pulled her skirts up.' Hannah's face was crimson. 'She struggled and tried to push him off. And then he stopped and stood up.'

'No sexual activity took place?'

Hannah shook her head. 'She was thankful when he got off her without actually... well, you know.'

This wasn't what I'd been expecting. 'Did Lord Timpson say anything?'

'He asked Lydia if she was a virgin,' Hannah whispered hoarsely. 'She told him that she was.'

'And what did Lord Timpson say?'

'He said that she was worth saving for his son.'

I clapped my hand over my mouth. 'What did Lydia do?'

'She didn't want to go back to the hall after that. She tried to pretend she was sick, but Pa was having none of it. Lydia stopped eating, she kept shaking all the time, but they made her go. I tried to tell her it was going to be all right. But then a few weeks later, Lord Timpson saw her crossing the courtyard to go home and stood in her way. He said he'd need her soon, and she'd have to do what she was told.'

'What did she think he meant by that?'

'Master Daniel was due home on leave, and she thought he was going to force her into having sexual relations with him. She was petrified. She didn't want to go back to the hall, but Ma made her.'

'And she...' I couldn't bring myself to say the words.

She dabbed at her nose. 'My parents were very religious. They told us that we would go to hell if we had relations with a man out of wedlock.'

I slumped in the chair and put my head in my hands. The sound of the front door opening jolted me upright. 'Will you tell your story in court? It could make all the difference to the trial.'

She shook her head vehemently.

Samuel Moffat walked in and stared at me in surprise. 'What's going on?'

'I just came to talk to Hannah.' I got to my feet, wondering if he knew the truth about Lydia's death. Now wasn't the time to ask.

'What have you said?' he demanded of his sister. 'She's a reporter. She works for that newspaper.'

Hannah stared at me in horror. 'I don't want anything about us in the paper.'

'I'm not here because of the paper. I promise.'

'Then why are you here?' Samuel moved towards me.

'Because people need to know the truth.' I was looking at Hannah when I said this. 'A life depends on it.'

'What truth?' Samuel demanded. 'Whose life?'

'You'd better go now,' his sister muttered.

'Please, Hannah.' A parting plea as I stumbled out of the door.

30

The courtroom pulsated with anticipation as the counsel for the prosecution got to his feet. Sir Nigel faced the accused.

'Lady Timpson, I'd like you to tell me what happened on the morning of the fifteenth of April this year. You say your husband asked you to go for a ride with him?'

'That's correct.'

'Was this usual?'

'No, we only normally rode together when we had company. It was rare for just the two of us to go out together.'

'What reason did your husband give for wanting you to ride with him that morning?'

'He said he wanted to discuss the location of the warehouses we planned to build by the canal.'

'Were you suspicious of his motives when he said this?'

'No. I knew Tobias wasn't happy about my plans to build on the estate. It was his ancestral home. I felt it reasonable to give him a say in the matter. I was pleased he was taking an interest.'

'So you rode out with your husband. What happened next?'

'We got to Blacksmith's Bridge and dismounted. I had my back to Tobias. I was trying to tether my horse, Bessie, but the post by the bridge was too low. I struggled and gave up. She's a docile beast; I didn't think she'd run off. When I turned round, Tobias had a shotgun in his hand.'

'And it was at this point that *you* attacked him?' Sir Nigel challenged.

'I did not attack him,' Lady Timpson replied coldly. 'He said something like, "Do you think I'd let you turn Crookham into one of your disgusting factories, you bitch." He pointed the gun at me, and I screamed. That's when my horse reared up on her hind legs.'

'What did your husband do?' Sir Nigel asked sceptically.

'He raised his arms as the horse's legs came down towards him. I pushed him away. I think I pushed his arms.' She faltered. 'It might have been his chest, I'm not sure. The gun went off. He stumbled backwards to the ground. I mean, into the water.'

Sir Nigel pounced at this hesitation. 'Which is it, Lady Timpson? Did he fall to the ground or into the canal?'

'He fell towards the bank and into the water,' she replied firmly.

'Did you check to see if he was injured?' Sir Nigel enquired.

'I thought he'd just fallen over. I caught Bessie's reins and managed to mount her. I was terrified he would come after me or shoot at me as I rode away. I kept going until I got to the stables.'

'When you got there, did you tell anyone what had happened?'

She shook her head.

'No.' Sir Nigel answered for her. 'You gave your horse to the groom and told him that Lord Timpson was still out riding. Is that correct?'

'Yes.'

'You returned to the hall and didn't tell anyone, your servants or children, that you'd left Lord Timpson dead in the canal.' He announced this as a statement rather than a question.

'I didn't know he was dead.' She focused on the jury. 'I had to get away from him before he got up.'

'What did you do when you got back to the hall?'

'I changed out of my clothes. Then I went to my study.'

'You didn't give a moment's thought to your husband?'

'I thought of nothing else.' She hesitated. 'I didn't know what to do. How could I face him after what had happened? He'd planned to kill me, that much was clear. I decided to tell him I was going to the police.'

'Weren't you concerned when he didn't come back for lunch?' Sir Nigel said in mock astonishment.

She shook her head. 'I assumed he was still thinking about what to do next.'

'What interests me, Lady Timpson, is what *you* planned to do next.' Sir Nigel puffed out his chest as he spoke.

'Write a letter.' She sounded more decisive.

'A letter. To whom?'

'The police. I intended to give it to my daughter, Constance, to keep. I would say to her that she should take it to the police if anything were to happen to me. I'd tell Tobias what I'd done.' Some of her old vigour returned as she described her plan. 'I'd make sure he knew that if he tried to harm me again, the police, and our children, would know who was responsible.'

'Did you write this letter?' Sir Nigel asked.

'I was in the middle of writing it when Daniel returned and told us what he'd found.'

'How did you feel?'

'Relieved. But I was also upset for my children's sake. They loved their father very much. And he loved them.' She looked up at Daniel and Constance.

'You didn't admit to them you were responsible for his death?'

'When I pushed Tobias away, it was in fear. I honestly believed he was alive when I left him.' She appealed again to the jury. 'I thought he'd scramble out of the water. It isn't deep at that stretch of the canal.'

'When you were told he'd drowned due to his head injuries, did you feel remorse?' Sir Nigel turned to the jury. 'You certainly didn't feel the need to go to the police and tell them what had happened, did you?'

'I was confused and frightened.'

'Were you?' Sir Nigel was at his most cynical. 'Or was it because what you've told us is a pack of lies? I suggest that it was you who asked your husband to ride to the canal that morning. And it was you who attacked him, pushing or striking him so hard that he hit his head and fell into the water.'

'I had no reason to kill my husband.' Lady Timpson's former arrogance was beginning to surface.

'You had every reason. He was squandering your money. He'd accrued massive debts. And he was opposed to you building ugly warehouses in the grounds of his beautiful ancestral home,' Sir Nigel said with a smirk.

'Sir Nigel, that was a statement, not a question,' Judge Radden interjected. 'Do you have any further questions for the defendant?'

Sir Nigel answered the judge but faced the jury as he spoke. 'I'm merely responding to Lady Timpson's statement that she had no reason to kill her husband. I've just given her two excellent reasons. On top of this, she has portrayed Lord Timpson as an abusive husband. Those are all powerful motives for wanting him dead.'

'Nonsense.' Lady Timpson was dismissive. 'I thought I had him under my control.'

I scanned the faces of the jury. They'd appeared sympathetic towards the frail figure that had entered the dock. But faced with Sir Nigel's hostile questioning, Lady Timpson's fighting spirit had been rekindled. They were now looking at her with slightly different eyes.

'You thought you had him under your control,' Sir Nigel repeated. 'How may I ask did you achieve this?'

'I took his sapphire,' Lady Timpson announced.

A murmur went around the courtroom. Daniel and Constance looked startled.

'What do you mean?' For once, Sir Nigel sounded uncertain.

Philip Johnson appeared equally perplexed.

'My husband had used the Star Sapphire as collateral against his debts for many years. I controlled Timpson Foods, which in turn financed Crookham Hall. It was the only asset he had.'

'You're saying you stole his sapphire?' Sir Nigel seemed to be feeling his way with each word.

Philip Johnson rubbed his temples. It was clear from his expression he hadn't been aware of this.

'No, I moved it.'

'Why...' Sir Nigel stumbled. 'Er, what prompted you to hide such a valuable item? An item that belonged to your husband?'

'To feel safe. If he depended on me for money, I had some control over his behaviour. I wanted to ensure he could never hurt me again. I never dreamt he'd try to kill me.'

'When exactly did you move the sapphire?' Sir Nigel was still on unsteady ground.

'In August 1914. One of our maids left suddenly. I knew he'd assume she'd stolen it. But he wouldn't be able to report its loss without alerting his creditors.' The note of triumph in her voice was unmistakable.

Elijah and I looked at each other in astonishment. No wonder Lady Timpson had worn it like a talisman.

The courtroom was silent. Sir Nigel took a sip of water and ran his hands over the notes on his desk. The jury looked at him expectantly.

'Sir Nigel, have you finished questioning the defendant?' the judge asked.

'Er, yes. Yes. No further questions, my lord.' Sir Nigel gave a polite bow.

Philip Johnson gave a slight shake of the head to indicate he had no wish to re-examine his client.

As it was Friday, Judge Radden decided to call a halt to proceedings early. The trial would resume the following week.

We left the court in silence.

31

'We're going to lose Mother too,' I heard Constance whisper to her brother.

'Don't say that, Con,' he replied.

Mrs Siddons hurried them into the waiting car.

Blinking in the sunshine, Elijah, Percy and I walked towards Winchester Railway Station. It was as hot outside as it had been inside the Great Hall. I realised how cocooned we'd been in the courtroom. It was like being shut off from the rest of the world and trapped in a horrible universe where only the trial existed.

'I'd say it's damned unlucky the jury now has all weekend to think about Sir Nigel's accusations and this business with the sapphire,' Percy said.

Elijah nodded. 'I think you're right. But you can't predict how a trial will run. It's never straightforward. More evidence is needed to be certain of a conviction.'

At Winchester Station, Percy caught the train to London while Elijah and I returned to Walden.

'That Percy seems a decent fellow,' Elijah remarked. 'You should go dancing with him.'

I laughed – it was the lightest moment of the day.

We found an empty carriage, and Elijah settled into the corner and lit a cigarette.

'Can you believe that about the sapphire?' I cranked open the window, then slumped down opposite him, aware of how stiff my body had become after sitting on a wooden bench all day.

'No wonder Lord Timpson asked his chums at Scotland Yard to try to find Rebecca Dent.' He took a long drag of his cigarette.

'There's still so much we don't know,' I complained.

'True.'

'And it all comes down to Rebecca. What if she ran away, but Lord Timpson found her and demanded his sapphire back?'

Elijah nodded. 'Lady Timpson certainly put her in a dangerous position.'

'Is Rebecca dead or alive?' I was frustrated at the lack of certainty. 'Lord Timpson could have killed her.'

'So could Lady Timpson. She had more than one reason for wanting her out of the way. The overheard conversation at Westminster, the possible affair with her husband. And now this ruse of making it seem as though Rebecca had run off with the Star Sapphire.'

I thought back to the strange meeting with Kathleen Hooper at the Lyons Corner House. I'd been so desperate to find out about my mother I hadn't asked enough questions about Rebecca. Why had Kathleen been so secretive about where she lived? I wanted to speak to her again, but I had no way of contacting her except through the place in Covent Garden where she worked.

* * *

The following day, I was back at Walden Station. I'd dug out Aunt Maud's letter to check the name of the dress shop Kathleen Hooper had given as her address.

Walking over Waterloo Bridge, I thought of the last time I'd strolled across it, hand in hand with Percy. That feeling of being young and carefree had been too fleeting. When the trial was over, I'd ask him if he wanted to go to the pictures again.

Not far from Covent Garden market, I found Hartnell's Boutique and spent a few minutes examining the dresses displayed on wooden dummies in the window. They were beautifully made. At the foot of each dummy lay a pair of gloves, stockings and shoes, carefully selected to be worn with each dress. I couldn't imagine myself ever wearing such a perfectly coordinated outfit.

I went inside to examine the rails that ran down both sides of the shop. The walls were painted in soft mauve and fitted at intervals with mirrors in varnished teak frames. A strong smell of lily of the valley didn't quite mask the odour of mothballs.

Each item was handmade, some decorated with carefully embroidered embellishments. I couldn't see any price tags, which must mean they were expensive.

'Can I help you?' A stately looking woman appeared from the back of the shop. She wore a fitted navy dress and matching bolero jacket. Her grey hair was combed into a neat bun on the top of her head. I recognised her as Mrs Hartnell, the lady who'd been sitting by the window of Lyons Corner House when we'd met Kathleen.

'I was wondering if I might have a word with a friend of mine,' I asked. 'Kathleen? Mrs Kathleen Hooper?'

'Mrs Hooper doesn't work here,' Mrs Hartnell replied in a precise, clipped voice. 'She brings Mrs Bowen's dresses in to us. That one's delightful, isn't it?'

I was standing next to a shimmery blue crepe silk evening dress. Laid over the top of the silk was a translucent fabric stitched with tiny glass beads surrounded by perfectly embroidered petals. 'It's beautiful.'

'Exquisite.' Mrs Hartnell beamed. 'You rarely see such precise needlecraft.'

Visions of purple and green sashes embroidered with sweet violets swam into my mind. I examined the dress. 'The tiny stitching is quite distinctive. I'm sure I've come across it before. Is Mrs Bowen a tall lady with long blonde hair?'

'No, Mrs Bowen has short dark hair. She is a tall lady, though. Not that we see much of her. Mrs Hooper tends to handle all her commissions and collects and delivers the garments.'

'It was Mrs Hooper I was hoping to see. I seem to have mislaid her address. Is she still in Catford?'

'Oh no, Mrs Hooper lives in Lambeth now.'

'Of course. Would you be able to give me her address?'

'I'm not sure. I suppose it would be all right. Didn't I see you with her the other day in the Corner House? With another lady?'

'That's right. My Aunt Maud. She and Mrs Hooper are old friends. Mrs Hooper wrote down her address and gave it to my aunt, but my grandmother threw the piece of paper away.' I leant forward and said confidingly, 'I think Gran did it on purpose.'

'Do you?' Mrs Hartnell appeared suitably intrigued.

'My aunt looks after Gran, you see.' I was enjoying my improvisation. 'But Gran can be so demanding. I don't think she likes Aunt Maud having friends. She wants her to wait on her all the time.'

'Your poor aunt has my sympathy. My own dear mother can sometimes be quite a trial to my husband and me.'

'Aunt Maud was so upset when she couldn't find the address, I said I'd see if I could find Kathleen for her.'

'Let me go and check my records. I'm sure I have it somewhere.' She disappeared into the back of the shop.

I examined all of the embroidered dresses until she returned. In neat, curling handwriting she'd written:

27 Victoria Street, Lambeth.

I thanked Mrs Hartnell and left the shop, my emotions gravitating between self-congratulation at my success and trepidation at what I might find in Lambeth. It was only a few stops on the underground. But how would Kathleen react if I just turned up on her doorstep? I walked towards the station. I'd decide what to do when I got there.

The guard at Lambeth underground station told me Victoria Street was five minutes' walk away. I soon found myself on a long, straight road with terraced houses on either side. Number twenty-seven was in the middle of a terrace.

Tall plane trees lined the street, and I stood behind one and looked over to the house on the opposite side of the road. A tall figure was moving around in one of the upper rooms.

After a while, an elderly lady with a Yorkshire terrier came out of the house behind me. The dog snuffled around the base of the tree, then cocked its leg. I hastily moved onto the pavement.

'Excuse me. Is that where Mrs Hooper lives?' I pointed towards number twenty-seven.

'She has rooms upstairs.' The woman smelt strongly of gin and tobacco.

'Thank you.' I backed away. 'I saw another lady upstairs. I thought I'd got the wrong address.'

'That would be Mrs Bowen.' The woman moved closer to me whilst her terrier sniffed my feet. 'They share. They're both widows.'

'Of course. Mrs Hooper did mention her. I'd quite forgotten. Thank you so much for your help.'

I crossed the road and squinted up at the first-floor window. A figure moved about, but it was impossible to make out who it was. The old woman was still watching me, so I walked towards the front door. If I was wrong, this was going to be very difficult to explain.

I rapped on the door and waited. It was opened by a broad man with a dark beard wearing a white shirt, undone at the collar, and coarse grey trousers with braces.

'Can I help you?' he asked in a cockney accent.

'Would it be possible for me to speak with Mrs Hooper?' The words came out in a rush.

He took a step back and bellowed up the stairs. 'Kathleen. Someone here for you.'

'Your lunch is getting cold, Arthur,' a woman shouted from the end of the corridor. A strong smell of frying bacon wafted from the house.

Kathleen appeared at the top of the stairs. She looked startled to see me but nodded to the man. He grunted and left us, obviously keen to return to his meal.

'Iris. What are you doing here?' Her fingers gripped the banister, agitation etched on her face.

I hesitated, suddenly doubtful. I'd spent so long searching for clues, perhaps I was seeing links where there weren't any. Knowing I could be making a big mistake, I took the plunge.

'I want to see Rebecca.'

32

'What do you mean?' Kathleen still gripped the banister, her knuckles white.

I persevered. 'Mrs Bowen, then.'

She glanced over her shoulder but didn't move from the stairs. I stood on the doorstep, not sure what to do next.

Then a voice from behind her called, 'Come in, Iris.'

A tall figure appeared at the top of the stairs and beckoned to me. Kathleen hesitated, then took a step back.

I went upstairs to the room I'd been watching from the street. A tailor's dummy stood in one corner, covered in some icy blue fabric. There was a sewing machine on the table and a basket full of coloured threads.

'I'll be in my room.' Kathleen disappeared down the corridor.

'I'm glad you came, Iris.' She gestured for me to sit in a faded armchair by the unlit fire. 'Kathleen told me you looked just like your mother. You have her beautiful brown eyes. And her hair. She would have liked your haircut. Very modern.' Her accent was more Hampshire than London.

I examined her as she lowered her angular frame into the

armchair opposite. She had short dark hair and seemed young; she could pass for twenty-five. Rebecca would be thirty-one. Was this the same woman who'd once had long blonde hair and taught me to embroider?

'You are Rebecca Dent, aren't you?' I was suddenly uncertain.

She smiled, then nodded. 'I call myself Grace Bowen now. Do you remember when I taught you to sew at your mother's table all those years ago? We embroidered little purple flowers onto our sashes.'

Relief flooded through me. I'd done it. I'd found Rebecca.

'How did you know I was here?' she asked.

'I went to Mrs Hartnell's shop. I wanted to speak to Kathleen again. She'd been so secretive – not giving my aunt her address. When I saw the garments you'd embroidered, the detail of the flower embellishments reminded me of the violets we sewed onto those sashes.'

'You're clever. Like your mother,' she said sadly. 'I'm sorry for what happened. I wish I'd spoken to you about it at the time.'

'Why didn't you? You could have come to see us.'

'I was afraid of your father's reaction. He was angry. And I was scared of people finding out I was a suffragette. I would have lost my position.'

'But you left anyway.'

She gave a slight nod but didn't explain. Instead, she said, 'Kathleen told me what made your mother jump into the river. It sounds like Violet. She would never hurt a soul.'

'You didn't want to go to Westminster with her, did you?' She looked so young. Yet there was a weariness about her that spoke of years of suffering. Had it all stemmed from that day? Was my mother's reckless protest the reason Rebecca had decided to walk away from her old life? 'Did Mother persuade you?'

'I let myself be persuaded. Violet was keen to do it. She said we'd be safe as the police would be patrolling the march at Buckingham Palace. She thought she'd be home with you and your father before anyone knew where she'd been.'

I felt a surge of relief at hearing this. Mother had just wanted to paint the grilles, hang her banner, and force those in power to acknowledge the suffragettes. But it had all gone terribly wrong. And not only for Mother.

'I wish I could change that day.' Tears glistened on Rebecca's face. 'I wish I'd confronted Lady Timpson there and then and left with Violet. I feel so guilty about her death.'

'Did you run away because of it? Or was it because of what you'd overheard?' I still couldn't understand why she'd stayed hidden all these years.

'No, it had nothing to do with that day.' She picked up a length of fine silver thread that had caught on the armchair. She twisted it around her fingers.

'Then, why?'

'I was scared.'

'Of Lady Timpson?'

'Of him.' It was almost a whisper.

'Donald Anstey?'

'No, not Donald.' She lowered her head. 'Lord Timpson.'

'Were you having an affair with him?'

Her head shot up. She gave a forced, choking laugh.

'No,' she said with venom. 'I did not have an affair with him.'

'Then why was he seen coming from your room?'

'Because he would rape me.'

I felt a tremor run through my body. The words I'd been about to say dried on my lips. 'But...' I stopped. After what I'd heard in court, why was this such a shock?

'You don't believe me?' She must have seen the incredulity I was trying to hide.

I had to admit that even after everything I'd learnt about Lord Timpson's character, I was still shocked by her revelation. It was hard to believe that charming, attractive man with twinkling blue eyes had been a rapist.

'It's just he seemed so...' I faltered. What was I trying to say? 'Nice, I suppose. He seemed nice,' I said weakly. Alice had used the same words. They'd sounded hollow then, yet here I was repeating them.

'He could be nice. He could be extremely charming.' Rebecca paused. 'I almost fell for him. Almost. It was clear he liked me in that way. But I couldn't risk losing my position at Crookham Hall. I told him to leave me alone – and he didn't like that.'

'Why didn't you go to the police?'

'Do you think they'd have believed me? The word of a maid against that of the charming Lord Timpson?' Her voice was ragged. 'You said how nice he was.'

I winced. Once again, I found myself having to make a rapid adjustment to the way I'd thought about this man.

'He was a monster,' she continued. 'He believed I was his property. I was a servant of the Crookham estate. Another of his possessions to do with as he pleased. I could do nothing to stop him.'

'So you ran away?' I realised she would have had little choice but to escape.

'I couldn't let him do it to me again. Not ever.' Her face contorted with pain. She pulled at the thread, digging it into her pale fingers.

'How did you get away?'

'Lady Timpson arranged it.'

I gasped. I'd been so stupid. I'd always suspected Lady Timpson knew more than she was letting on. Her constant refusal to search for Rebecca had made me think she didn't want her to be found. But it had never occurred to me she'd helped her disappear.

'Why did she do that?'

'I tried to blackmail her. I feel ashamed now, but I was desperate. I told her what I'd heard in the House of Commons. Said it would ruin her if it came out.'

'She helped you to keep you quiet?'

'No. She laughed it off. She told me I could tell whom I pleased, no one would believe me.'

'But she still helped you to run away?' I was intrigued and horrified at the same time.

'She asked me why I was so desperate to leave Crookham Hall. From the way she looked at me, I got the feeling she already suspected. So I told her exactly what Lord Timpson was doing to me.'

'What did she say?'

'Nothing. She just nodded. A slight nod to acknowledge what I'd said was true.' Rebecca gave a small, mirthless laugh. 'I hated her at that moment. She didn't even seem surprised. How could she let him get away with it? I wanted to scream at her.'

'Why didn't you?' I would have wanted to hit her.

'Because then I saw the look in her eyes. And I knew.'

'Knew what?'

'That he'd done it to her too.'

I thought of Lady Timpson's testimony in court, and sweat formed in my palms.

Rebecca leant her head against the back of the armchair. 'My hate turned to pity then. I felt defeated. I'd thought it was because I was a servant with no power. But she was a lady. He took what he wanted from women, whoever they were. It made no difference to him.'

'How did you escape?'

'She arranged everything. Gave me money and new clothes. She even found a place for us all to live. Kathleen and Leonard and me. It had to be a busy London borough so that we wouldn't be noticed.'

I thought of all the servants milling about the busy courtyard at Crookham Hall. 'But how did you manage to leave without being seen? Lady Timpson wasn't even there that day. The police records say she and Lord Timpson were away in London that weekend.'

'She'd given me a key so I could leave by a side door of the hall rather than go through the servants' quarters. I'd hidden it under the floorboards in my room. She left a train ticket in her own bathroom and some hair dye and scissors. I went there first to cut my hair and colour it. I left my locks hidden in her chest of drawers.' Her hand rose to touch the bare skin at the nape of her neck. 'No one saw me leave. I walked to Walden Station and took the last train to Waterloo. Lady Timpson was waiting for me. She'd paid a cab to take me to the house where Kathleen and Leonard were already living. She'd given them money and clothes for me.'

Since learning of Rebecca's disappearance, I'd imagined a dozen different scenarios of what could have happened to her. I'd never come close to guessing the truth. Everything I'd learnt in the last weeks about Lord Timpson had forced me to dramatically change my opinion of him. I was now having to completely readjust my view of Lady Timpson.

'I became Mrs Grace Bowen, the lodger. We hadn't planned what to say next. But with the war, it became easy. Everyone's husband was away fighting. We told people I was a widow; that my husband had been killed in action, and I didn't go out much as I was grieving. I felt guilty about that, especially when people were kind. So many young women were widowed. I felt a fraud. I am a fraud, I suppose.'

'But Lord Timpson had the police out looking for you?'

'We moved around frequently at first. But once the fuss died down, we began to feel safer. Then Kathleen got a telegram to say

Leonard had been killed in action. She became a widow too.' Rebecca blinked. 'The couple downstairs, Arthur and Molly, were kind and let us board here.'

'It must have been hard.' I couldn't comprehend the ordeal they'd been through.

'We struggled with Leonard gone. But Kathleen found outlets for my work, places like Mrs Hartnell's boutique.'

'Couldn't you have asked Lady Timpson for help?'

'It was too risky. We'd agreed to have no further contact with each other.'

'Why didn't you tell Donald Anstey what was going on?' From what I knew of him, he was a decent man. My father thought so. 'He would have helped you. He was in love with you.'

Rebecca bowed her head, rubbing the bridge of her nose. She gave a sigh as if conflicted. 'Because of Violet.'

'I don't understand.' I stared at her in confusion. What did my mother have to do with this?

A small head peeked around the door of the adjoining room.

'Did you call me, Mummy?'

33

'I named my daughter after your mother.'

A fair-haired child of about five peered at me with large blue eyes.

'It's all right, darling. You can go back to your drawing.' Rebecca got up, steered the little girl out of the room and closed the door. Then she went over to a small stove in the corner and began to heat some coffee.

The implications of what I'd seen kept me glued to the armchair. I watched Rebecca's tired movements, noting her thin arms and trembling hands as she placed two cups of coffee on the small wooden table.

'Is Lord Timpson her father?'

Rebecca nodded. 'Donald and I were never together in that way.' She lowered herself into the armchair.

'I'm sorry. Sorry for everything you've been through.' I massaged my temples, trying to ease the throbbing in my head.

'It's a relief to tell someone.' She sank back, her weariness evident. 'Kathleen and Leonard were the only people who knew. And Lady Timpson.'

'That must have been a shock to her.' I could imagine Delphina Timpson's reaction to the news that her husband was going to father an illegitimate child.

'I'm sure she had no desire for anyone to know her husband had made one of the servants pregnant,' Rebecca said as if reading my thoughts.

'Did you tell Lord Timpson?'

She nodded. 'I thought it might stop him from touching me again. It didn't.' The pain returned to her face. 'He said it was my fault. He was even more brutal than before.'

I was hot with fury. I couldn't believe what I was hearing. 'What did he expect you to do?'

'He said he'd make arrangements for me to see someone who would get rid of the baby.'

The callousness of the man was breathtaking. I sipped the bitter coffee, trying to absorb what I'd heard. I'd knocked on the door of 27 Victoria Street with some trepidation, not knowing what I'd encounter. I certainly hadn't anticipated anything as cruel as this.

'When I heard he was dead, it was such a relief. To know he'd never come looking for me or Violet. I thought about going to the police. But...'

'You're scared of people finding out?'

'I'm worried for Violet. What will people say? And I'm scared to tell the police about my part in the protest and the blackmail.' Her hands shook as she clutched her cup.

'They don't seem interested in old suffragette cases now. And despite what Donald told them, the police don't have any real evidence of Lady Timpson bribing an MP. It's unlikely she'll mention your blackmail attempt.'

'No, I don't suppose she will. Do you know what she said when

I thanked her?' Her eyes grew distant, seemingly reliving that moment six years earlier.

I shook my head.

'She said I needn't have tried to blackmail her. She said she would have helped me anyway. When I asked her why, she said, "Because I was once helpless. And I remember the fear."'

I was silent. Lady Timpson may have been sincere in what she said. But it hadn't stopped her from taking advantage of Rebecca's disappearance to implicate her in the theft of the Star Sapphire. But now wasn't the time to mention that if I wanted to persuade Rebecca to testify. Instead, I told her what Lord Timpson had done to Lydia Moffat.

'Oh my God. That poor, poor child.' She wailed. 'I feel so guilty. If I'd reported him, she might still be alive. I should have been braver.'

I watched her tears fall and hated the fact that I was about to make her life even more difficult. But I had no choice. 'I was in court each day for the trial. It's not going well for Lady Timpson. If she's found guilty, she'll hang for murder. Your story makes her version of events much more credible. I'm afraid I couldn't persuade Hannah Moffat to testify.'

She shuddered. 'I never believed it would come to this, otherwise I would have acted sooner.'

'You'll talk to the police?'

'I should have spoken up before now. But I thought my situation was unique. Trapped in the lair of a wicked lord like some gothic novel. But since living in London, mostly in the poorer quarters of the city, I've realised it's the same everywhere. Whether you're a servant in a grand house or a young woman in a factory, most people turn a blind eye to the abuse that goes on around them.' She shook her head. 'I'll talk, but I'm not sure anyone will listen.'

I couldn't pretend it would be easy. 'The defence lawyer is likely to want to put you on the stand. He needs to strengthen Lady Timpson's case. But the prosecution will cross-examine.'

'That's what scares me.' She sat up straighter. 'But I don't have a choice. If she goes to the gallows, I'll live with the guilt for the rest of my life.'

'There are people who will help you. I think Donald is one of them.'

'I treated him badly. But when he went away to Scotland, I felt abandoned.' She fingered the gold locket around her neck. 'What could he do anyway? When war was declared, I knew I had to leave. Donald planned to enlist and when he went away, I'd have no one. I had to take control of my life.'

'Did he give you that locket?'

She nodded. That she was wearing it indicated she still cared for him.

'I asked Donald why he went to Scotland. He showed me a ring he'd inherited from his grandmother. He went to see his parents to get it and to tell them he was going to ask you to marry him.'

I saw the pain flare in her eyes. Then she buried her face in her hands and wept.

After a few moments, she lifted her head. 'I wanted to wait for him to return, but I couldn't. It was too much.'

'He'll understand,' I said. But would he? I didn't know him well enough to be sure.

'I thought about telling him. But... Why ruin his life? I decided he'd be better off without me.'

'He lives in Walden now. He moved there to try to find out what happened to you.'

'I read he was standing in the by-election.' She paused. 'Will you talk to him for me? I know it's a lot to ask, but if I go to the police, I'm not sure what they'll do. They might arrest me.'

I didn't think they would, but I had to acknowledge it was a possibility. What would happen to Violet if Rebecca was charged? I felt somehow responsible for this child who bore my mother's name.

'Tell him what I've told you.' She sounded more determined. 'Then ask him if he'll see me. I'll understand if he doesn't want to. But if I give evidence at the trial, it will be in the newspapers. He deserves to hear the truth before that happens.'

I didn't relish the task. But someone had to talk to Donald before news of Rebecca's reappearance became known. I couldn't let him find out from a newspaper. And it would be too distressing for him to meet her again without some forewarning.

'I'll speak to him.' I stood. 'Don't go to the police yet. I'll talk to Lady Timpson's barrister first. He'll probably want to come and see you.'

'Thank you for finding me, Iris.' She pulled me into a weak embrace, and I felt the frailty of her body. 'It's been so hard.'

* * *

The following morning, I walked to Church Road to call on Donald Anstey. But first, I needed to talk to Elijah.

Fortunately, it was a warm day, so we sat in the garden rather than his smoke-filled parlour. I relaxed for a few moments, enjoying the July sunshine. Elijah wasn't much of a gardener. The patch of ground my mother had once dug over to grow vegetables was now covered with bramble. I closed my eyes, remembering Mother's slender hands delicately sowing rows of tiny seeds.

The sound of a striking match roused me. I yawned. I hadn't slept much. Rebecca's story had kept replaying in my mind, and now I had to relate it to someone else.

'What were you doing in London yesterday? Out with young Baverstock?'

'I wish I had been.' I yawned again.

'What then?'

'I found Rebecca.'

His face was grim. 'Alive?'

I took a deep breath and told him.

'Bloody hell,' was all he said. Several times. When I finished, he was shaking his head in disbelief.

'I've spoken to Mrs Siddons, and she's arranging for Philip Johnson to meet with Rebecca. Do you think he'll ask her to give evidence?'

'Almost certainly. He needs the jury to believe Lord Timpson was capable of killing his wife. Her story confirms he was a violent man. I'm surprised Lady Timpson hasn't told Philip herself.'

'She doesn't know where to find Rebecca. They agreed to have no further contact. I also get the impression she doesn't want Constance and Daniel to know they have an illegitimate sibling.'

'Lady Timpson needs to start telling everything she knows. When the jury hears this, they'll be more inclined to believe she was defending herself and that Lord Timpson was the instigator of his own death.'

'Do you think Rebecca will be charged with any offence?'

'Can't see Cobbe trying to convict her of anything now. But I'll have a word with Horace to see if he can exert any influence there. I'm afraid her biggest problem is going to be Sir Nigel Bostock. He won't give her an easy time in the witness box.'

'She's suffered enough.'

'You believed her? I can't see why she would make it up. But I wasn't there to hear her story.'

'Yes,' I replied with conviction. 'If you'd seen her face, you wouldn't need to ask.'

He nodded. 'Poor woman. And poor bloody Anstey.'

'I'm not looking forward to telling him.'

'I'll come with you if you want. Though I'm not sure he'd want me there. It might seem like we were interviewing him for the paper.'

'If Father were home, I would have asked him to come with me. He gets on well with Donald. As it is, I think I should go alone.'

'Can't you wait for Thomas to return?'

I shook my head. 'He's away for a few weeks. If I don't tell him now, Donald may end up hearing about it in court.'

'Come back here afterwards. I'll have a brandy ready in case you need it.'

'I'll be fine.' But would I? I had no idea how Donald was likely to react.

Half an hour later, I was seated in the shabby parlour of Donald Anstey's tiny cottage. He stared silently out of the window. He hadn't moved from this position for some minutes.

I wanted to offer some words of comfort, but I couldn't think of any. I owed it to him to be patient, but eventually I couldn't stand it any longer. 'Would you like to see Rebecca?' I asked.

'Why didn't she tell me?' he said yet again.

'Because she didn't want to ruin your life,' I repeated. We'd been through this several times.

'She ruined my life by walking out without a word.' His sorrow was mixed with anger.

'She felt she had no choice. You must understand how desperate she was.' I was sorry for Donald, but what Rebecca had been through was worse.

He didn't reply.

'What would you like me to tell her?'

'Nothing. I have nothing to say to her.'

'I'm sorry.' I stood to go.

He was still sitting in the same position when I let myself out. I walked up the road to Elijah's cottage.

'I will have that brandy.'

34

With trepidation, Elijah and I returned to court the following week. As expected, Philip Johnson had been permitted to call Rebecca Dent as a witness.

Donald Anstey watched from the gallery. Although it would be painful for him to listen to the evidence, I felt it might help him to hear her own words.

When an elegant blonde woman took the stand, I realised with a start that it was Rebecca. Her short dark locks had been dyed back to their original colour. She was wearing an outfit I guessed she'd made herself, a well-cut blue suit and cream blouse with an embroidered collar.

She appeared cool and poised as she took the oath.

Philip Johnson got to his feet. 'Miss Dent. You went to live at Crookham Hall in 1904, after your mother's death, when you were employed as a laundry maid. How old were you at that time?'

'Fifteen.' Rebecca spoke clearly.

'You later became a housemaid. But it was when you were promoted to the role of Head Housemaid that Lord Timpson began to prey on you?'

'Yes.' She gave a slight nod. 'My work then took me into the main rooms of the hall, and I would often see Lord Timpson.'

'He began to pay attention to you?'

'He would make flirtatious remarks. Usually about my figure or my hair. I had long hair in those days.'

'Did any of the other servants hear these comments?'

'No, he would only make them when we were alone.'

'Did he touch you on these occasions?' Philip Johnson's voice seemed to get lower and more serious with the gravity of each question, yet every word was audible throughout the courtroom.

'He sometimes touched my cheek or my hair. Once he ran a hand over my breasts.'

'How did you respond to this?'

'I would try to leave the room straight away.' Rebecca answered each question in a precise manner.

'How did Lord Timpson react?'

'The more I resisted, the more persistent he became.'

'Then, on the twenty-eighth of May 1914, he entered your room at night, is that correct?'

I glanced at Constance's glacial expression. Whilst she appeared to be steeling herself for what was to come, Daniel simply looked sad. I had a feeling he already suspected what his father had done to Rebecca.

'I was asleep. I heard a noise and woke to find his hand over my mouth.'

'That must have been extremely frightening for you, Miss Dent.' Philip paused. 'I appreciate this will be upsetting for you, but can you tell us what Lord Timpson did next?'

I noticed Donald Anstey's eyes never left Rebecca's face.

'He grabbed at my breasts. Then he pulled his trousers down and pushed my nightdress up. He raped me. This happened on four other occasions.'

She recited these events calmly, with none of the palpable distress I'd witnessed when we were alone together in her small sitting room. I could understand why. She didn't want to bare her soul in a courtroom full of strangers. But I hoped the jurors wouldn't find her too unemotional.

'Sometime in August 1914, you went to see my client, Lady Timpson, to ask for help. Is that correct?'

'Yes, it is.'

'You told her what her husband was doing to you?'

'I did.'

'Did she believe you?'

Rebecca nodded.

'Were you surprised by this?'

'Yes, I was. I'd been scared to talk to her, thinking she would call me a liar. But I was left with no choice.'

'Weren't you afraid of losing your job?'

'I was pregnant.' Several gasps were heard around the courtroom. 'I would have lost my job anyway when it became known.'

'But my client, Lady Timpson, came to your rescue?'

'Yes. She knew I was in danger, and she helped me escape. She gave me money and found me a safe place to live.'

'Did Lord Timpson know you were carrying his child?'

'Yes.' She gulped. The mask began to slip, and her pain was evident. 'He came to my room, and I told him in the hope that he wouldn't touch me again.'

'And did he touch you?' Philip Johnson asked.

'Yes.' She took a deep breath. 'He punched me in the stomach and then raped me.'

Daniel closed his eyes. Constance's cheeks were wet with tears. A few of the jurors seemed doubtful but most looked horrified.

Rebecca continued. 'Afterwards, he told me he would arrange for me to undergo an abortion.'

'But you decided to have the baby?'

'Yes. At that time, I didn't think I would be able to keep it. Once I was settled in London, I was going to arrange to have the baby adopted by a decent family.'

'That didn't happen, did it?'

'No.' She looked directly at Philip.

'When you were delivered of a baby girl, you wanted to keep her?'

'My friend had told me not to hold the baby. She said I should let the nurse take her away as soon as she was born. But I couldn't resist. I'd carried her for all those months. I wanted to see her.' Rebecca seemed to be willing her listeners to understand. 'Just to hold her for a moment before I let her go.'

'And you changed your mind?'

'I knew then that it was my responsibility to care for her. It was February 1915. No one could say how long the war would go on for, and I didn't know where she would end up. I couldn't abandon her. Not with so much turmoil in the world. I decided that we'd stick together, no matter what.'

Philip nodded. 'One final question, Miss Dent. Why do you think Lady Timpson chose to help you?'

'Because he'd done to her what he'd done to me.'

Constance's head was bent low whilst Daniel stared down at his mother, a helpless expression on his face.

'No further questions, m'lord.'

Sir Nigel got to his feet. The courtroom seemed to hum with tense expectation.

He began by asking Rebecca if she'd been happy at Crookham Hall. She replied that she'd been grateful for employment and a roof over her head.

'You didn't enjoy your work?' Sir Nigel asked with an affected air of surprise.

'No, not particularly.'

'You had *aspirations*?' He emphasised the word to make it sound like a childish notion.

'I wanted to become a seamstress.'

'So, you decided to disappear overnight and start a new life?' He gestured with his arm to imply this was some carefree, impulsive action on her part.

'As I have explained, I ran away to escape from Lord Timpson.'

'So you would have us believe. Perhaps it would be truer to say you ran away because you were unmarried and pregnant and wanted to escape the consequences.' He smirked at the jury as he said this.

'Lord Timpson raped me,' she replied through gritted teeth. 'It happened more than once. The first time was on the twenty-eighth of May 1914.'

'You had been employed at Crookham Hall for nearly ten years. But you say the first time your employer decided to force himself on you was in May 1914, after previously having paid no attention to you.' Sweat was glistening on Sir Nigel's brow.

'He had paid attention to me before that date. But I had always avoided being alone with him. In May 1914, I was promoted to Head Housemaid and given my own room. That's when Lord Timpson started to attack me. Before this, I'd shared a room with another maid.'

'I find it hard to believe that on an estate as large as Crookham Hall, the Lord of the Manor would be aware of his servants living quarters,' Sir Nigel mocked.

'I believe Lord Timpson knew where everyone slept. It was his kingdom. He liked to control every aspect of it.' Her cool, poised manner was back.

'Do you have any evidence of your claims? Any eyewitnesses? Did anyone hear you cry out when these attacks were supposed to have taken place?' Sir Nigel theatrically took out a large white handkerchief from his pocket and mopped his brow.

'They happened late at night. I couldn't cry out because he would smother my mouth.'

'I'm sorry, Miss Dent, but your story is not credible. A man of Lord Timpson's means would hardly sully himself with a mere servant. I think you've taken advantage of his death to fabricate these lies in order to excuse your irresponsible behaviour.' Sir Nigel sounded like he was reprimanding a child. 'First, you waste police time by running away because you were pregnant. Now you try to tarnish the reputation of a nobleman. However, I believe the members of the jury will have the sense to see through your lies.'

'They are not lies.' If Sir Nigel was trying to rile her, he wasn't succeeding.

He suddenly changed tack. 'Did your employer know you were a suffragette?'

'No.' She looked uncomfortable.

'You kept your illegal activities hidden?' He gave a conspiratorial wink in the direction of the jury.

'My activities were largely confined to helping out in the office when I could. I didn't feel my employer would be particularly interested to know what I did on my days off.'

'Really?' Sir Nigel puffed out his chest. 'The police received a visit from a Mr Donald Anstey that would indicate otherwise. He told them you took part in a suffragette protest on the twenty-first of May 1914, when you broke into the Houses of Parliament and caused extensive damage. Because of this protest, one of your fellow suffragettes died. Whilst this poor woman was fighting for her life after having fallen into the River Thames, you were hiding inside the Members' Lobby of the House of Commons, eavesdropping on a conversation between the accused and an unnamed MP. Isn't that true?'

I went rigid at this account of my mother's death. Rebecca looked up at the gallery but not at Donald. Her eyes met mine. 'It's true that I was there. It's true that I saw Lady Timpson and hid. As a result, a dear friend died.'

'But according to your boyfriend, Mr Anstey, you did more than hide. You stayed there to witness Lady Timpson agreeing to pay money to this MP in exchange for a list of sites that the Society for the Promotion of Nature Reserves wanted to protect. This politician was offering to help Lady Timpson purchase this land at a knockdown price.'

'Objection.' Philip Johnson was on his feet. 'My client has not been charged with any offence relating to this matter. Lady Timpson often visits Parliament and is friends with many MPs. There is no evidence to suggest any impropriety on her part.'

'You digress too far, Sir Nigel,' Judge Radden warned.

'I'm just trying to establish the dubious nature of Miss Dent's character. I do not believe she went to Lady Timpson with her cock-and-bull story and was believed as readily as she claims. I suspect an element of blackmail may have been involved.' He inclined his head in acquiescence. 'But I respect your wishes. No further questions, my lord.'

Sir Nigel sat down, but the damage was done. The jury was now aware of Lady Timpson's underhand business dealings and Rebecca's possible attempted blackmail.

35

'I have matters to discuss with counsel in my chamber.' The judge rose. 'Therefore, we will resume tomorrow.'

'I'm surprised Sir Nigel didn't mention the Star Sapphire,' Percy remarked. 'He could have claimed there was a conspiracy between Lady Timpson and Rebecca to hide it.'

'Probably decided not to risk it,' Elijah replied. 'The fact that Lord Timpson never reported it missing supports Lady Timpson's version of events.'

They headed outside to smoke in the sunshine. I was about to follow them down the stairs when I heard someone call my name. It was Rebecca.

'You were so brave.' I hugged her. 'And so calm. I would have lost my temper with that odious man.'

'I'm glad it's over.' She gave a weak smile. 'I appreciate you going to see Donald for me. Was he very upset? I'd hoped to have a chance to speak with him.'

'A little. It was a lot to take in.' I'd written to tell her about my conversation with Donald, diplomatically describing his reaction as one of shock. Now I wished I'd been more honest about how angry he was. He could make things a lot worse for both Lady Timpson and Rebecca. The full story of the overheard conversation wouldn't do much for Lady Timpson's reputation. And his account of Rebecca's role in the protest could prompt a criminal charge.

I was about to ask her if she'd spoken to the police when Daniel and Constance emerged from Philip Johnson's room. They stiffened when they saw Rebecca.

Daniel took a step towards her and cleared his throat. 'Miss Dent. I appreciate how difficult it must have been for you to give evidence. I'm sorry for everything you've been through. What I want to say is...' He hesitated. 'There's always a place for you at Crookham Hall should you want it. And your child.'

Constance's expression showed how appalled she was by this invitation.

'That's kind of you.' Rebecca managed a slight smile. 'But I have no wish to come back to the hall.'

Constance's relief was plain.

'I hope the jury reaches the right verdict and your mother is home soon,' Rebecca continued.

Daniel nodded and thanked her. Constance said nothing.

* * *

The court resumed late the following day, with Judge Radden making a surprise announcement.

'The defence has applied to call another new witness. Despite Sir Nigel's objections, I have decided to allow it. I think it's of sufficient relevance to the case.'

All eyes in the courtroom were on this new witness as she made her way to the stand, looking petrified. It was Hannah Moffat. She wore an old blue linen dress that had been mended many times. By contrast, Samuel sat in the gallery in the same smart corduroy jacket he'd worn to give evidence.

With thin, shaking hands, she took the bible and said the oath. I felt my own hands tremble in sympathy.

'Miss Moffat, is it correct that your younger sister, Lydia Moffat, was employed at Crookham Hall as a laundry maid in September 1916?' Philip Johnson's manner was calm and soothing.

'Yes, sir.'

'Was she?' I heard Daniel whisper to Constance. He would have been away fighting at the time.

'I've no idea.' She shrugged.

'Did your sister go to live at the hall?' Philip asked Hannah.

'No, sir. She stayed at home with us. But she had to get up early and go in each day. She used to walk across the fields to get to the kitchens.'

'How old was she at that time?'

'Fifteen.' The handkerchief in Hannah's hand had once been white but was now a dull grey colour.

'How long did Lydia work at Crookham Hall?'

'For about six months, sir.'

'Was she happy there?'

'She was at first. She was very happy when she got the job. The wages were good, and the hall was so grand. She used to talk about the kitchen and what food they'd eat. But after she'd been there for four or five months, she said she didn't like it any more.'

'Did she tell you why she didn't like it?' Philip Johnson was taking his time.

Hannah hesitated. 'Not at first. She just said she didn't want to go back there. But Ma told her she had to. We needed her wages, you see.'

Philip lowered his voice. 'But she confided in you, didn't she? You knew why she didn't want to go back.'

Hannah turned crimson and nodded.

I saw Constance bow her head as if shielding herself from what was to come. Daniel was gaping helplessly at the witness box.

With gentle prompting from Philip, Hannah told the story of Lydia's encounter with Lord Timpson and her fear of what would happen when Daniel returned home on leave.

My heart bled for Daniel as the courtroom stared at him. Even Constance turned to him in dismay, and he shook his head vehemently at her. Sir Nigel reviewed his papers, ignoring the horrified reaction of the jurors.

Philip Johnson left a long pause, allowing Hannah's testimony to sink in before asking, 'Did Lydia carry on working at Crookham Hall?'

'Yes, sir. For a while. Then she...' Hannah stopped and sniffed.

'Take your time, my dear,' Judge Radden advised.

'Then she...' Her voice became a whimper. 'We found her in the barn. She'd hung herself up with a rope.'

Sharp intakes of breath echoed around the courtroom. I saw Samuel wipe his eyes with the sleeve of his jacket.

'Your sister took her own life?' Philip Johnson said softly.

Hannah nodded, brushing away tears with the grey handkerchief.

'What drove her to do such a thing?'

'Our parents had taught us that if we had knowledge of a man out of wedlock, we would go to hell. I told her that she wouldn't. Not if something happened to her that wasn't her fault. I told her God would forgive her.' She gave a loud sob. 'But she didn't believe me.'

'So, at just fifteen years old, your sister, Lydia, decided to take her own life.' Philip Johnson turned to face the jury as he made this statement.

Hannah nodded, tears streaming down her face. 'I'd promised

to help her. But I didn't know what to do. Samuel was away fighting. Isaac, our other brother, had been killed in France. We couldn't tell Ma or Pa.'

'I hate him. I hate him,' I heard Daniel say to Constance. She held his hand tightly.

'Thank you, Miss Moffat.' Philip Johnson gave a slight bow. 'You've been very brave. Unless my learned friend has any questions, you may stand down.'

She breathed an audible sigh of relief.

'Just a couple of questions, m'lord.' Sir Nigel got to his feet. Hannah gripped the edge of the witness box.

'Miss Moffat. Apart from yourself, did your sister tell anyone else of her predicament?'

'No, sir,' she whispered.

'Could I ask you to speak up, Miss Moffat,' Judge Radden said kindly. 'The jury must be able to hear what you are saying.'

She nodded.

'She confided in no other family member?' Sir Nigel demanded. 'Why didn't she tell your father? Surely he would have protected her?'

'She was too scared. Lord Timpson used to give Pa money.' She added in a scared voice, 'I don't know what for.'

I frowned, glancing over at Samuel. He'd sunk down into the bench, his shoulders hunched. If he'd believed his father's story that the money was for access rights to the estate, why hadn't Hannah?

'That was kind of him,' Sir Nigel said as if this somehow mitigated what we'd just heard. 'So no one can corroborate your story?'

'I don't understand.' She looked at Judge Radden for help.

'Sir Nigel is asking if there's anyone else who knew what went on between your sister and Lord Timpson. Did she, or you, tell anyone else what happened?' the judge explained.

'No, sir.' Hannah shook her head.

'Four years have passed since your sister died,' Sir Nigel continued. 'Yet you waited until today to tell her story. Why was that?'

'I heard what he did to the other maid, Rebecca Dent.' She sounded more resolute. 'I wanted everyone to know Lydia's story too.'

'Did you? Or perhaps you saw an opportunity to make some money after you'd read all about the case in the newspapers,' Sir Nigel said with a contemptuous sneer.

'Objection.' Philip Johnson rose from his seat.

'But I haven't asked anyone for any money.' Hannah looked bewildered. 'I just wanted people to know what he did to Lydia.'

'No doubt the more salacious newspapers will fall over themselves to pay you for your lurid tale,' Sir Nigel scoffed.

Hannah stared at him in horror. I doubted she would speak to a newspaper. But I wondered about Samuel. Where had he got the money to buy his new jacket and the chickens at the farm?

'That is not a question. It is an inflammatory statement,' the judge interrupted. 'Members of the jury, there is nothing to suggest that Miss Moffat has anything to gain financially by giving evidence here today. Sir Nigel, do you have any further questions for this witness?'

'No, m'lord.' Sir Nigel waved his hand dismissively at Hannah. She stepped down from the witness box, stumbling in her haste.

'I'd love to punch that man in the face,' Percy whispered.

'Sir Nigel or Lord Timpson?' I asked.

* * *

After some discussion with counsel, Judge Radden agreed the summing-up process should begin the following day.

As soon as we'd filed out of the court, I went in search of

Rebecca. I found her sitting on a bench in the corner of the lobby, her arm around Hannah Moffat. Both women had been crying.

'It wasn't your fault.' I heard Hannah say.

Before Rebecca could reply, Samuel Moffat appeared and tugged at his sister's arm. 'We're going home.'

Hannah wiped her eyes and followed her brother out of the Great Hall. I took her place on the bench beside Rebecca.

'I feel responsible for what happened to Lydia Moffat. She was only a child. I should have done more to stop him.' Rebecca clasped the handbag on her lap.

A tall figure cast a shadow over us. 'You aren't responsible for what he did,' Donald Anstey said with vehemence. 'You couldn't have stopped that monster. He would have talked his way out of it.'

'He's right,' I said.

'Rebecca.' Donald twisted his hat in his hands. 'I'm sorry.'

'There's nothing for you to be sorry for, Donald.' Her voice shook. 'I should have told you.'

'You felt you had no choice. I understand.'

'I thought I was doing the right thing for everyone by leaving. I want you to know how terrible Leonard felt about not confiding in you. He always wanted to tell you, but I wouldn't let him.'

Donald gave a brief nod. 'I was sorry to hear of his death.'

'We thought we were doing the right thing for everyone.' She stood. 'I must get back to Violet.'

'May I walk you to the station?' he asked.

She hesitated, then nodded. Cautiously, she took the arm he offered.

'Miss Woodmore?' he said.

'I'll wait for Mr Whittle,' I replied.

He gave me a brief smile. I followed them to the top of the steps of the Great Hall and watched them walk away, arm in arm.

36

The next day, we gathered back in court. All the evidence had been presented. This hideous sequence of events was drawing towards its conclusion. All that was left was to hear the summing up of counsels and Judge Radden. The final act would be the release of Lady Timpson. Or her death sentence.

I was tired and tense. I could only imagine how Daniel and Constance were feeling. Both had dark shadows under their eyes.

Sir Nigel got to his feet. 'Members of the jury. In the last weeks, you have heard evidence regarding Lord Tobias Timpson's profligate ways – his gambling and philandering.'

'Philandering?' I was outraged. How could he call the brutal rape of a woman philandering?

Elijah shook his head in disbelief.

'But how seriously can we take these accusations? It is clear to me that at some point Miss Dent attempted to blackmail the accused. Is her testimony to be taken seriously? I think her credibility is in serious doubt. Next, we come to the story of poor unfortunate Lydia Moffat, as told to us by her sister, Hannah. But did Lord Timpson even know who Lydia Moffat was? I'm quite sure he would have been completely unaware of the existence of the laundry maid.' He smiled at the jury. 'I think we can safely ignore the fanciful tale of Miss Hannah Moffat.'

I was glad Hannah wasn't in court to hear this arrogant dismissal of her evidence.

Sir Nigel went on to portray Lady Timpson as a domineering woman who ruthlessly demolished any obstacles in her path. He said she'd decided to kill her husband because his womanising and gambling were becoming an embarrassment that could cost her what she desired most – a seat in the House of Commons.

He hooked his thumbs in his gown. 'You've heard Lady Timpson speculate that her husband had intended to shoot her and then claim that poachers attacked them. That's an interesting theory, is it not? I wonder, what made Lady Timpson think of such a thing?'

Elijah made a 'humph' sound. It was clear where Sir Nigel was going with this.

'Because perhaps that was what Lady Timpson had planned to say,' announced Sir Nigel. 'Could she have planted the shotgun at the scene? Maybe she had intended to ride back to the hall, crying in distress, claiming they'd been set upon by poachers and her husband injured? But.' He paused for emphasis. 'Something went wrong. It would be foolish to speculate as to what that was. Only the two people present at Blacksmith's Bridge that morning know the truth. And one of them is dead.'

Sir Nigel ended his speech with his customary arrogance, telling the jury this was a case of premeditated, cold-blooded murder, and it was their duty to return a guilty verdict.

Philip Johnson stood. 'Members of the jury. This case rests on whether Lord Tobias Timpson was a violent man. A violent man who had decided to murder his wife. But why he would want her dead?' He paused, then banged on the desk, making the jurors jump. 'Because his wife had told him "no". And this is a man who doesn't like to be told "no". We've heard in this courtroom how he reacts to that. He uses brute force to take what he wants anyway. I pity any woman or girl that Lord Timpson took a fancy to, for their bodies were no longer their own. They became mere objects to be brutalised by someone who considered himself to be above the law. Lord Timpson was born into a life of privilege. He believed he was entitled to take whatever he wanted.'

Philip outlined how it had been Lord Timpson who'd planned the events of that morning, planting the danger of poachers in people's minds. It was he who had purchased a shotgun and concealed it under Blacksmith's Bridge with the intention of shooting his wife and claiming they'd been set upon by villains.

He went on to praise Miss Dent and Miss Moffat for their courage in sharing their stories, emphasising that neither woman had been financially motivated – and that Lady Timpson had been brave to reveal the truth about her brutal marriage.

'These are the sad facts of Lord Timpson's death. He died as a result of his own evil intent. My client was left with no other recourse but to defend herself against his vicious attack. And now, the only course of action left for you is to acquit her of all charges.' Philip Johnson made a slight bow to the jurors before taking his seat.

* * *

During the short recess, Mrs Siddons ushered Daniel and Constance into a private room and left them there. When Philip emerged from the courtroom, she took him by the arm to discuss something she clearly didn't want Daniel or Constance to hear.

'What do you think that's about?' I asked Elijah.

'Preparing what to do in the event of a guilty verdict. The judge will have to go straight to sentencing.'

'Can't Philip appeal?'

'That could be lodged later. But Daniel and Constance must be prepared. If the verdict is guilty, the judge will issue a death sentence.'

I shivered.

We shuffled back into the public gallery to hear the judge's summing up.

'Members of the jury, you have listened patiently to the testimonies put before you.' Judge Radden's words were slow and deliberate as he recounted the evidence that had been presented during the course of the trial.

The courtroom was hot and airless, and by the time the judge reached his conclusion, sweat was glistening on the foreheads of the jurors.

'At the heart of this case is the defence's claim that Lord Timpson was a cruel, violent man,' the judge explained. 'You heard testimony from Lady Timpson to this effect. You also heard the evidence of Miss Dent and Miss Moffat, which was offered to substantiate that claim. If you believe these women were telling the truth, then this goes some way in supporting Lady Timpson's version of events. The prosecution did not call any witnesses to suggest that Lady Timpson has ever been a violent woman.'

The judge clasped his hands together as if to indicate the weight of his next words. 'As you know, in English law, an accused person is held to be innocent unless proved otherwise. The defence doesn't need to prove Lady Timpson's innocence. However, the Crown must prove her guilt. Therefore, unless you are satisfied beyond all reasonable doubt that the defendant is guilty, it is your duty to return a verdict of "not guilty". Are you all clear on this point?' he asked the jury.

The twelve jurors nodded.

'In that case, I am now going to ask you to retire to consider your verdict.'

* * *

'I don't know about you, but I could do with a drink,' Percy announced.

Mrs Siddons had whisked Daniel and Constance away. We would all return to the courtroom each day until a verdict was reached.

'That's the most sensible thing I've heard you say,' Elijah replied.

Percy led us to a pub on the banks of the River Itchen, not far from the Great Hall, and ordered three beers. This was his old stomping ground from his days at Winchester College. His parents still lived in the city.

We sat outside, watching brown trout swim in the clear water.

'I'd say that was a fair summing up.' Elijah took a swig of beer.

Percy handed him a cigarette. 'The problem is, although the jury may believe Lord Timpson was a rapist, there's no proof he was a killer.'

'But there's no proof Lady Timpson's a murderer either,' I retorted.

'Except for the fact that it was her husband's body found floating in the canal and not hers,' Elijah pointed out.

'Say it had happened the other way around, as Lady T claims it was meant to.' Percy trailed his hand in the river. 'Say Lord T shot Lady T dead and then rode to the hall and told everyone poachers had attacked them.'

'He'd probably have been believed,' I said.

'In which case, would he have got all her money?' Percy asked.

'And full control?'

'Money, yes. But maybe not the business,' Elijah retorted. 'I suspect Lady Timpson has left that to Constance and Daniel, but he was probably confident he could manipulate them.'

'Everyone would have believed him, and no one would ever have known what he did to his wife, or Rebecca or poor Lydia Moffat.' I simmered with fury on their behalf. 'There would have been no repercussions, and he'd have been free to carry on preying on women.'

'He relied on his position to protect him.' Elijah let out a long exhale of smoke. 'But in the end, retribution took its course.'

'Did Daniel suspect something wasn't right?' I asked Percy.

'Not when he was younger. But when he was away fighting, he had a lot of time to think. We all did.' He ran his fingers through his hair. 'When he returned to Crookham Hall, he was a grown-up. And he began to realise what his father was like.'

'Because of his behaviour towards women?' Elijah asked.

Percy nodded. 'He would encourage Daniel to... to...' He floundered. 'Take more of an interest in girls. Sexually, I mean.'

'Rape them?' I said in disgust.

'He encouraged him to take what he wanted. It revolted Daniel. Then when you came asking about Rebecca, it dawned on him why she might have run away.'

'Did he question his father about her?' I remembered the row Olive had overheard between them.

'Yes. And got a clout for it. It was enough to convince Daniel his father was somehow involved.'

'Christ.' Elijah drew on his cigarette.

I shook my head in disgust. 'God knows how many women he molested over the years. We need more female politicians, judges, lawyers and police – to stop men like him from getting away with it.'

'It's the absence of female jurors that's the problem in this case.' Elijah swirled the dregs of beer around the bottom of his glass.

'You think they'll believe Sir Nigel?'

'Surely not.' Percy drained his beer.

Elijah frowned. 'I've seen it before.'

* * *

We returned to the Great Hall the following morning. The wait was tedious, with no way of knowing how long the jury would take to reach a verdict. But in the middle of the afternoon, we were summoned back into court.

We all rose as the judge entered. Lady Timpson looked up at Daniel and Constance and gave a weak smile. She nodded as if to say she was strong enough to handle whatever was coming. I couldn't help but admire her nerve. My own knees were trembling.

The clerk mopped his brow and then stood to address the jury. The temperature was creeping up to eighty degrees Fahrenheit.

'Members of the jury, have you reached a verdict?'

'We have,' the foreman replied.

'Is it a verdict upon which you all agree?'

'It is.'

'How do you find the defendant? Guilty or not guilty?'

'Guilty.'

Constance gasped. Daniel covered his face with his hands. Their mother gazed at them – her eyes filled with tears. Suddenly Constance's strength seemed to dissolve, her body went limp, and she fainted. Percy dived forward and caught her in his arms just before she hit her head on the wooden bench.

'We will go straight to sentencing.'

The clerk placed the black cap before the judge.

37

'What does Superintendent Cobbe expect you to do?'

Ben had asked me to meet him at Blacksmith's Bridge.

'Review all the evidence.' He frowned. 'The problem is there's not much to review.'

I could see what he meant. Apart from admiring the scenery, there wasn't much else to look at. The canal was motionless and opaque, its banks overgrown with wildflowers and bramble. It wasn't the most likely setting for an attempted murder.

'Does the superintendent think she's innocent? Or is he just reacting to the backlash against the verdict?'

'He never wanted to prosecute her until he had more proof. He needed more time to gather evidence. But he didn't have much choice: it would have looked like he was favouring the aristocracy if he'd let her off.'

Philip Johnson had lodged an appeal, but without new evidence, it would be difficult to get the conviction overturned. Stories had appeared in national newspapers revealing fresh allegations of attacks on women by Lord Timpson. It was difficult to know if they were true or not. But even if they were, the jury had decided that, no matter what they knew of the deceased, Lady Timpson was the one to premeditate his murder.

'I think after what came out at the trial, he's more inclined to believe Lady Timpson's version of events, though he hasn't said as much,' Ben continued. 'But he still feels she's not being entirely honest.'

I agreed with Superintendent Cobbe. I didn't think she'd intended to kill her husband, but I got the impression there was still a lot we didn't know about what went on that morning at the bridge.

Ben gestured around him. 'I need your analytical mind.'

'The only physical evidence is the shotgun.' I contemplated the murky depths of the canal. 'How deep is the water?'

'About five feet at the deepest point.'

'And nothing was found here except the shotgun? You said there were some items that Lord Timpson would have had on him?'

'A pocket watch, cigarette case and lighter. There's no sign of them. They could have fallen out of his riding jacket as he fell and be hidden in the undergrowth.' He peered into the water. 'Or be stuck in the mud down there.'

'But you would have found them when you searched the canal. And the banks weren't so overgrown in April. Surely, they would have been spotted.' I looked around. 'Where do you think he hid the shotgun?'

'An area was trampled around here.' He walked to the foot of a willow tree. 'Lady Timpson was trying to tether her horse to that post next to the bridge. Lord Timpson would have known she'd do that, so we can work on the assumption that he concealed the shotgun here. Allowing him to fire at close range.'

'But it can't have been there for long. It wouldn't have been that well-hidden, and leaving it out in all weathers would have risked damaging it.'

'I don't think Lord Timpson can have bought the shotgun himself. With all the publicity around the case, if someone had sold it to him, they would have come forward by now.'

'You think he got someone to buy it and hide it for him?'

Ben considered the shacks on the other side of the bridge. 'Someone who needed money and didn't ask any questions.'

I followed his gaze. 'If it was one of them, they're not going to admit it.'

'We've questioned all the local gun suppliers, but it could have come from anywhere.'

'What about Samuel Moffat? In court, Hannah said that Lord Timpson used to give her father money. She made it sound like a regular payment. Perhaps he did the same for Samuel? Do you still have Lord Timpson's financial records?'

'Only the ones that relate to his debts. I believe Mr Laffaye still has the household ones.'

* * *

'Well, my dear, what is it you want to know?' Horace asked.

He and Elijah were sitting with glasses of brandy in hand, looking at me like a pair of indulgent uncles.

'How frequently did Lord Timpson give money to the Moffats?' I asked.

'I wasn't aware that he did,' Horace replied.

'It was something Hannah Moffat mentioned when she was in court. She said that they wouldn't have survived unless Lord Timpson had given her father money. I've heard Samuel mention it as well. He seemed to think it was over access to the estate from their land, but Daniel said that wasn't true.'

'She was probably talking about cash in hand for odd jobs, that sort of thing. I'd be surprised if there was any formal arrangement.' Elijah took the cigar Horace offered him.

'Could I take a look at the financial records?' I persisted.

'By all means.' Horace inclined his head towards a desk in the corner of his immaculate living room. 'They're all there.'

There were more journals than I'd expected, and I started to scan the pages quickly. I wasn't sure how long Horace would tolerate me sitting at his desk. But he and Elijah seemed happy enough chatting together, comfortable in their relationship.

I wondered when they'd become a couple, because that's obviously what they were. Not that they could ever publicly be together, but it was clear that privately they'd decided to throw their lot in with each other.

Ignoring them, I concentrated on the task at hand. It took me nearly half an hour to spot the entries I was looking for, and when I traced them back, a horrible truth began to dawn.

'Did you find what you were looking for?' Horace asked when he saw me sit back and close the journals.

'Yes, thank you.' I deliberately made them wait.

'Are you planning to share this information with us?' Elijah asked sardonically. 'Having just taken up Mr Laffaye's valuable time?'

I swung around in my chair to face them. 'Lord Timpson made a payment of fifty pounds to Ned Moffat every month.'

'And?' Elijah said in exasperation.

'These payments go back twenty-two years. They started in 1898. The year Samuel Moffat and his twin brother, Isaac, were born.'

'Oh,' Horace exclaimed.

'Bloody hell,' Elijah said.

* * *

'Are you sure you want to do this?'

I took a deep breath and nodded. It was seven years since I'd last stood outside the gates of Holloway Prison, waiting for my mother to be released. Mrs Siddons waved at the guard, and we were allowed to enter.

The clicking of our heels echoed as we walked through tiled corridors. Thousands of women had passed through these hallways, including my mother.

Lady Timpson was waiting for us in a tiny square room with white painted walls. She was seated on one side of a pine table that smelt as if it had been scrubbed with carbolic soap. The wooden chairs scraped on the floor as we sat opposite her.

A prison wardress with iron-grey hair and a neutral expression stood by the door. I wondered if she'd been there when Mother was imprisoned. Had she been one of the wardresses who comforted the young women who sobbed at night? But the next day held them down whilst they were force-fed?

'It's good to see you, Sybil.' Lady Timpson reached out to take her hand.

'Keep your hands on your lap,' the wardress ordered.

Mrs Siddons squeezed the trembling fingers before they withdrew. 'Philip believes he can get the death penalty commuted.'

'I hope so. It would be too much for Daniel and Constance.' Lady Timpson gave the impression of having given up for her own sake. A reduction in sentence would mean a lifetime in prison instead of the gallows.

'The police are reviewing the evidence. Something new may come to light that could get your conviction overturned.' Mrs Siddons tried to sound optimistic.

Lady Timpson gave a slight nod but showed no interest.

'It's possible someone else bought the shotgun and concealed it by the bridge,' I said. 'Someone who was paid to do it.'

She gave no reaction.

'When you examined your husband's financial records did you ask him about the payments he made to the Moffats?' I asked. 'The payments that started the year of Samuel and Isaac's birth?'

She gave a half-smile.

Mrs Siddons leant towards her. 'Did he tell you what they were for?'

'Not at first. But it didn't take much to work it out. I knew Samuel was the same age as Daniel. I confronted him over it, and he admitted he'd made Mary pregnant. He didn't go into the sordid details, and I didn't ask. Ned Moffat had been struggling with the farm, and Tobias persuaded him to marry Mary and say the twins were his. When I decided to stand for election, I told Tobias the payments had to stop. Ned and Mary Moffat were dead – there was no need for them to continue. It would look suspicious if anyone found out.'

'How did he react?' I tried to hide my irritation at her lack of concern for Hannah and Samuel Moffat.

'He was angry. But I refused to back down. A small crumb of revenge.' A gleam appeared in her eyes.

'Do you think Samuel Moffat would have helped Tobias procure the shotgun?' Mrs Siddons asked.

Lady Timpson shook her head. 'I don't think he knows the truth about his parentage. Tobias wouldn't have told him. My husband never publicly admitted to any of his indiscretions.'

Indiscretions was a polite way of putting it. To my frustration, she seemed to have little interest in helping us to uncover new evidence, despite Mrs Siddons' best efforts.

I left the prison feeling as despairing as Lady Timpson.

* * *

'The barn finally fell down?'

Hannah Moffat shook her head, placing a cup of tea in front of me. 'Samuel took a sledgehammer to it and finished it off. It's where Lydia died.'

I wondered where Samuel and his sledgehammer were at that moment. 'What are you going to do?'

'Sell. Samuel's right. Too much bad stuff has happened here.' She looked around the kitchen. 'Might as well tear the whole place down and start again.'

I contemplated the scrubbed shelves and jars arranged in neat rows. This was the room she'd miss the most, despite the drama she must have witnessed there. The kitchen was the heart of the home, and I was sure some uncomfortable conversations had taken place around the battered table. Conversations she'd be reluctant to share with me. But a life was at stake, and I had to try.

'Did Samuel hide the shotgun by Blacksmith's Bridge?'

'No.' But it wasn't said with much conviction.

'I don't think he knew why he'd been asked to do it.' I touched her arm. 'He'd been lied to, hadn't he?'

She hesitated, then broke down. 'I was scared to go to court in case it all came out.'

'What all came out? What did Samuel think the shotgun was for?'

'Daniel won't handle guns. Not since he came back from the war. Lord Timpson said he needed to persuade him to start shooting again. He said that Daniel would refuse to come riding with him if he thought they were going hunting. He gave Samuel the money to go and buy a shotgun and told him where to leave it. He said he planned to ride up there with Daniel to give him some shooting lessons.'

'But Samuel saw him ride up with Lady Timpson instead?'

She nodded. 'Then he heard the gunshot. He came back here in a right state. I asked him what the matter was. He told me what he'd done. Said he couldn't understand why Lady Timpson had been there, not Daniel. Then it dawned on him what Lord Timpson had really wanted the shotgun for.'

I felt a surge of triumph at finally learning the truth. But it was short-lived. Hannah's word wouldn't be enough. I'd need to get Samuel to admit to what he'd done to get Lady Timpson's conviction overturned.

'Idiot.' Hannah's exasperation showed. 'I told him he was an idiot for trusting that man. He said I was being stupid. That's when I lost my temper.'

'Is that when you told him what Lord Timpson had done to Lydia?'

She nodded. 'I should have done it before.'

'When the police were gathering evidence, they obtained Lord Timpson's financial records. They were mainly interested in his debts. But I noticed there were some entries that related to payments to your father. You mentioned them in court?'

She picked up a dishcloth and folded it neatly but didn't reply.

'Do you know what they were for?' I guessed from her expression that she did.

She was guarded. 'Do *you*?'

'Lady Timpson told me that when she confronted her husband over them, he admitted the truth.' I watched Hannah refold the dishcloth. 'How did you find out?'

'Pa told me when he was dying. He said to go to Lord Timpson and threaten to tell everyone if the payments stopped. But he didn't know what that man had done to Lydia. I was too scared to go. Samuel was still away fighting. When he came back and took over the farm, he had some notion the money was for access rights. But that was some nonsense Pa had told him years before.'

'Why didn't you tell Samuel the truth after your parents died?'

She blushed. 'The payments were still coming in.'

'But this year, they stopped. And that morning, you told Samuel the real reason for them.'

She shuddered. 'It all came out. I couldn't stop myself; I was too angry.'

I jumped at the sound of hinges creaking and heavy boots on the flagstone floor of the hallway.

She looked at me nervously. 'You'd better go.'

I shook my head.

Samuel ambled into the room in his socks. When he saw me, he came to an abrupt halt. 'What are you doing here again?'

'I came to talk to you about the shotgun you bought for Lord Timpson.' I attempted my best impression of Mrs Siddons at her most composed, but my hands were shaking. I put my teacup down with a clatter.

He didn't move for a moment, and the room was silent. Then he sunk into a chair. 'That bastard set me up. He was going to tell them I did it.'

'I expect he told you where to get the shotgun from?' I wanted to hear his story.

He nodded. 'Oh yes. A place down in Portsmouth. He planned to lay the trail right to my door. What an idiot. I didn't know what he was like. I thought he was a decent bloke, like Daniel. He said he was sorry his wife had stopped paying us, but she controlled the money. He said he'd try to help in other ways. Pay me for doing odd jobs and stuff.'

'This was one of those odd jobs?'

'He gave me money to go down there and get the gun. Said he'd give me more later on.' He snorted. 'All I'd have got later on was the hangman's noose.'

'Why didn't you go to the police when you found out he'd lied to you?'

'They wouldn't have believed me. It would have been me in the dock instead of her.'

'But you knew she was innocent.'

'I thought she'd get off. She's a rich, stuck-up cow. It was her who stopped those payments.'

I tried to sound commanding. 'Go to the police and tell them what you just told me. The fact that you bought the shotgun proves Lady Timpson is innocent. If you don't, I will. Your chances of avoiding prison will be better if it comes from you.'

'He didn't care that I'd hang.' Samuel stared into his lap, his hands dangling loosely by his sides. 'My own bloody father, and he didn't give a damn.'

'If he only gave you the money for buying the gun, where did you get the money you've been spending on chickens and new clothes?'

His head shot up. Hannah clasped her hand to her mouth.

'Did you take the pocket watch, cigarette case and lighter from Lord Timpson's body?'

'I didn't think he was dead.'

'You couldn't have done that easily if he was in the water.' I thought back to Sir Nigel's cross-examination of Lady Timpson. After saying her husband had fallen to the ground, she'd corrected herself, insisting he fell towards the bank and into the water.

'I never meant to kill him. I wanted to humiliate him. Make him feel as worthless as he made me feel.'

'So you pushed his body into the water?'

'Please don't tell the police,' Hannah begged.

I clutched the sides of the passenger seat as we sped towards Crookham Hall.

Mrs Siddons had succumbed and bought a motor car, which she insisted on driving herself. At high speed.

We'd been invited to the hall for an interview with Lady Timpson. After legal wrangling, Philip Johnson had managed to secure her acquittal, based on Samuel Moffat's statement that he'd purchased the shotgun for Lord Timpson.

Constance was keen for the family to try to re-establish themselves socially for the sake of the business and had asked me to write an article giving her mother's side of the story.

'Delphina's very fragile. She doesn't want to talk about Tobias's death, but she wants to explain the situation she found herself in.' Mrs Siddons turned to look at me.

I gripped the sides of the leather seat tighter, wishing she'd keep her eyes on the road. 'I'll try to do her story justice,' I muttered.

'How do you intend to structure the piece?' She tooted the horn and waved enthusiastically at someone.

I hoped we wouldn't pass too many of her acquaintances. I preferred it when she kept both hands on the steering wheel.

'I'll start by showing how idyllic Lady Timpson's life appeared from the outside. Lovely family, beautiful home. Then describe how Tobias Timpson's violence would have remained a dark secret if he hadn't tried to kill her. Without the trial, we would never have known what he did to her or Rebecca and Lydia Moffat. I want to highlight that.'

'Poor child. That man was a monster.' She shuddered. 'I never expected that.'

'They were all so powerless. That's what I want to get across.' I'd sketched out the article in my head. 'I'll touch on the prejudicial press coverage, but I can't overdo that aspect because Elijah wants to try to sell the article to some of the nationals. I'll end by reflecting on how Lady Timpson, the victim in all this, could so easily have been executed.'

Mrs Siddons nodded. 'Good. I'm speaking in Parliament on the abolition of the death penalty. I want to use this case as an example. It would have been a sad reflection on our judicial system if Delphina had gone to the gallows.'

* * *

Constance came out to greet us. To my surprise, she put her arms around me.

'Thank you, Iris, for giving us Mother back. I know it was down to you that Samuel Moffat went to the police.'

We chatted in the warm September sunshine. I could see Constance had lost some of the poise I'd once envied. She seemed more hesitant and less sure of herself. So much had happened in the six months since my first visit there. Lady Timpson may have been acquitted, but this once glamorous and powerful family were in ruins. Maybe not financially, but socially, their world had been torn apart.

'How's Daniel?' Mrs Siddons asked. 'Is he here?'

'He's with Mother. He's become very withdrawn, like he was when he first came back from the trenches. He's still trying to come to terms with... with everything.'

'Give him time. It's been a terrible ordeal for you all. How is your mother?'

Constance shrugged. 'She spends most of her time in her room.'

'Does she want to see us?' Part of me would be relieved if the answer was no.

'Yes. After the trial, I thought she'd be reluctant to speak of those things again.' Constance appeared perplexed. 'But it seems to have unlocked something within her. She wants to get it off her chest. The things Father did.'

'That must be hard for you,' Mrs Siddons said.

'I want to support her, take care of her. But I don't want to hear any more.' She put her hands to her ears. 'I loved him. Father, I mean.'

'Of course you did,' Mrs Siddons reassured her. 'And he loved you and Daniel.'

'But he was so cruel to other people. I feel guilty.'

'Why should you feel guilty?' It was infuriating how Lord Timpson's actions had caused others to question their own culpability. 'You've done nothing wrong.'

'Memories start to fall into place. You realise why he did certain things that you didn't notice at the time. I feel so stupid. I had no inkling of what he could be like. Even Daniel knew more than I did. I thought... Well, I thought I was so clever.' She shook her head. 'What a fool. A privileged child, ignorant of the suffering of others.'

'That's not true,' Mrs Siddons said. 'You didn't know because your mother protected you.'

'I wish she hadn't. It wouldn't have come as such a shock. Instead, I'm left wondering what's real and what's not. The life I thought I had has gone forever.' She frowned. 'But I don't want it back. I don't want to live that way any more.'

'You plan to make changes?' I said.

'Starting with Timpson Foods. Mother's signed the business over to me. I won't have young children working in our factories. And I plan to increase wages. But I need to make sure we have the money first.'

'What about Daniel?' Mrs Siddons asked.

'He'll inherit Crookham Hall. But he'll lose it unless I can make the business work. I couldn't bear that, not after everything he's been through.'

'You two will manage if you stick together,' Mrs Siddons said.

'We'll survive somehow. But I'm not sure Mother will.'

Mrs Siddons took her arm. 'Let's go and see her.'

We followed Constance up a wide staircase and along a corridor to Lady Timpson's private sitting room. It was beautifully decorated in duck-egg blue with heavy gold silk drapes at the windows.

Lady Timpson sat in a cushioned armchair, staring into an unlit fireplace. The drapes were partially drawn to shield her from the glare of sunlight.

Daniel sat in a chair next to her. He gave a weak smile. I noticed his usually tanned skin had become paler.

'Mother, Mrs Siddons and Iris are here,' Constance announced.

Lady Timpson squinted up at us through watery eyes. For a moment, she looked confused and then seemed to remember who we were.

'Sybil, how lovely to see you.'

'Delphina, you're looking better.' Mrs Siddons kissed her on the cheek.

This wasn't true. She hadn't regained the weight she'd lost during her time in prison, and her short-sleeved summer dress revealed thin, pale arms.

We sat on the small sofa opposite Lady Timpson's armchair. The air was still, and it was uncomfortably warm in the room.

I was uncertain how to begin the conversation. But then Lady Timpson spoke. 'You warned me about him, Sybil. I should have listened to you.'

'I take no pleasure in being right.'

'He was a brute. A charming brute.' Lady Timpson gave a hollow laugh. 'So attractive. I fell for those twinkling blue eyes.'

I expected her to continue, but she fell silent. For a long time, the only sound was the ticking of an ornate gold clock on the mantelpiece. I began to think she'd forgotten we were there.

'Of course, I knew why he wanted to marry me.' Lady Timpson suddenly came back to life. 'He needed money. And he knew I craved a position in society. We understood what the other wanted. It could have been sordid, but he was so charming about it.'

'Were you in love with him?' Mrs Siddons asked. 'I've always wondered.'

'I was infatuated by him in those early days. He was so attentive. Loving, even, when we courted. I was no great beauty, I was flattered.' She smiled at the memory. 'He was everything I wanted. Handsome and titled.'

'He was a charming man,' Mrs Siddons said. 'If my husband hadn't told me what he knew of his character, I would have been taken in by him.'

'I knew he didn't love me,' Lady Timpson continued. 'Once we were married, I didn't expect him to be faithful. I assumed we would live fairly independently of each other.' Her lips trembled. 'I never expected the violence. It was such a shock. I was a fool for not believing what you'd told me, Sybil. I thought it was just gossip. That's what I wanted to believe. I never thought he'd raise his fists to me.'

She looked as if she was going to dissolve into tears. Instead, she abruptly composed herself. 'But there it was. That was what I'd married. I wish I hadn't shut you out of my life, Sybil. It would have been nice to have had someone to talk to.'

'Did you suspect he pursued other women?' Mrs Siddons asked. Since the acquittal, even more newspaper stories had appeared alongside speculation over how many women Lord Timpson could have attacked over the years.

'I thought he confined his activities to his London clubs. I never dreamt he would force himself on one of the servants. Not on his own doorstep.' Lady Timpson was contemptuous.

'But you believed Rebecca when she told you he'd raped her?' I asked.

'I was horrified. I was scared then that there were others. I had no idea about the poor little laundry maid.'

'But you still used Rebecca's disappearance as a way to protect yourself.' I couldn't help saying it. 'You made it look like she'd stolen the Star Sapphire.'

Mrs Siddons shot me a warning glance.

'I saw it as a way to help us both.' A hint of Lady Timpson's steel resurfaced.

'Without the sapphire, Lord Timpson came to you for money?' I said.

'Exactly as I predicted.' She gave a slight smile. 'It wasn't much, but it was a vengeance of sorts.'

'Did you ever think about leaving him?' I asked, out of curiosity more than for the sake of the article.

'Many times. But I was trapped. He would never have agreed to a divorce. And he would have publicly humiliated me if I'd tried to leave him. The best I could hope for was to distance myself from him as much as possible. Over the years, that's what I did. Things became easier once the children were older. He was a good father in his way. We even had some happy times together.'

Constance smiled and squeezed her mother's hand, but Daniel seemed unconvinced by this last statement.

Lady Timpson looked towards her son. 'I'm sorry I left you to find him. Even th-though you hated him, I...' she stammered. 'It must have been distressing for you to have found him like that.'

'I didn't hate him then.' Daniel looked miserable and confused. 'I do now. But, oh God, I don't know what I think any more.'

His mother gripped his hand. 'It was a terrible accident.'

The fear in her eyes confirmed my suspicion. 'When you rode away, where was your husband lying?'

'He was in the canal.' She said it so quietly I had to strain to hear.

I felt Mrs Siddons nudge me. This was not what the interview was supposed to be about.

'Not lying unconscious on the ground?' I ignored the pressure of Mrs Siddons elbow on my ribs.

'No. That's not right.' Lady Timpson's breathing had grown heavier.

'You think he fell into the water after Mother rode away?' Daniel asked.

'Don't say any more, Daniel.'

I had to put her out of her misery. 'It wasn't Daniel.'

'But, but...' she stammered.

'Iris.' Mrs Siddons warned me.

'Samuel Moffat rolled your husband's body into the canal.'

39

'What are you talking about?' Daniel demanded. 'I don't understand.'

'Your mother thinks you found your father where she left him,' I said. 'Unconscious at the foot of Blacksmith's Bridge.'

'But...' he spluttered. 'But I found him floating in the water.'

'Samuel Moffat?' Lady Timpson's breathing was growing even more laboured. 'Samuel Moffat?'

'He ran away when he saw you coming that morning, as he said. But he was confused. He was expecting to see Daniel, not you. Then he heard the gunshot. He went back to the farmhouse and told Hannah what he'd done. She was angry and thought it was time Samuel learnt the truth about his sister, Lydia, and the real reason behind the payments to Ned.'

'What payments?' Constance asked. 'I don't understand.'

In a low voice, Lady Timpson told them the truth about Samuel and Isaac's parentage.

Daniel and Constance gazed at her in horror.

'Samuel...' Mrs Siddons was struggling for words. 'Samuel Moffat killed his own father. Is that what you're saying?'

Lady Timpson covered her eyes with her hands.

'Samuel realised he'd been set up,' I continued. 'He went back to the bridge and saw Lord Timpson lying on the ground. He couldn't resist going through his jacket and taking the pocket watch, cigarette case and lighter. Then, on impulse, he pushed him into the water. He never intended to kill him, just to humiliate him.'

'But why would you say you pushed Father in the canal if you hadn't?' Constance was looking at her mother with ill-concealed fury.

'I thought Daniel...' Lady Timpson trailed off.

'Why?' Daniel stared at his mother in disbelief. 'Why would you think that?'

'I'd heard you the day before. Arguing with him about Rebecca Dent. I thought you knew...' Lady Timpson turned to me accusingly. 'You stirred it all up, coming here and asking about her.'

'You argued with Father about Rebecca? Why didn't you tell me?' Constance demanded of her brother.

'I'd seen the way he was around her. The way he looked at her.' Daniel was bitter. 'But I was naïve then. I never dreamt he'd forced himself on her. But when I came back from France, I saw him in a different light. I knew then he must have done something to her.'

'When you said you'd found him in the canal, I thought...' Lady Timpson's face sagged. 'I left him on the ground. I couldn't understand how he'd ended up in the water. I didn't think anyone else would...' Tears rolled down her cheeks.

'All this because of Samuel Moffat?' Constance's voice was tight with rage. 'The hell we've been through?'

'I had to protect Daniel,' Lady Timpson pleaded. 'I knew he'd been in love with Rebecca. I thought he'd decided to punish Tobias for what he'd done to her.'

'How could you think that?' Daniel said again.

'Everything we've been through. The trial,' Constance shouted. 'Why didn't you just tell the truth?'

Mrs Siddons turned calmly to me. 'Are you sure about this?'

'Samuel admitted it.'

'But why? Why did you suspect him?' Mrs Siddons asked.

'I was curious to know where he'd got the money to buy a new jacket and some chickens.'

'Chickens?' Daniel was incredulous. 'You suspected him because of chickens?'

'They've lived in poverty for a long time. They would have sold anything of value ages ago. Suddenly, Samuel had money, but it was clear Hannah wouldn't spend any of it. She had nothing new to wear. I suspected she refused to take it because she knew Samuel had got it from stealing.'

'But it could have been the money he was given for buying the shotgun,' Mrs Siddons suggested.

I shook my head. 'He was only given enough money to buy the gun. The rest was to come later. Of course, it wouldn't have. Lord Timpson would have made sure he was arrested for murder.'

'Unbelievably cruel.' Mrs Siddons pursed her lips. 'To do that to your own son.'

'I'm going to tell the police,' Constance announced. 'He should be punished for what he did to Father.'

'Your father died as a result of his own evil intent.' I repeated the words Philip Johnson had used in his summing up to the court. 'If you go to the police, your mother will have to explain why she lied in court. She's already confessed to pushing your father into the water. I'm not sure anyone will believe her if she changes her story and says she left him lying on the ground.'

'If I'd have known.' Lady Timpson's eyes followed Daniel, who strode over to the window.

'If you'd have known, you'd have told the truth?' I asked.

'You've no idea what I've been through. And that boy goes unpunished.'

'When you thought it was Daniel, you didn't think he should be punished.' I wanted her to understand the inequality of their situations.

'He's my son. He's so young. I thought it was an impulsive act. A moment of madness. Done in anger.'

'It was. Samuel was angry and confused over everything he'd just learnt. His world had been turned upside down.' I looked at her directly. 'And he wouldn't have been so desperate if you hadn't stopped the payments they'd come to rely on.'

Lady Timpson groaned and put her head in her hands. 'He should be punished.'

'He is being punished. He's devastated.' I'd become an unlikely champion for Samuel Moffat, but I'd seen the fear and desperation on his and Hannah's faces. 'If Samuel goes to prison, Hannah will be left with no one.'

'It's over, Mother.' Daniel's voice held more authority than I'd heard before. 'We have to forgive. God knows this family has caused the Moffats enough damage. We need to take responsibility for our part in this.'

'I don't condone what Samuel did,' Mrs Siddons said softly. 'But I can understand his distress. I intend to proceed with my plan to buy the farm from him so he and Hannah can make a fresh start.'

'Constance.' Daniel turned to his sister. 'I intend to do what I can to make amends to the Moffats and Rebecca Dent for the damage that has been done to them. I would like you to help me.'

'I will,' Constance replied. 'But I agree with Mother that Samuel should be punished.'

'And I believe he should be forgiven,' Daniel countered. 'If he were to hang, it wouldn't be justice, it would be vengeance. Violence breeds more violence, and this has to stop now.'

For a long time, no one said anything. Sunshine poured in from the tall window, illuminating dust particles in the air. Lady Timpson stared into the empty fireplace. I listened to the ticking of the clock.

Constance contemplated Daniel, and her fury seemed to dissolve. She joined him by the window. 'I agree.'

Mrs Siddons regarded Lady Timpson. 'You have to pity the poor boy, Delphina.'

Lady Timpson inclined her head. 'I ignored your advice last time, Sybil, to my cost. This time, I will do as you ask.'

40

'Your article is in all the papers.' Elijah pushed a bundle of newspapers at me. 'I thought you'd be overjoyed.'

'I am.' I flicked through the pages of one without reading.

'You don't look it. Mr Laffaye is delighted. You might even get a pay rise.'

'I didn't tell the whole truth.'

'Is that what you think you should have done?'

'Isn't that what journalists are supposed to do?'

'Then why didn't you?'

'I didn't see what it would achieve. I don't think what Samuel Moffat did was right, but. Oh, I don't know...' I sighed. 'I'm not sorry Lord Timpson is dead. I hate him for what he did to Rebecca and Lydia Moffat. And Lady Timpson would never have been safe whilst he was alive. He would have carried on preying on her and other women.'

'We can't know what he would have done.'

'He'd got away with his crimes for so long, I think he felt invincible,' I argued. 'And if his plan to kill Lady Timpson had worked, Samuel would probably have been hanged. His own son.'

'Then why do you think you should have told the truth about Samuel?'

'Because isn't that what a journalist should do? Tell people what's really going on. Not collude with lies.'

He didn't answer immediately, and I sat back and listened to the rhythmic sound of the printing presses below.

Eventually, he said, 'I think you did the right thing. In your shoes, I would have done the same.'

'Would you?' I felt relief at his words. 'Why?'

'For the same reasons you did. There have been times when I've faced moral dilemmas over what to write. I like to think I've never lied. But I have omitted certain facts if I think they'll cause too much harm or distress.'

'The article was never meant to be about Lord Timpson's death anyway. My intention was to use what came out at the trial to illustrate how powerless women are in certain situations. I wanted to tell Rebecca's story. And Lydia Moffat's.'

'You achieved all that. It was a good article. If you'd revealed Samuel's part, it would have become a trial by newspaper for a crime that Lady Timpson had already admitted to. It would have detracted from your message. Instead, your article clearly showed why things have to change; why there have to be more women in positions of power to fight this abuse.'

I nodded, my mood lifting.

He reached for his cigarettes. 'You have to decide what type of journalist you want to be. Some are happy to print downright lies and don't give a damn about the consequences. Others become slaves to the principle of truth at whatever cost. Then there are the rest of us, trying to use common sense and take a pragmatic approach. Sometimes you have to make difficult decisions. When you make those decisions, you need to show compassion. That's what you did.'

I picked up the newspaper and, for the first time, felt some pride. 'Thank you.'

'You're a suffragette's daughter. You should know you need to focus on what you can change, not on what you can't.' He waved his cigarette at me. 'Now put it behind you and go out dancing with young Baverstock. That'll take your mind off things.'

* * *

I placed the dress I planned to wear on the bed. Twenty-five years earlier, my mother would have stood in this very room, doing the very same to go and see Thomas Woodmore.

I picked up the wooden box Aunt Maud had left on the chest of drawers. I didn't think she would have thrown away Mother's suffragette pins and badges, but it was still a relief when she said she'd kept them for me.

I took out the silver and enamel Holloway Brooch of a portcullis shot through with an arrow. It had been given to my mother after her first time in Holloway Prison. Next to it was a tarnished medal that hung from green, white and purple striped fabric. This was the one that caused me the most pain. It was awarded to suffragettes who went on hunger strike to protest against being jailed as criminals rather than political prisoners.

I hastily wiped away a tear at the sound of a tap on the door. 'Come in.'

Aunt Maud came and sat down on the bed next to me.

'I know they upset you.' She picked up one of the badges. 'But you should be proud of what your mother achieved.'

'I am proud of her. I just wish she was still here. I miss her so much.' My voice cracked.

She put her arm around me. 'You can always come back here to live, you know. If you're unhappy in Walden.'

'I'm starting to feel more at home there. But it helps to know I can always stay with you and Gran.'

'Where are you off to tonight then?' I suspected she was changing the subject to mask her disappointment.

'I've arranged to see Rebecca. Constance and Daniel have asked me to deliver a letter to her. I'm going to meet young Violet again.'

'Don't be too late, will you?' She glanced at the dress laid out on my bed.

I wished I'd hidden it. I'd planned to put a coat on before I went downstairs so they wouldn't notice what I was wearing. 'No, I won't be. But I'll take my key in case, so I won't disturb you or Gran.'

She left the room, and I sat down at the dressing table. I patted some powder on my face and applied a tiny amount of rouge to my cheeks. I slipped a lipstick into my purse. I wouldn't dare use that until after I'd left the house. Gran would pounce if she saw me wearing lip colour.

I knocked hesitantly at the door of twenty-seven Victoria Street. I wasn't sure if Kathleen would welcome seeing me again after the way I'd deceived Mrs Hartnell into giving me her address.

But when she answered the door, the transformation was astonishing. She seemed lighter, her expression open and friendly. The relief at not having to hide any more was evident, and she chatted happily as she showed me upstairs. It was clear Kathleen and Leonard Hooper had sacrificed a lot to keep Rebecca and Violet safe.

'Rebecca already has a visitor.' She gave me a wink before disappearing into her room.

To my surprise, I found Donald Anstey seated in the armchair by the fireplace. Violet was on his knee. The little girl's wide blue eyes looked at me with suspicion. I couldn't help thinking of Lord Timpson.

I handed Rebecca the letter from Daniel and Constance and sat down opposite Donald so I could play with the child.

Rebecca brought over some coffee, then sat down and opened the envelope. When she finished reading, she folded up the sheets of paper and tapped them on the side of her chair. She seemed to be weighing up the contents.

'What does it say?' Donald asked.

'They want to give me money to help with Violet's upbringing. They also ask if they can see her.'

I knew Rebecca never wanted to set foot in Crookham Hall again. Who could blame her?

'What are you going to do?' I asked.

'Decline. It's kind of them, and I do appreciate their offer of financial help. But I don't want them to meet Violet. It would be too confusing for her. How could I explain who they are? The Timpsons may offer financial stability, but they would be reminders of the violence that brought her into the world. I want to protect her from that.'

I could understand why Daniel and Constance wanted to provide for their half-sister. Perhaps even get to know her. But I could also see how difficult that would make life for Rebecca. I watched the little girl play happily with Donald's necktie. He seemed delighted by the child.

'I finally got around to asking Rebecca to marry me,' he said with pride.

'I said yes.' She held out her hand to display the diamond and emerald ring that Donald had shown me.

Violet seemed pleased by the change in her mother's expression and beamed.

'I'm glad for you.' If anyone deserved some happiness, it was Rebecca. And Donald.

'Once I've finished work on the housing project with Mrs Siddons, we're going to move to Scotland, not far from my parents in Dundee,' he said.

Rebecca smiled. 'It will be a fresh start for us.'

'Will you write to tell me how you're getting on?' I felt a proprietary interest in this little girl who'd been named after my mother.

'I will.' She hesitated. 'If you promise not to give our address to the Timpsons. I know they mean well, and I'm sorry to have to ask, but I don't want Violet to have any association with them. I want to protect her from the past. Do you understand?'

I nodded. More secrets. But Rebecca had suffered enough. She'd earnt the right to bring up her child as she saw fit.

We talked about their future plans, and I noticed that Kathleen wasn't the only one to have undergone a transformation. Donald spoke animatedly with none of his usual ponderous pauses. His air of weariness had lifted, and he looked like a much younger man.

I didn't want to intrude on their rekindled relationship, so I rose to leave. I had a relationship of my own to attend to.

'That's a pretty dress you're wearing,' Rebecca said. 'Are you going somewhere nice?'

'Just to a dance with a friend.'

* * *

I opened the door to the Foxtrot Club, and music blasted my ears. I made my way down a set of steep steps to the basement. The band was playing a tune I wasn't familiar with, and the floor was covered with people dancing wildly. I was shocked by the shortness of the skirts some of the women were wearing. You could glimpse their thighs as they danced. I hesitated, then saw Percy heading towards me, grinning broadly. I gave my coat to the hatcheck girl.

'I didn't think you were going to come.' He pushed his hair over his forehead. 'You look jolly pretty. But as you know, I think that about most girls.'

I laughed, breathing in the heady fragrance of cigarettes, alcohol and sweat. It was going to be an interesting night.

'Do you want to dance?' he asked.

The music was infectious, but the dance moves were far more exuberant than any I'd seen before.

'I'm not sure how.'

'I can teach you. It's easy. You'll love it.'

'I can't stay too late.' I took his outstretched hand.

'Let's not waste a moment.'

We took to the dance floor, and whilst I'm not sure I mastered any of the moves, I enjoyed being close to Percy. As he swung me around in his arms, I felt a lightness I hadn't experienced before.

Eventually, I held up my hands in surrender. As much as I wanted to be like these modern women who didn't give a damn, I couldn't make my body move with quite the same abandon.

'I'll get you a drink.' Percy took my hand. 'I've been hoping to see you for ages. There's something I want to talk to you about.'

Although he chose the booth furthest from the band, he still had to move in close so I could hear him. I felt a flutter of nerves at his hot breath on my neck.

'I'm embarrassed to say it. You'll think me mad, but...' he began.

'But what?' I smiled. 'Come on, tell me.'

'Since spending all that time together at the trial...'

'Yes?'

'I think I'm in love with Constance.'

ACKNOWLEDGMENTS

I'd like to thank the following people for their encouragement and support: my parents, Ken and Barbara Salter, for everything. Special thanks to Dad for his help with historical research. Thura Win for his advice and eye for detail as no. 1 beta reader. Jeanette Quay for acting as a sounding board during the many years of novel development. Barbara Daniel for giving so much of her time to read my novels and offer positive advice and editorial guidance. Anstice Hughes for her feedback and kind comments on an early draft of this book. Lesley McDowell for her excellent manuscript assessment of a very early draft and her encouragement to persevere with the novel.

I enjoyed researching this book as much as I did writing it. I'm indebted to the numerous people, books, libraries, and museums that contributed to my knowledge of this period.

I'd like to thank Dr Clifford Williams, Force Historian, for kindly answering my questions.

Thanks to Roger Cansdale of The Basingstoke Canal Society for sharing his knowledge of the canal's history. The books produced by the society were a useful source of information.

In the summer of 2018, I visited the Voice & Vote exhibition in Westminster Hall. The exhibition and accompanying book, Voice & Vote: Celebrating 100 Years of Votes for Women, provided valuable information and inspiration. The permanent suffragette exhibition at the Museum of London was another useful resource.

MORE FROM MICHELLE SALTER

We hope you enjoyed reading *Death at Crookham Hall*. If you did, please leave a review.

If you'd like to gift a copy, this book is also available as an ebook, digital audio download and audiobook CD.

Sign up to Michelle Salter's mailing list for news, competitions and updates on future books.

https://bit.ly/MichelleSalterNews

ABOUT THE AUTHOR

Michelle Salter writes historical cosy crime set in Hampshire, where she lives, and inspired by real-life events in 1920s Britain. The first book in her Iris Woodmore series, *Death at Crookham Hall*, draws on her interest in the aftermath of the Great War and the suffragette movement.

Visit Michelle's Website:

https://www.michellesalter.com

Follow Michelle on social media:

twitter.com/MichelleASalter

facebook.com/MichelleSalterWriter

instagram.com/michellesalter_writer

bookbub.com/authors/michelle-salter

Poison
& Pens

POISON & PENS IS THE HOME OF
COZY MYSTERIES SO POUR YOURSELF
A CUP OF TEA & GET SLEUTHING!

DISCOVER PAGE-TURNING NOVELS FROM
YOUR FAVOURITE AUTHORS &
MEET NEW FRIENDS

JOIN OUR
FACEBOOK GROUP

BIT.LYPOISONANDPENSFB

SIGN UP TO OUR
NEWSLETTER

BIT.LY/POISONANDPENSNEWS

Boldwood

Boldwood Books is an award-winning fiction publishing company seeking out the best stories from around the world.

Find out more at www.boldwoodbooks.com

Join our reader community for brilliant books, competitions and offers!

Follow us
@BoldwoodBooks
@BookandTonic

Sign up to our weekly deals newsletter

https://bit.ly/BoldwoodBNewsletter